REVEALED IN FIRE

Also by K.F. Breene

REVEALED

IN FIRE

By K.F. Breene

Contact info:
www.kfbreene.com
books@kfbreene.com

PROLOGUE

"WE'VE GOT MORE of them! Hurry up, let's go," Devon said, jogging toward the bedroom. "The others will meet us there."

Charity swore under her breath, her spoon stopping mid-stir in the simmering sauce on the stovetop. "More demons? How many nights in a row is that?"

She dragged the pan off the burner, then turned off the cooktop and oven. Dinner would have to wait. Again.

Devon ran from the bedroom in rip-away basketball sweats, shrugging into a T-shirt as he went. "Too many. They're springing to the surface like weeds." He grabbed his phone from the table and shot her an impatient glance. "Vlad has been busy."

"I'm coming, I'm coming." She sprinted to the bedroom, changed into athletic sweats, and grabbed her sword from a holder on the wall—easy access. "Roger can't think it's all still Vlad though, right?" she asked as she hustled to the front door. "Because Penny said the circle she found two days ago didn't look like the others.

It was ancient. A couple of other circles were like that, too. And yeah, I know Vlad is ridiculously old, but it's weird that some of the circles would look different from the others."

Penny was the co-leader of the new Mages' Guild, which she ran alongside her partner, Emery. They'd been helping the shifters control the upsurge in demons since they'd come back from the fae lands, what the magical people called the Flush. Vlad had had a meeting with Lucifer not long before, and then it was like a tide of demons coming to the surface. They acted like his little minions, causing havoc, guarding him when he turned humans into vampires...

"It probably isn't all Vlad, no," Devon said, "but he's still doing plenty. He has always been a thorn in Roger's side, but this has gotten ridiculous."

They got in the car, and Devon took the turns at a breakneck pace, whipping past the trees.

"Where are they?" she asked.

"Near downtown. We need to get rid of them before everyone sees them."

"At least my dad is close by," she murmured.

Up until recently, Charity had thought she was just a girl, like any other, and her focus had been on blending in instead of standing out. But she'd learned she was a princess of the warrior fae, and several of her people had left their ancestral land to follow her into the Brink, her natural father among them.

He was living in a modest house in downtown Santa Cruz with a sizable yard. She'd encouraged him to move further into the trees, but he was reluctant to go until he perfected his garden. Given things grew slower in the Brink than in the Realm, there was no telling how long that would take.

"Yeah, Roger contacted him first."

They reached the end of the windy two-lane road, and Devon hung a right. His eyebrows pinched together as he slowed, heading into traffic. The sun was still out, and while vampires couldn't go out in daylight, demons had no such hang-ups. In fact, the person or persons summoning them seemed to purposely do so at the most inconvenient times possible. He cut left, the tires squealing.

A "detour" sign stopped through traffic, sending them around the block. Dwindling light showered the empty street beyond the barrier. No human officials waited around the sign or the barrier, because it hadn't been set up by them.

Devon leaned forward over the steering wheel, slowing. "Based on what Roger said, this is the place. Or near enough."

"Looks like the mages are already on the scene. The Guild is responsive, I'll say that much." Charity clicked off her seatbelt and wrapped her fingers around the handle of her sword, adrenaline firing.

Devon eased the car past the barrier and pulled over to the side of the road. They jumped out, urgency speeding up Charity's movements. Devon hurried out of sight to change, but she didn't wait for him. He was faster in his wolf form; he'd catch up.

Halfway down the street, Kairi, her fighting assistant, stepped out of an alleyway and joined her. A large black wolf raced past them.

"What do we have?" Charity asked by way of greeting, adding a nod.

They turned, following Devon's lead, and headed down a long driveway between two houses. They passed two mages rustling through their side-body satchels.

"One of the demons left the backyard and has already been sent back to its maker," Kairi said. She pointed to the right, where Charity's father, Romulus, waited with Halvor, his fighting assistant. The wooden gate to the backyard stood open. Just before it, Devon joined his pack. The others had already changed, too. The largest of them, Steve in his lion form and Cole in his even bigger yeti form, loomed in the back. "It was of lesser power, and they think…"

Her words drifted away as Charity got within range of her father. He turned, his eyes crinkling as he beheld her. Unlike the man who'd raised her, he was always pleased to see her, just as she was to see him. Everyone always commented on how much they looked alike.

"It seems the demon who wandered out of the backyard was meant to draw us in," her father finished, adjusting the strap of the sheath holding his sword to his back. "These aren't acting like the others we've seen."

"Vlad's?"

"*Any* of the others. They are much more powerful, for one, those waiting in the yard. Three of them."

"What kind of circle was used?"

Romulus shifted. "That is one of the differences—there is some sort of air blockade. We can't get far enough into the yard to see. Steve the Lion"—the way the fae pronounced the names and titles of the shifters always made it seem like they were capitalized—"said he's seen magic like it before, but not from demons. He didn't elaborate, wanting to wait for Devon, but he thinks if we all work together, we should be able to break through. The mages cannot help, though. They are not powerful enough, it seems."

Charity frowned. Whether called by Vlad's people, Vlad himself, or whoever was doing the more ancient circle magic, the demons had never been so powerful that just three of them would pose a serious problem. Usually it was their quantity that posed the threat.

A memory surfaced, the details told to her mostly secondhand because she'd been in the throes of magical poisoning at the time. Demons battling in the Realm, sent there to find a woman traveling with a vampire that had infiltrated the Underworld months before. They had wanted to know if Charity was that woman. They'd wanted to take her down to the Underworld to question her. They'd been powerful, those demons. As powerful as these?

"Have the demons spoken?" Charity asked, sword at her side and begging for action.

"No," Romulus replied. "They do not smile and laugh and taunt, like the others. They are waiting quietly. Patiently. They know we will go to them, and they are content to wait."

Her frown stayed in place. These definitely seemed like a different breed of demon. Or maybe now they just had different orders. The circle from whence they came would be a telling factor.

"Well," she said, scanning the bushes and grass beyond the open gateway. The shifters still stood to one side of the opening, but she couldn't see the demons from her vantage point. "Let's take care of it. Is there an opening on the other side?"

"Yes."

"And the owners?"

"No sign of them."

Charity nodded, because that was pretty normal. The owner of the house had probably ended up starting a new life as a vampire whether they'd wanted to or not. That, or they'd become vampire food.

She connected gazes with Devon. Their magic rushed back and forth between them, pleasing and exciting, both of them feeling the song of battle. She jerked her head, indicating she'd take the other gate. He dipped his head, meaning he understood.

Between the shifters and her new family, she'd had to get good at reading subtle physical cues. It was the way her people communicated, and the only way shifters in animal form could.

"How was your day?" Kairi asked as they made their way toward the back. Charity's dad and Halvor followed, and the other fae on scene peeled away from their positions, filing in behind them.

"Great, thanks," Charity answered.

"School went well? You had a test today, did you not?"

Charity's sophomore year was rough, what with this second job for the shifters and her position among her people. "Yeah. It was a little harder than I was expecting, but I think I'll get an A."

"Fantastic, Third," Kairi said as they rounded the back of the fence and reached the gate. "That's great news."

Charity pulled the latch and pushed the door open. Halfway through, it bumped against empty air. She reached forward and felt the area, confirming it was indeed a blockage. A glance back, and her father stepped up to lead. She was the liaison between the warrior fae and the shifters, but he was their leader, second in line for the throne. Not to mention he was well trained for battle and she was still learning.

He pulled his sword with smooth economy, his subtle body language calling Halvor to his side. Charity edged over, giving them more space to work with, and Kairi fell in behind them. Charity and Halvor lifted their swords too, and they held as one, waiting for the wolf call that would unite the forces.

A single note rose into the air, the beautiful song of Devon's wolf, containing power and authority and the drumbeat of battle.

Electricity rolled through Charity's veins. As one they struck, their swords hitting the invisible mass. Her father pushed forward his other hand, and a thin stream of blistering fire—hellfire—slammed into the demon's magic.

"Summon the lightning, my darling," Romulus said, his magic eating through the blockage.

Heat prickled across her skin, and she pulled lightning down from the sky, tiny points hitting the wall in front of them. Halvor struck it with his sword again.

A *gush* blew her hair back, the magic releasing. The wall gone, Charity stepped forward with her father, and

Halvor fell back, the other fae quickly enclosing him in the center of their people, their special fighting style.

As a group, they rushed into the backyard, hearing growls from the other side. No roars from Steve, though. Nothing that would have the neighbors calling the cops. Hopefully.

Three demons waited in the middle of the space, forming a triangle.

A moment of déjà vu washed over Charity, calling up a vision out of nowhere.

She staggered to a stop, and then suddenly she was standing within a line, under the eternally orange sky of the Realm. Devon and Roger stood to her left in wolf form. Her father waited on her right, pride shining brightly in his eyes. Her people and the shifters spread out behind them, waiting for her command to start forward. She felt the expectation of it.

A song drifted on the air. Drumbeats. Her heart quickened.

She'd had this vision before—her people had called it her quest. Except this time, it wasn't Vlad and a man with slicked-back hair, surrounded by demons and vampires, opposite her on the battlefield...

This time, the warrior fae were facing off with the elves and a collection of various magical folk spread out behind them.

Between the two groups, to the right, stood a cluster

of three people leading a larger group. Their faces had been blurry in her last vision, but this time they were crystal clear. Reagan stood in front, wearing leather pants, army boots, and a fanny pack, and Penny and Emery were just behind her, the three forming a pyramid like the demons in this backyard. The similarity of their positioning was uncanny.

Opposite Reagan stood a group of vampires. She recognized the leader as Darius, Reagan's beau, an elder vampire with almost as much power and prestige as Vlad. Charity had only seen him once before. He'd shown up in the Brink a couple of months ago—right before Reagan had disappeared off the face of the earth.

In a moment, the image cleared. The smell of mud and blood and the crisp morning bled away. The hazy orange sky faded into blue.

"Charity, darling, are you okay?" Her dad had stopped to peer anxiously at her face.

"Another vision," she said, panting. "The quest has changed."

Her dad blew out a breath. "The Red Prophet said it would be so. We will analyze it tonight. Come, let's best these creatures now, before the Alpha Shifter steals our glory."

Charity laughed, running forward. She reached the first demon as Devon lunged at another. Air wrapped around her and squeezed. Breath halting, she called the lightning, raining it down on the disgusting creatures. They had stubby horns, hooves for feet, and she watched in disgust as a snake crawled out of a hole in the far left one's side and slithered up its chest.

The snake bit the creature, and the scores and burns from her lightning stitched back up at incredible speed.

"What the..." Charity wheezed, fear worming through her.

Romulus hacked the air around her as Halvor launched out of the cluster of fae and attacked the third demon even as Steve got there. A white wolf, Yasmine, went flying, thrown by an unseen hand. Andy followed. They slapped the ground and kept rolling.

The demons didn't push their advantage. Over the din, in a scratchy voice like thousands of insects running across a hardwood floor, the snake-bitten one said, "You are not the one. It must be the other."

Romulus stepped into her line of sight and shot a small blast of hellfire at the hardened air around her. The hellfire barely sliced through it, the effort not enough to release her.

Romulus's eyes widened. That was certainly...disconcerting.

He pumped in more power as Kairi and Hallen hacked at the invisible binding, pouring power into their blades. The magic finally released in a gush of wind, and Halvor, Steve, and Cole tore and cut their demon in half, the creature just standing there and accepting its fate.

No time to lose, Charity shot a ball of electricity at her demon as her father joined his efforts with hers. Hallen darted in to slash. Kairi got in a strike too, and Devon and the rest of his shifters focused on theirs. It took all of them to overcome its tough hide.

With the considerable effort, in no time it was over, and that was largely because the demons didn't fight back, not in any real way. Even still, with all the power at their disposal—a Second and Third fae Arcana, a pack alpha almost as powerful as the alpha of the entire North American pack, and people like Halvor, Steve, and Cole—for it to be this challenging to end three demons who'd just stood there…

Romulus stared at Charity for a moment.

"What?" she asked, still panting.

"Since you were the only one restrained, they must've been assessing you," he said. "They found you wanting."

You are not the one. It must be the other.

"A band of demons was looking for someone in the Realm," Devon said, newly changed and striding over. The rest of the shifters regained their human forms.

Charity nodded, relaying what she'd been thinking earlier.

"This group didn't need to question her, though,"

Devon said, wiping sweat from his brow. "They had more power than the others. It sounded like they figured out really quickly that she wasn't the one they were after."

"Except…we killed them," Charity said. "The question has been left unanswered. Again."

"There really is only one super-powerful—and bangin'-hot—lady who wastes her time with vampires, isn't there?" Steve said, looking at Devon. "Who we saw wield incredible power when battling the Mages' Guild? Magic like we just witnessed…"

"Except no one has mentioned a thing about it since that time in the Realm," Devon returned. "We've encountered a lot of demons since. None have mentioned looking for that woman."

"Yeah, but…" Steve shrugged. "Those were low-powered types, sent up in numbers by Vlad. These were more similar to the type in the Realm, possibly sent by the Lord of the Underworld himself, or one of his minions. A few months is nothing to an immortal of Lucifer's caliber. Seems like a moment. A snap of the fingers."

"If that's true, I can't imagine it'll be much longer until they find the right woman," Devon murmured.

Silence washed through everyone as they realized the implications.

"We need to take this to Roger," Devon said after a

moment.

"And probably no one else," Steve replied. When everyone glanced at him, he shrugged again. "I'm no good at politics, but if this is to do with *a woman and her vampire sidekick that we all probably know,* it'll involve a cunning elder vampire that I doubt anyone wants to tango with. That's why Roger gets paid the big bucks. He'll want to handle this himself."

"I agree." Romulus looked over his shoulder, and Charity knew he was checking to make sure the mages were still waiting at the front of the house. "This does not go beyond us. We will present it to Roger and decide if there is more we should do."

"Second." Halvor held out a curled-up brown scroll with a blood-red seal. "I found this on one of them."

Romulus took it from him, then studied the seal for a long moment before running his manicured finger along the edge, breaking it open.

"Do you recognize the seal?" Charity asked, scooting closer.

"No. It reads, 'The Great Master requests an audience with his heir. Summon her.'"

CHAPTER 1

THE SKY WAS a light, fluffy shade of purple, and a
lone vulture sailed through it lazily. The scavenger
looked down on the scene below, a twisted wooded path
leading nowhere, flanked by manic clowns, their
pointed teeth dripping with blood and their mouths
curled up into horrible sneers. Up ahead, an elephant
perched near the path, a large bullet hole in its neck and
its chest awash with deep, flowing crimson. It was about
ten minutes from bleeding out. I'd make sure it died
right next to Cahal, whose favorite animal was the Brink
elephant.

All of this was for Cahal, the incredibly tough warrior druid who was duty-bound to his lethal skill set
until he found his perfect mate, something that would
release him from his curse and allow him to settle down
with his mate and produce plump children, or whatever
he planned to get up to. Maybe he didn't want kids.
Maybe he just wanted an elephant. It was hard to say
with him.

The best assassin in the world, and he thought the

duty was a curse. What a tragedy.

I'd offered to trade his lot in life for mine.

No dice.

I cracked my knuckles and patted my thigh, looking for one of my daggers, only to remember I didn't have them. Dang it, that was right—no weapons allowed for this training. It was magic only.

Taking a deep breath, I fashioned another vulture and waved it to life above us, sending it toward Cahal. He was waiting along the path somewhere, underneath his least favorite color, surrounded by one of the only things that made his bowels watery, near his favorite animal in the stages of bleeding out.

Some might call me a real asshole for shoving the guy's worst nightmares in his face. Those people would be right. It was great fun watching him squirm. Just as fun, probably, as kicking my ass was for him. At least, I assumed that was why he always did it with such gusto.

"Here we go." Magic pumping through me, I started to run along the path, speeding up the gestures and jeering of the clowns. Maybe that would distract Cahal a little, and I could get a few more punches in before he threw me against a tree.

All of this had been fashioned with my magic, of course. The clowns weren't real. I would never shoot an elephant—I liked those big sons of bitches. Purple sky? Weird. But my father could construct worlds, and I needed to learn how to do it too. I'd gotten pretty good at it, much to Cahal's unwavering delight.

He didn't love my sarcasm, though.

A pasty-white swamp monster jumped out from behind a clown, its mouth open and saliva dripping from the wicked fangs in its black gums. It—or *he*, in this case—spread his clawed hands and prepared to get his ass handed to him.

I flung air like it was knives, opening slashes in the sides of his chest, my aim now a work of art. Which was good. I didn't want to kill my boyfriend, after all. He was great in bed, so it was worth being cautious.

A block of air punched him in the kisser, and then I was on him, sweeping his legs out from under him before fashioning a sword made of air. I hacked down, but he rolled at the last moment, hopping up and stabbing his claws forward. I arched, barely missing a few puncture holes before I slapped him with air and sent him flying. He scraped the solid air with his claws, but my power was pulsing at a demonic mid-five level, edging closer to hitting level six, which was where my father sat, at the top of the hierarchy. It would take Darius a while to get through that air, and by then I'd be facing a god-touched druid, the likes of whom the world had never seen.

At least, I liked to think of him that way. It made me feel better when he bested me.

A clown jumped on a pogo stick to my right, somehow staying on while waving her arms in the air and squealing. What a freak show. I might be laying it on a little thick.

Around a reaching bush covered in lollipops—Cahal was trying to ditch the sugar, worried about his boyish figure—the path opened up, and there he stood, a blindfold over his eyes, holding a wicked black sword with a curved blade. Light gleamed off the point, the moonlight bright enough to paint that nightmare.

I sent a small whip of magic, snapping the blindfold off him. The cloth fell away as he turned slightly to face me. Another blindfold waited under the first, secured tightly to his head. He could always sense the direction of my magic. It was really annoying for sneak attacks.

"Really hate those clowns, huh?" I said, because it wasn't his first encounter with them.

"You have an uncanny ability to unsettle your opponent and gain the advantage," he said, bending his knees just a little in preparation for my attack. "I needed a way to protect my eyes from witnessing your horrors."

"My horrors? You mean my face? I haven't lost my eyebrows in *weeks*…"

He launched forward, not giving me an opportunity to peel off that second blindfold. He moved so fast that he basically blurred. He wrapped his magic around his body, shadows clinging to him, moving and changing and tricking my eyes. I pushed forward to meet him while calling up daggers of air. I was just preparing to throw them when they dissolved into nothing.

Swearing under my breath, I called up fire. Still nothing happened.

"When did Penny get here?" I ground out, because only Penny knew the spell for deadening my magic. "This just became an incredibly unfair fight."

Cahal's wicked sword cut through the air, and I bent backward to miss it. The blade caught a piece of my hair and sliced it right off. I was just glad it hadn't gotten close enough to shave my whiskers. Also that I didn't have any whiskers.

Turning the arch into a slide, I scraped the dirt and punched upward as I moved under him. My fist connected with his package hard enough to lift him into the air.

"*Eeeiiii.*"

The sound he made didn't seem quite human.

I popped up on the other side of him and worked Penny's spell, which hovered around the clearing like a fart. If I burned it from the outside in, I could usually get rid of the thing.

Cahal staggered, the very first time I'd ever seen him do so. Not wasting my advantage, still working Penny's spell, I sprinted forward and considered a one-two punch to his melon. That would get him back in the game, though. He had an amazing ability to ignore injuries in order to keep busting heads. Right now he was wallowing in his bruised manhood. I wanted to make the most of his distraction.

So I ripped his blindfold off.

Clowns danced into the clearing, blood oozing down their chins and dripping onto the ground. The fluffy purple sky rained candy canes, bouncing around us on the gumdrop-studded ground. The wounded elephant laboriously limped down the path, pathetic in its dying, its gaze pleading.

Cahal's eyes rounded and then darted around, horror slacking his jaw.

Bingo.

I'd gotten today's world-building perfectly right. It had taken a couple of months for me to suss out all his hates, fears, and dislikes, but this payoff was worth it.

Penny's spell dissolved away, and I commenced a full-scale attack, kicking Cahal while he was down. It was the only way to take on this freaking druid. It was intensely hard to make him say uncle.

Air-throwing stars ripped into his flesh. Fire burst to life under his feet and grew quickly, the heat sweltering. I was one of very few magical creatures who possessed the ability to use hellfire, but that would actually kill him. No go.

I created a spear with air, instead, and threw it at his

stomach. He could heal like a vampire. Like me. He'd live if it skewered him.

His sword swished in an arc, though, cutting through my magic and actually deflecting the spear.

"I still don't understand how you can do that," I said, tossing more air-throwing stars and then two more spears, keeping him occupied while I tried to burn him at the imaginary stake.

He did a hot-footed dance, his sword whirling like a tornado, flinging away all my efforts. I smashed air down on top of him, but before I could flatten him to the ground, he punched upward. His fist connected with the solid air, and the sheer strength of his will stopped its downward trajectory.

"You are losing power because you're using too many magical elements at once," he said, his voice quavering with the effort. He gave a mighty heave and shoved the magic off, still dancing gracefully within my flames as he moved across the squishy gumdrops, the fire trailing him. "Reduce the various elements of your magic and focus on the kill strike."

"Any hint on which I should reduce?"

"This horrible world you've created would be nice."

Good hint.

I cut out the fire, not hot enough to do lasting damage (on purpose), and stopped the air assault. He paused for a moment, and a gleam lit his eyes. He nodded slightly. I'd read him correctly. He was too good for half-baked assaults. They would never beat him, something I hadn't properly learned in the past. He'd always fight me until I ran out of steam, and then he'd pummel me.

Messing with his mind, though…

The elephant gave a mighty wail as it shrank down to a baby elephant, crying for him, stumbling his way. On the other side of the clearing, I created its mournful mother, the building of even this small world taxing but fun. I called it a win every time Cahal reacted, even slightly. If he flinched, it was the equivalent of a normal person screaming and curling up into a ball.

The fluffy purple sky shifted down, enveloping us, and chocolate welled up and flowed in little eddies and streams around us, carrying marshmallows on top.

He licked his plush lips, his eyes darting again. Then…he smirked. It was the first I'd ever seen him do it.

"You're pretty hot when you grin. Has anyone ever told you that?" I built up my power, circling him slowly.

He stalked toward me, wariness in his eyes, his grin fading. Then his gaze darted to the wounded baby elephant. He had a few heartstrings hidden deep down inside of him, it seemed.

"Don't like when someone mentions your appearance, huh?" I badgered. "Have you gotten a complex from women treating you like a side of beef all your life?"

His gaze bored into mine. "You are world class at sensing and exploiting weaknesses."

"I've had to be. Working in a magical community while hiding my magic... It helped me develop a sort of"—I flung an air spear at him that erupted in fire at the last moment; he swung his sword in a graceful circle, deflecting it—"penchant for survival." I grinned. "People don't focus on you so much when they're battling their own demons."

"You should not actually throw the air with your hand. You don't need to, and it alerts me to your plans."

"*Riiight...* Put that on the list of items to practice."

"Yes." And then he burst into movement, zipping across the clearing like a phantom, shadows draping around him, making it hard to track his movements.

I threw up an air shield, and then made copies of the baby elephant. Yeah, I could do that. I stamped those suckers all around us as Cahal tried to bash through my shield with his expert sword moves.

"Help them," I pleaded. "Don't let them die."

He crashed into my air shield as I readied another elephant calf behind him. His eyes darted, and he jerked away from the one nearly at his side. It made him bump into the apparition behind him, but his back pushed through the image. They weren't solid, and I didn't know how to infuse enough air into them to make it so. Not yet. It was a work in progress.

I backed it away.

"They're dying," I hollered, putting as much drama into it as I could. Blood gushed, the little babies faltering, and his body tightened.

And then I crashed a second wall forward, smashing him in between them.

He flattened against the wall in front of me. His sword sliced into his forearm, and his cheek smeared against the hard air. Red-tinged spit dribbled out of his smooshed lips and leaked around his chin.

"Say uncle," I yelled, using all my power to keep him put, shaking with the effort as he tried to buck and create some room for himself to escape. "Say uncle!"

He tried to buck again, and I dumped all I had into my magic, no longer focusing on keeping the world intact around us. The fluffy sky started to dissolve like cotton candy in the rain. A leg fell off an elephant, and it hobbled before bending to breaking knees.

"Yield!" he mumbled through still-smooshed lips.

"I said say *uncle*, not *yield*. You have to say uncle or I won't let you out."

Another elephant crashed to the ground, and the illusion of blood spread across the ground. My faltering magic couldn't hold the original design. This was so much more gruesome than what I'd created.

Cahal jolted, his eyes wide as he caught sight of it. He bucked wildly, the wall pushing back.

"No you don't." I gritted my teeth and balled my fists, needing to visualize the air pressing against him. "Not this time. I will not lose at the final moment and get beaten up for my efforts. I will win this time. *Say uncle!*"

Another elephant crashed to the ground. I gave a fourth a little push to do the same, since Cahal was obviously reacting to the sight of them hitting the dirt, lifelike or not.

"Uncle," he finally said, going limp. "*Uncle.*"

I tore the air away, panting. Working quickly, I tore the rest of the scene down, letting my magic dissolve back into the world, raining down through the moon-soaked night like acid across a painting. Darkened grass took the place of the gumdrops. Just over a berm, the liquid-black ocean shimmered as it lapped against the flat sands. The twisted wood cleared to a landscaped and carefully tended front yard, little potholes dug into it from my boots or my scuffle with Darius. A large mansion wavered into view behind us, the pool in front of it lit from within with eerie blue light. When Darius had organized a retreat to hide me away from the world, he'd done it like he did everything else—in style.

Cahal wiped his lip with the back of his hand, his eyes burning into mine.

"The rules of uncle are clear and finite." I held up my hands and took a step back. "Once you say it, you are declaring yourself the loser of the fight, and you cannot resume the attack after you're freed. That would be cheating."

"You always cheat."

"Only when you're not looking."

He paused for a moment. "How'd you know about the elephants?"

"Yeah, bud. What's the deal with that? You really don't like to see elephants suffering, huh?"

His stare raised my small hairs, something very few people could do.

I jerked my head toward the house, seeing Darius hadn't just recovered but was already dressed and pristine and waiting for us behind the bar. Emery sat in a chair with his ankle resting on his knee, watching as Penny lazily swam through the water. They'd laid the power-siphoning spell for me and then gone about their leisure time. How nice for them.

"You mentioned that elephants were your favorite animal," I said, "and you tensed for a fraction of a second, so I thought I might play off that. I had no idea you'd go full-scale soupy about it."

"Soupy?"

"Yeah, you know..." I sagged my shoulders, slumped forward, and pouted.

"No. It is not clear."

"It affected you, basically."

"Would've been easier just to say that at the get-go."

"And miss out on a colorful explanation?" I grinned at him as we climbed the steps leading up to the pool area. I stopped there and turned toward the ocean, breathing in the warm, salty air and taking in the lovely view, knowing it looked even better in the day, the clear turquoise waters sitting beneath the royal-blue sky. "I literally want for nothing right now. Through Darius, I have all the money I could ever possibly need. I have a life of luxury. I have love and support. Most people would find this a dream come true."

"The struggle of life defines you. You are not a pampered pet; you are a savage hunter. You were born to it. You were bred for it. You yearn to throw off the robes of secrecy and reach for your destiny."

Here he went again, with his visions of grandeur. I didn't bother arguing. He never seemed to hear me when I said that my sole desire was to go home to my comfortable house in New Orleans, take up my old job of bounty hunting, and chase some shifters around for sport. I missed taking pleasure in the little things, like trying to force the overly loud were-yeti to call me ma'am, just for funsies, and checking in with my neighbors, a surly crew who would kill for me. Not that my friends wouldn't kill for me—they had—but it didn't mean as much in the magical world. Humans digging an unmarked grave meant bros for life. Or...bras, in this case, since I was a chick.

"You cannot hide here forever," Cahal finished.

"I know. The plan is to hide until I am better acquainted with my magic. Which is really coming along, thanks to you. It's lucky for me you saw my father training one of his heirs." Not so lucky for my half-brother, though. His other half was human, and he'd died a miserable death in the Underworld.

"You asked about the elephants." He fell silent for a while. "They are my favorite, yes, though my pain in seeing their death only...makes me soupy—"

"There you go. Now you're getting it."

"—because of my relationship with you."

"I'm not following."

"That is because you are incredibly impatient, and I have not yet explained." His *look* suggested violence, and since I wanted to hear this, I pursed my lips in a show of silence. No baiting the druid when I wanted info. I'd learned the hard way. "I knew the last heir, as I've said. Not terribly well, but well enough that I was invited to watch him blossom under Lucifer's care in the Dark Kingdom—"

"Wait." I turned and put the edge of my hand against his arm to stop him. "*You* were in the Dark Kingdom?"

"Yes."

"You got past the fog?"

"This was before the treaty your father was backed into by the elves. There was no fog. Any creature could come and go as they pleased, enjoying the sights, as Lucifer intended."

"The treaty…" My perfect recall system, something I'd gained from my bond to Darius, brought up what he was talking about. Darius had been schooling me on all the politics—stuff I didn't really want to know but probably should learn just in case. They were long, boring lectures only made bearable because of the frequent breaks he took to pleasure me. "Right, right. Lucifer tried to carve out a space in the Realm for his son, who was deteriorating in the Underworld because of his human side—he didn't have the lineage of the gods like I do. The elves denied him. If Lucifer's son had wanted to simply live in the Realm, under their rule, that would've been fine—or so the records say—but Lucifer wanted to create his own territory in the Realm. They tried to kick him out, he decided he'd just take their throne, and after a long, bloody battle, the elves forced him to return down below and his son stupidly followed. The son died, Lucifer was pissed, but the treaty held. What about the lack of oxygen, though? How'd you deal with that?"

"Again, that wasn't an issue at the time. Now, however…" He paused. "I am god-touched, as you know." Something he didn't often speak of because it would make him a target for other magical people who wanted the same gifts. It was the same sort of magic Penny had stolen from a horrible little goblin we were sent to get rid of, and then shared with Emery through their bond. "My power can have a nulling effect on Lucifer's, just like Penny's spells null your magic."

"And that's why you can withstand my fire to some degree, and push away my walls."

"Unless you correctly apply your power, yes. The fog and air weren't a problem at that time, and now I can successfully walk through his fog and breathe in the inner court of the Dark Kingdom, even though his spells mask the air. He cannot use magic to deny me access—"

"Wait, wait…" My hand was back against his arm. "They *mask* the air? There is actually air in the center of the kingdom?"

"He does not live in a vacuum-sealed bubble. Of course there is air."

"I hear you—I realize that you are calling me dense—but seriously, how was I supposed to know that? Physics in homeschool didn't cover the Underworld." I blew out a breath. "Wow. That's a shocker. So wait…Penny and Emery can get into the Underworld since they have the god-touched magic?"

"Yes, though they shouldn't, unless you or Lucifer strip away the magical pitfalls designed to impede their kind. There are magical traps for those who don't belong that being god-touched won't totally nullify."

"Huh."

"Getting back to the point…" he said, and I curled my lips inward. "The Underworld changed the heir significantly, and not just because the magic corroded his human side. Power corrupted his mind.

"When I think back on it, I must admit that the heir started out wanting. If he were in your position now, the only thing he'd want was *more*. More riches, more luxury, more power. He'd lord his good fortune over others. In your position, he'd force your friends, the natural dual-mages, further into the vampire's employ so as to control them. Or, at least, that's the kind of person he became."

"And you were the friend he tried to force?"

"More of an acquaintance, but yes. He asked me to be his guard, and I refused. He tried to lure me with riches and power. Another refusal. The next lure was women—their version of women, at any rate. Then he tried to beguile me into a contract, which was the most laughable attempt of all. It showed his ignorance of how my kind work. And finally, he tried to force me."

"He tortured an elephant?"

Again came the *look*.

"It's not that I'm impatient," I replied, "it's that you take forever to get to the point."

"It is not your impatience that is the problem at the moment—it is your thinking capacity. There are no elephants in the Underworld."

"You've learned Darius's trick of how to pleasantly call me an idiot."

"Yes." He waited for me to frown at him before going on. "Julius trapped me for a full year, beating me every day, trying to break me and turn me to his cause."

"Wow. There goes your friendship. But, obviously, he wasn't strong enough to break you."

"No one has been strong enough to break me, though many have tried."

I widened my eyes at that. It occurred to me that I knew very little about the deadly man standing beside me, and suddenly I wanted to amend that fact, if only because it sounded more interesting than living in the lap of luxury.

"Your father, who had allowed his heir free rein in what he called 'side pursuits,' finally stepped in and commanded I be released. He did not like what his heir had turned into, I could tell, both because Julius was slightly...unhinged—"

"Just *slightly*?"

"—and because he was ineffective."

"You mean he didn't have the power to break you."

"Correct. He was an embarrassment on two levels."

"My dear old dad isn't such a good guy, I take it."

"He exists in balance. He can love and hate, lust and kill. Like you. Like me. He looked at his child the way humans look at theirs. His son was…getting soupy…"

"Nope. Missed the mark that time."

"Lucifer tried to get help for his son. He thought the Underworld was responsible for breaking Julius down. That the human side of him was too weak for the Underworld. And in some ways he was right, but as I said, I suspect power also corrupted him. Regardless, that is why Lucifer sought refuge for his son in the Realm, as any parent would."

"He also let his son torture an innocent acquaintance for a year…"

"We're not all perfect."

"Wow. I think you are out of balance, because your level of forgiveness is on par with an angel."

"I am in balance."

Shivers covered my body. I didn't want to know the darkness that clearly lurked within him.

Well…kind of didn't, and kind of did. I just didn't want it directed at me.

"Do you ever chase shifters around for sport?" I asked. He gave me a funny look, but I waved it away. "Never mind. It also should be noted that Lucifer would've rather gone to war to get what he wanted than take the obvious solution and send his son back to live in the human world."

"A parent would move heaven and earth for their child. Lucifer is no different."

I squinted, because yes, he was different. My mother had sacrificed big time to keep me safe, and Penny's mother had done the same for her. Neither of them would have turned a blind eye if we'd started torturing people in our rooms. My dear old dad would not win any awards for father of the year, and I wouldn't put it past him to torture me to bring me to heel. Clearly the practice was tolerated, and I knew for a fact that Lucifer's power had a larger range than mine. If anyone could break me, I had every reason to believe it was him.

I sighed. "We still have not covered how elephants could possibly fit into all of this, since they also do not exist in the Realm."

"*Now* your impatience is the problem. After I was released, I washed my hands of Julius. I left the Underworld and did not look back. I haven't been there since."

"You hold grudges. Got it."

"Julius showed his displeasure by mutilating the elephants that roamed freely on my Brink property and delivering them to my doorstep. I'd saved those elephants from...what we'd call poachers now. They had refuge on my estate. They were the closest thing I had to family, as alone as I am in this life. It was like mutilating a pet, in a way, but more meaningful. I grieved heavily that I was the ultimate cause of their demise."

"Hmm. So my using elephants was a pretty low blow."

"Certainly not as low as punching me in the nut sack."

"It's lower, believe me. I'll punch a dick any ol' day and twice on Sunday. I do not care. Take that as a warning. But seeing me re-kill your not-pets must have been rough. My bad."

"The memory has faded. My worry is less about seeing a fake elephant die than it is about an heir who would kill a defenseless animal out of spite. Those elephants represent my fear of what you may become."

CHAPTER 2

I BRACED MY hands on my hips. "That was quite a truth bomb. But not to worry—I don't want to lord my power over people. I'm happy living in the Brink, and even though it seems like I have everything I could possibly want, it is at the expense of my freedom. I'd prefer to be left alone and get on with my life. You're in no danger of losing not-pets. Not from me, anyway."

"What is your freedom worth? Your friends' lives? Your beloved's?"

"Darius calls me his beloved, not the other way around. I'm not nearly old enough to use that term of endearment. But no, my freedom is not worth any of those things, which is why I went down into the Underworld rather than letting my father come find me up here."

After being in Cahal's company every day for the last couple of months, I could read the subtle nuances in his blank stares. I'd just answered a question.

"Surely you knew that those rumors were about me," I said, turning and heading toward the others. It had taken a while, but my elephant question had been answered. Time to get back to being pampered in luxury. Man, my life was dull.

I couldn't even go annoy other vampires, even though this place was a sort of refuge for them. Usually they'd bring a whole host of humans and eat and bang and do whatever else vampires got up to when the boss wasn't around. Since I was being hidden here, however, the campus was closed for "renovations," something Darius did every few years anyway. It was just me, him, a druid who didn't know staring was rude, and now my mage friends. That was it. None of them would run if I chased them. What kind of sport was that?

"I could really go for a shifter bar right about now," I murmured.

Everything okay? Darius thought as I neared.

Since I had demon magic that could pluck thoughts out of people's heads (unless they knew how to shield me), we could speak telepathically, one-way radio style. The bond between us also allowed the sharing of emotion, and that seemed to provide Darius with all the guidance he needed to guess my thoughts. With anyone else, that would have made me nervous.

"Yeah. Cahal was just telling me that he worried I'd get recruited by my dad, lose my mind, and try to kill his elephants. The guy is a real downer as far as those things go."

Without further comment, Darius handed a straight whiskey in a plastic red cup over the mahogany bar. He could tell that I wasn't in the mood for crystal and ice cubes and finery. I nodded in thanks, my gaze lingering on his beautiful hazel eyes, green specks floating within them, and felt my heart squish.

I was in this majestic hideout for a reason, yes. It just wasn't the reason everyone thought.

On the surface, I had consented to this little getaway so I could learn and practice and stay away from the public eye. But in reality, I was allowing Darius to protect me in the best way he knew how. I was here for him, and for my friends, who would rush into danger to protect me. Who wouldn't listen if I told them to run to safety.

Growing up, it had been just my mom and me. We only had each other, and because she'd always feared what would happen if I entered the larger magical world, I had contented myself with learning my magic and sticking to the woods or the tiny town where we bought supplies.

She'd died when I was nineteen, and I was so shocked and shaken by the loss that I'd continued to hide what I was out of practice. But that hadn't stopped me from seeking magical work. I could've fudged the paperwork for a human job, or worked under the table somewhere. I could've earned money away from the magical world.

But instead I became a magical bounty hunter.

Hiding from danger wasn't in my blood. It just wasn't. I couldn't stay in this place forever.

I loved Darius, though, with all my blackened heart. I loved my dual-mage friends Callie and Dizzy, though I would only admit it in drunken hug-fests, and I loved my natural dual-mage friends, who managed to visit me a few times a month even though they had a Mages' Guild to help run and new recruits to train. I even strongly liked the prickly and incredibly closed-off druid who beat my ass on the regular. For them, I would stay here, out of harm's way, and out of trouble.

At least until the screws in my noggin started to come loose.

I blew out a breath, vacating the bar so Cahal could grab a drink, and plopped down on the sunless sun chair next to Emery.

"Hey," I said.

"Hey." He glanced at my red cup. "You can take the girl out of the bad neighborhood…"

"Darius hasn't figured out how to break me of my desire to slum it in this fine place."

"You're the challenge he never knew he needed."

"Something like that." I watched Cahal accept a sparkling glass of pink stuff in a crystal goblet. Pastel pink was the guy's favorite color, but he hated pastel purple. I did not get it. At least he didn't love yellow. That color made me want to punch things. "So what's happening in the world at large?"

Emery heaved a deep breath and leaned back a little. "Demons. They're cropping up—"

Darius was beside us in a moment, the speed with which he got there at odds with the slow, deliberate way he pulled a chair around, cognac gently swaying within the snifter he held.

"They're cropping up all over the country," Emery continued, and as if on a five-second delay, I felt a nasty spell hover in the air.

I grinned at the natural mage, a guy used to fighting for his life on the run. He wasn't someone to spook, at any rate.

"You're quick," I said, "but he would've had you."

"I have a bad habit of letting down my guard around him," Emery murmured.

"You must know that I wouldn't harm you," Darius said, unperturbed, as he sat beside me. He took a sip of his drink, something he only allowed himself to do if he knew I would be on hand to give him blood should he need it.

I shivered with the memories of how pleasant it was to be his blood donor.

"There are never any certainties with a vampire," Emery returned, and he had a point.

"Who's sending the demons?" I asked, watching Penny do laps in the pool. Her slinky little bikini had likely been picked out by Marie, Penny's biggest fan and Darius's very fashionable vampire child.

"Yeah, that's the question." Emery rubbed his nose. "They're being brought up by different summoners. Some of the circles are simple, and others are ancient in design. Dizzy is studying those with great interest. He knows how they work, but he's getting more info on the details and the time period they were in vogue. That should help us trace the creator."

It's Ja, Darius thought, referring to the extreme elder vampire Penny had unintentionally awoken. *She is using those demons as a distraction, as protection, and as trusted workers. She has illegally bonded two that I know of, neither of which have been able to get her through the fog barrier in the Underworld.*

Bonding with demons was pretty gross if you asked me—I'd much rather fight them—but then, she *was* a vampire. Different set of *ew* factors, I guessed.

"Does anyone else know?" I asked him, purposely keeping my words vague. Emery shouldn't want to piece this together, something he clearly realized from the way he entwined his fingers over his stomach and let his gaze drift away. It was wise to stay away from vampire politics. I would've if I could've, but my bond with Darius meant I had no choice but to be involved.

No. Not even Vlad, I don't think. I wonder if she purposely revealed her hand to me. She has a grasp on politics and survival the likes of which I have never seen. Her experience is clear, and it's just as clear she is jumping back into the thick of it. She has a plan, but I do not know what that is.

"So two types of circles calling demons?" I asked.

"A lot of different circles, actually," Emery said, rejoining the conversation. "All power levels, which suggests several different mages, witches, humans—whoever—are doing the calling. Probably at the behest of Vlad. Other than the ancient circles, nothing really distinguishes them. A few of the demons have been called to distract shifters from changing parties, but most of them seem to be…" Emery glanced at me.

"Trying to goad me back into the world of the living?" I finished. "Trying to make me out myself to the demons?"

His nod was so slight that I wondered if he'd meant to nod at all. He knew this was a sticking point with Darius.

Sure enough, I felt a flash of anger through our bond.

Darius and Vlad had always maintained a respectful distance from each other when it came to their professional endeavors. As a courtesy, they did not step on each other's toes. There were two reasons for that, one being that Vlad had made Darius. There was a connection there, even though vampires who had reached elder status no longer had to offer their maker a percentage of their income or any sort of fealty.

The second reason had to do with the type of vampires they were. Making it to elder status was no small feat. It required a cunning individual who could "play the game" through the ages and adapt with the times. It required a ruthless sort of mind backed by a great team. Vlad and Darius both had this, and they'd always known better than to go up against each other. Until now.

Apparently, I was motivation enough for Vlad to cross the line.

Well, more to the point, *my father* was motivation enough. Vlad wanted Lucifer's favor. He wanted him in his corner when he tried to overthrow the elves.

He was absolutely stepping on Darius's toes, and it had not gone unnoticed. The only thing was that I didn't know what Darius planned to do about it. I had somehow given him back his humanity, and he was loath to actively go against his maker, a sentiment Vlad didn't share regarding his child. Darius was between a proverbial rock and a hard place.

I planned to let him sort it out himself. Vampire politics were no fun. The little I knew gave me a headache.

"He has been trying to find where I've stashed you." Darius calmly sipped his drink. "If not for the natural dual-mages' magical concealment"—he nodded at Emery, giving his thanks—"he would've already found us."

"That must really piss him off." I pushed up with the intent to get more whiskey.

Darius was up in a flash and reaching for my cup. Emery flinched.

I laughed this time. "Still too slow, bro. So. Some of these demons are being called by Vlad and his minions, others are called by...this other being." I bit my lip to keep from mentioning Ja's name. "But you said there are probably human and mage summoners, too. Do you think Vlad and the other ones are controlling them all, or are there more people behind this?"

"It's likely Vlad," Emery said, "though we have limited proof. The types of demons are...mostly the same." I caught his slight pause. "They are being called at inopportune times, though, and for that you need someone who can go out in the sun. Vlad has a lot of people on the payroll—getting someone to do his bidding wouldn't be a problem. Though a few have been...stronger than the others."

"How much stronger?" I asked.

"Quite a bit," he replied. "And seemingly without the agenda as the others. Not inclined to cause mischief, but more to look around, we think."

"Look around?" I asked.

Emery stared at Penny. Cahal shifted where he stood off to the side.

"Ah," I said, really good at reading these people at this point. "Daddy is making house calls, only he doesn't know which house to visit, so he's sending his minions to search for clues."

"We don't know for sure," Emery admitted. "We've had some powerful demons pop up from rudimentary circles. It's as if they've pushed the intended demon out of the way and hitched a ride to the surface. Not even the ancient circles could call demons of this magnitude. Not on purpose. We have no proof, but while the powerful ones have popped up everywhere, there are higher concentrations in Seattle, New Orleans...your old neighborhood..."

I accepted my refilled cup from Darius. "You mean my *current* neighborhood, with the house that I very much still own and live in? I *will* go back there."

"You will have no need of such a—"

I held up a finger for Darius. "Don't start."

"If you emerge—"

I swung my hand to stop Cahal. "You either. It is my home, I love it, and I will go back there. End of story."

Silence fell over us.

Until Penny got out of the pool. "What'd I miss?"

"Nothing." I waved her away. "Vlad being a pest, demons hitching rides—the usual."

"Oh yeah." Penny grabbed a towel and wrapped it around herself. Emery jumped up and offered her his chair, circling around the pool to pull another one over. She gave him a dopey smile usually reserved for lovesick lambs before sinking into it, her hair in a wet and twisted ponytail. "The latest ones coming up are hard to kill. Emery and I helped take out some of the ones in Seattle. It's pretty strange. If the shifters don't have some of their more powerful pack members on the case, or help from another powerful magical creature, like mages or fae, then those suckers just have a look around, mind their business, and bugger off. They act differently than the ones summoned by Vlad's people and whoever's responsible for the ancient circles—which is probably Ja, because that vampire seems to have a thing for me. I cannot shake her."

Darius stiffened. Clearly that was information he hadn't been given. Emery's grimace said he would've liked to keep it under wraps, probably to use as currency with Darius, but Penny had a habit of messing up everyone's plans. I liked her more for it.

"They aren't in the area to fight," Penny said. "Seems like they're playing detective or something."

"Again, we have no proof," Emery said.

I laughed. "Give it up, Emery. She's giving away all your secrets. Penny picks up on magical intent, and she can tell those demons are not after violence, like the others. They're looking for me."

"But not finding you," Darius said.

"They won't find you here unless they capture Emery and me and torture the information out of us." Penny looked around.

Darius instantly rose. "Forgive me. What would you like to drink?"

"Oh. Just a—"

"Shot of tequila," I said quickly.

Her dark look made me grin. I hated that she couldn't stay all the time. She really was a great distraction.

"Sparkling water," she said to Darius.

"She means Mexican sparkling water. In other words, a shot of tequila. With a worm," I added.

She leveled a finger at me, but it wasn't her middle one, sadly. She probably wanted it to be, though. "Number one, that's not even accurate, and number two, I am not going to get drunk this time, so don't even try."

She most definitely was going to get drunk. I loved drunk Penny, mostly because of how worried Emery got that she'd tango with me and do something crazy. The unpredictability was a hoot.

But seriously, what I wouldn't give for a shifter bar. Drunk Penny and a bunch of meathead shifters trying to throw their weight around, only to end up running for their lives from yours truly. That could cure anyone's boredom.

"I doubt a demon could capture either of you," Darius said, and delivered a sparkling water, the traitor, before sitting down again.

"Even if they did, they couldn't crack me." Ferocity rang in Emery's voice.

"Sorry, Reagan, but they might crack me." Penny's large blue eyes looked at me sorrowfully. "I'm not as tough as Emery."

I waved her away. "I wouldn't expect you to try. If someone grabbed you, including Lucifer, I'd show up myself and rip you free. Don't worry about it."

"The time will come when you will tire of hiding—"

"Nope." I held up a finger to Cahal. "Still on a timeout with all of that. Not now, bub. We're having a nice time, just now, trying to talk Penny into drinking too much and doing something crazy."

She shook her head adamantly and clutched her water with both hands.

"If you will excuse me." Darius rose gracefully, and I watched the play of muscle under his black button-down shirt, his pecs popping and his shoulders straining the fabric. "I will put something on for dinner."

I smiled devilishly at Emery. "Just watch. He'll put on something that Penny absolutely loves so that she'll forget to keep the rest of your secrets."

CHAPTER 3

"**S**ORRY," PENNY SAID to Emery. They sat on a love seat in the grand ballroom, next to a little table holding their drinks. Darius spun Reagan around the dance floor, their fluidity and grace effortless, their moves incredible. Reagan's hips sashayed like they had a mind of their own, and Darius's shoulders shifted and flexed as he led her in a series of intricate steps. Both were dressed to the nines, Reagan in a low-cut, sparkly dress that accentuated her curves and showed off her muscular legs and butt, and Darius in a pristine, tailored tux showing off his stellar physique. Reagan had even ditched her army boots for small, dainty heels she turned up with various dance steps. They were both knockouts in their own right, and it was hard to tear one's eyes away from them when they were together, especially with their mastery on the dance floor.

"I cannot believe Reagan learned to dance like this in a couple of months. Like...that's crazy," Penny murmured.

"I can't believe Darius got her to dress up. I almost

don't recognize her," Emery responded. "Actually, if I didn't know it was definitely her, I don't think I *would* recognize her. She had help with the dancing, though."

"I know, but even with Darius teaching me, I wouldn't be able to pick it up that fast. Not even remotely."

"I mean, she has that perfect recall." He glanced at Penny. "She's always been athletic, too. That probably helped."

She smiled up at him. "Does it almost make you want to bond a vampire?"

"No."

She laughed and slipped her hand onto his thigh, hoping he didn't immediately fling it off. It wasn't like him to do something like that, but still, she deserved it. Darius had made this incredible *coq au vin* paired perfectly with some sort of red wine she still needed to get the name of—she'd barely been able to think with how delicious it had been. On her best day, she'd never cooked a meal like that.

Then, the wine flowing freely, the delicious flavors exploding in Penny's mouth, Darius had started peppering innocuous little questions into the conversation. His interest always seemed polite and not obtrusive, but Emery's hand would suddenly tighten on her knee, and she'd have to rein herself in from spilling mage business. Or her personal business. Or whatever else Emery didn't think vampires should stick their noses into. She knew Emery always worried that Darius would find a way to strengthen his hold over them, and considering Reagan agreed with him, and had given her *that look* over dinner, she'd obviously spoken too freely.

"I'm really sorry, Emery," she said again, softer this time.

He glanced down at her before slinging his big arm around her shoulders and pulling her close. "Were you apologizing to me for something specific a moment ago?" He chuckled and kissed her head. "I thought that was random."

It was true: she did just randomly apologize for things these days. But honestly, there were so many people around all the time lately, what with the endless training and meetings required to organize and structure the new Mages' Guild, that it seemed she was always running into someone. So when she bumped into someone—or even a wall or chair at this point—she apologized out of reflex. It was easier than paying attention.

"Why are you apologizing?" he asked. "You have nothing to be sorry for."

"About dinner. I didn't realize he was plying me for information, or I would've zipped my lips and just refused to talk to him. Sorry if I gave away your plans or anything."

He shook his head and squeezed her again, looking up as the music changed to a tango. Darius effortlessly altered his bearing, waiting a beat for Reagan to catch on, and then they were strutting, Darius's legs reaching between hers, and then he was turning, dipping her, his upper body following, their mouths inches apart, their passion swelling to fill the room.

"This feels like a private moment," Emery murmured, but he didn't look away.

Emery was right, it did feel like a private moment, and yet, just like him, she could not tear her eyes away. Even as the couple straightened up, Reagan's legs all but wrapped around Darius's, their middles pressed close, their gazes eating each other up, Penny found that her eyes were stuck. They were so beautiful, the way they moved together, strong and powerful and sure, perfectly synced even though one was a master and the other a pupil.

"I want to learn how to ballroom dance," she murmured.

"Yeah. Good call," Emery replied.

She laughed and snuggled closer. "It might take us a little longer to look that good, though."

"The fun is in the journey. But seriously, you didn't give away anything important. Actually, you probably helped us out. I need more information about Ja's interest in you, and I didn't want to have to trade information for it. Vlad is basically stalking Charity and her dad because he wants the warrior fae on his side. I assume Ja wants you for the same reasons, but you and I are tied together. You can't do anything huge without me helping, and the same goes for me in relation to you. So why is she so focused on you while completely ignoring me? There is a game afoot, but damned if I can figure it out. Hopefully Darius will have some ideas."

"Yeah, she creeps me out. The daily flowers wouldn't even be nice from you. It's too much. Stop killing things and then trying to decorate my table with the corpses, you know what I mean?"

His body shook as he chuckled. It was one of those times when he didn't seem to realize she was being serious. Thankfully, he knew what kinds of gifts she preferred—flowers that could be planted and power stones that seemed like they were living. Those things were much better than cut flowers, in her opinion.

"But Reagan didn't seem to think Darius should have that information," Penny said as Reagan and Darius strutted closer, the push and pull of the tango one of Penny's favorite types of ballroom dancing.

"She would've told you to shut it if you were saying something that would negatively affect you, though I'm not totally sure if that rule applies to me." He paused. "Based on the way he was talking to you, it hasn't occurred to him that I *know* you can't keep secrets, and we wouldn't have come here if there was something urgent that you couldn't share. Given his usual insightfulness, I'm guessing he's incredibly distracted. He basically just clued me in to his anxieties and vulnerabilities. That is valuable info regarding an elder vampire. I can use that to my advantage if I need to."

"But you won't."

"Unless he makes a play to trap you in some way, no. I just like assurances." His voice softened. "I told you I'd keep you out of vampire hands, Turdswallop. I mean to keep that promise, by any means necessary."

She fought a smile at the nickname, because even though it was ridiculous and embarrassing, it reminded her of when they'd first met. Of when they first fell in love.

"You've gotten really good at politics," she said. "You're almost as good as Darius."

"Survival is a strong motivator." He squeezed her again, pensive for a moment. "I think Darius is beside himself freaked out about Reagan. My guess is a lot more work is going into hiding her than we see here. He's wound pretty tightly. This isn't just a play for an asset… He *actually* loves her."

"You knew that."

He wobbled his hand. "I heard that, but all this time, I mostly thought he was playing a good game. He's an *elder*—that's their whole life, playing a good game to get what they want. But after seeing all this"—he waved at the dancers—"and our talk at dinner, and..." He shrugged. "Hard not to be a believer. Somehow, Reagan made that vampire more of a man than a beast. It should not be possible."

"Just because people have always said it isn't? By that logic, a mage, a natural mage, shouldn't do magic like a witch."

He looked down on her, the soft light of the ballroom infusing his beautiful blue eyes and softening his ruggedly handsome face. "Touché."

"What we should be thinking of is how can we get the other vampires to become real boys. And girls."

His eyes turned shrewd and drifted back up to Darius as he twirled Reagan, a classical song coming over the built-in speakers and prompting them to change things up. "Hmm."

"You're going to try to figure that out and leverage it over the vampires, aren't you?" Penny said.

"No. *We* are going to figure it out and leverage it. Remember what I said? Anything huge requires both of us. If we can figure this out, it's big enough that I might be able to wiggle out of my affiliation with Darius so we can completely stand on our own."

Penny just shrugged. She wasn't worried about where she stood with Darius. Not with Reagan in the mix, at any rate. Reagan might enjoy shoving Penny into danger, but she had never thrust her into something she couldn't handle, not without stepping in if things went pear-shaped. Reagan would never allow Darius to corner Penny, or trap her, or hurt her.

Still, pinpointing the reason Darius had found his humanity could make a huge difference for the Brink *and* the Realm. Penny would help for that reason.

She took a deep breath and thought about getting another glass of wine.

"She seems genuinely happy," Emery said after a while, Darius pulling Reagan closer as the music slowed. "Did you want to dance, by the way? I know you didn't earlier, but—"

"And have them completely show us up? Are you kidding me?" Penny laughed. "No. I'm tired from the flight. I'm looking forward to just chilling for a couple of days. Reagan's not allowed to get up to any mischief here, so I'll get a real break. And no, she is not genuinely happy."

"No? What am I missing? She has never struck me as the type of girl to fake her emotions."

"Usually she's not. And she's not faking her love for Darius. It's just…" She shrugged. "People always think Darius is the dangerous one of their pair. They see an elder vampire and think she's the one in need of protection. That they shouldn't mess with her because of *him*. But that's not it at all."

"I'm not following."

"Do you know what would happen if someone hurt him, for example?"

"She'd kill them, I imagine."

Penny leaned away so he could see her lifted eyebrows. "Yeah. Kill them. At the *very* least. If they kidnapped him?" She whistled, which almost sounded like a raspberry. "If he got into trouble, she'd *handle it*, know what I mean? Like…dynamite and earthquakes kind of handling it. Like, burn down a town and—"

"I got it, I got it." Emery grinned.

"Don't laugh. I'm serious. She would go absolutely nuts. You think she's unhinged when she gets bored? Well…" Penny hit him with a poignant look.

He laughed and put up his hands. "She's territorial, I got it."

"She's more than territorial. Once she trusts, she's a ride-or-die kind of person. She would never let any harm come to Darius if she could help it. Me either. She'll always have my back. Our backs, I guess, though you are basically marrying into it."

"I hope to, at any rate." He rubbed his thumb across the power stone in the ring he'd given her when he proposed. The stone purred in contentment. It liked him more than Penny, she was pretty sure. "Though…ouch." He smirked.

"You know it's true. You're in her circle of protection because of me."

"So, for your sake, she'd blow the world to save me?"

"I mean…Emery, she would kidnap a person's family and hold them for ransom. She might even skin a pet or something, I don't know. She's nuts, man. Don't mess with her loved ones. She's not rational—"

He fell away from her, leaning against the arm of the sofa, laughing. "I got it, I got it."

"I know that you're laughing at me, but you have no idea. If you'd been on as many bounty hunter gigs with her as I have, you'd know that the woman has no sense of self-preservation. Literally none. She's not here to protect herself, and she's not here for vacation, like we are. She's here because the people who love her want to keep her safe, and she worries that if she leaves, she'll drag us all into danger. Then she'd have to, like, light cars on fire or something, I don't know. Burn Roger's house down, though that might just be for fun."

His big body shook with laughter next to her, and he wiped his eyes. Penny cracked a grin, because the last *had* been a joke. Reagan knew better than to mess with Roger. Hopefully.

"Did she say this?" Emery asked, finally calming down.

"She hasn't admitted it, but I see it more and more every time we visit. I think she really hates it here."

"That's crazy. This is literally paradise. I would give my left nut to own this place and hang out here whenever I felt like it."

"Ew. That's the thing, though. You'd choose when to hang out, and when to go back to your life. She doesn't have a choice, and I think it's eating away at her. I was sheltered for most of my life, and now, after getting a taste of the magical world, I would wither and die if I had to go back to that. She's never been sheltered before. Not really. She was sequestered away, but from the sounds of it, her mother exposed Reagan to plenty of danger so she could learn her magic. Her mother found a balance. And that was easy when no one knew she existed, but with so many people out there, looking for her…"

Emery sobered and leaned back toward Penny. "Yeah, I suppose."

"She can't hide here forever, Emery," Penny said quietly. "Even if so many people weren't actively trying to flush her out, Darius can't keep her hidden forever. He's good, but he's up against the literal creator of hell."

"The Underworld isn't hell—"

"Well, the demons we've been fighting sure *look* like the harbingers of hell, so excuse me for the confusion. Show me proof to the contrary, and maybe I'll believe it."

"You're right, though. Even if she wanted to stay

here forever, and you say she doesn't, Darius wouldn't be this on edge if he had everything locked down."

"I mean, even if no one finds her, sending all those demons is like tapping her on the shoulder. She knows she can help put them down. We have the situation under control right now, but the second those demons get too much for us to handle, she'll step in. You know she will."

"Will that be with dynamite and earthquakes, or will it—"

She elbowed him. "It's not funny!"

"I know, I know. I'm sorry. I've seen her in action. It's just your deadpan certainty of it that makes me laugh."

Penny had no idea why, but she let it be. He'd only try to explain, and then start laughing again when she didn't get it. She wondered if her dad, whom she was apparently most like in personality, had always been the butt of jokes when he was alive. She'd asked her mom once, but had been told, "Don't be ridiculous. No one made fun of him!" Given her tone, Penny had figured that probably meant *yes*, so she hadn't asked for specifics.

Emery wrestled the smile off his face. "It's hard to feel the gravity of the outside world in this place. Anyway, yes, I suspect you're right. You spoon-fed Darius everything we know about Vlad's plans and motivations. Hopefully it'll help him shrug off any lingering sense of duty he might have toward his maker. If those two go head to head, it'll be a test to see if the pupil has outstripped the master."

Penny's stomach twisted. Looking over, she watched Reagan glide across the dance floor. Darius often called Reagan *mon ange.* My angel. That was exactly what she looked like right then, her face tilted up to him with a serene smile, her dress sparkling and flowing around her legs, her handsome prince (of darkness) holding her hand while his other arm encircled her back. An angel…or a princess.

But then, she *was* a princess. In blood, if not by name.

Penny's gaze flicked to the druid, draped with shadows in the corner of the room, watching as well. He'd drifted away after dinner, and she hadn't realized he'd turned up here until right this moment. She wondered what part he'd play in the unfolding situation, or if he'd say goodbye when this phase was at an end and he had nothing left to teach.

She hoped he stayed. There was a calm certainty about him that put Penny at ease. When he stood sentinel, she couldn't imagine anything unwanted coming in.

Then again, he'd been hard-pressed to keep up with them in their battle with the former leaders of the

Mages' Guild. He wasn't used to Reagan's unpredictability, and even though he trained with her, it didn't
seem like he'd become accustomed to her tricks. Maybe
even he wouldn't be strong enough to save them.

Penny steeled her resolve. Whatever happened,
whatever wickedness came knocking on their proverbial
door, Penny would stand by Reagan. She would guard
Reagan's back, even if it meant plunging her soul into
hell to do it.

CHAPTER 4

A THUD PULLED me up to consciousness. The hard warmth of Darius curled around me in the soft bedding. Thick black curtains covered the windows, cinched tight. They were closed, which meant the sun was still out. A look at the clock on the nightstand confirmed it—late afternoon.

I listened for a moment. If the wards had gone off, the alarms would be blaring. Given Penny and Emery had set those wards, I was not at all concerned about a breach. It seemed far more likely that Penny had tripped over something upstairs and possibly tumbled down the stairs. You just never knew with her. She could move quickly, fight effortlessly, and really pack a kick when she wanted to, but sometimes the fight against gravity was too much for her.

Hearing nothing else, and sensing no magic, I turned within Darius's arms and slid my hands downward. I trailed my fingertips over his chest, feeling the grooves of muscle and then the hard plane leading to the fun factory. I lightly kissed his strong jaw while wrapping my fingers around his quickly hardening length.

His groan made me smile. I leaned against him, and he fell onto his back, sucking in a breath as I stroked. I slid my lips across his neck and pulled a leg over his hip, releasing my hand in favor of rubbing my slickness against him.

I made my kisses more aggressive, sucking in his warm skin as I made my way toward his mouth, sliding my hands back up his chest and curling them around the back of his neck. He responded eagerly, cupping my butt and lifting, the weight nothing to him. His tip dragged against my slit as he positioned himself and then abruptly pulled me back down.

Delicious sensation bloomed, and I pulled up to sitting, closing my eyes. I swirled my hips as I rose and fell, taking him all in and then backing off, our slow lovemaking every bit as exciting and erotic as I'd come to find our dancing. As I'd come to find all the things we did together.

Warmth seeped into my chest and I quickened my pace, crashing down onto him now, his fingers on my nub, massaging so fast that it felt like a vibrator. I moaned with the ecstasy of it and then leaned to prompt a change in position.

He rolled with me, pressing me into the mattress and settling between my thighs. I wrapped my legs around him, opening my mouth to his kiss and moaning when he swept his tongue through.

"Bite me," I breathed, digging my fingers in as I pulled them across his muscular shoulders and down his strong arms.

He kissed along my jaw, thrusting his hips rhythmically. A dull ache pressed against my artery, followed by the sharpness of teeth. In moments, his vampire's serum pumped through me, overcoming the pain and flowering into a delicious sensation, heightened by the feel of him sliding into me. He drew deeply and my stomach fluttered. I wrapped my arms around him, knowing this was the height of intimacy for a vampire and craving the closeness of it. Craving him.

He pulled away, pumping into me harder. I swung my hips up to meet him.

Crash.

I flinched and adrenaline flooded me.

"It's just Penny," Darius murmured. He kept going, not at all troubled by the interruption. Vampires weren't really worried about others seeing their intimate moments.

Sure enough, around Darius, I could just make out Penny staggering like a drunk, holding her shoulder and looking pleased with herself. She'd just busted in the top half of the unlocked double door.

"Hah! I did it, I—Oh gross. Oh no, oh gross. Oh my

God I'm so sorry—" The door wobbled, the top hinge loose, as she tried to yank it shut. Since it was listing now, it banged off the top half of the other door and bounced back. "Snap dragons, farting frogs! *Why won't it close?*"

Another attempt, another bang.

"Benedict Cumberbatch's toe ring, this stupid thing!"

Darius was off the bed in a flash, grabbing the door and pushing it into place.

"Suffering ding-dongs—no!" Penny's footsteps echoed down the hall.

Barely a second passed before Darius was again over me, pressing against my thighs. But I couldn't stop laughing. He didn't resume, instead looking down at me with twinkling eyes.

"She probably had an actual reason for being here," I said, the laughs still coming. I hugged Darius and then wiped a tear out of my eye, but the thought of her horrified expression started the laughter again. Darius moved off me for a moment so I could hold my stomach and let the laughter come. "Did you see the look in her eyes when you went to the door?" I shook with it. "She's only ever been with Emery. She is not equipped to handle a drive-by cocking."

"She did seem embarrassed, yes."

I let the laughter subside, knowing I needed to go

find out what she wanted…as soon as I finished with Darius, which I had every intention of doing after I let myself savor the memory of Penny's reaction one last time. When the laughter subsided again, I swung a leg over Darius and guided him into me.

"Hmm," I said, sitting down. His eyes were hooded. "Now, where were we?"

He cupped my breasts, and a sudden urgency overcame me. I sped up as he ran his thumbs over my budded nipples. Pleasure and feeling bombarded me. Sensations overwhelmed me. I clenched my jaw as the onslaught reached a crescendo and then pulled me under and drowned me in bliss. I shook, calling out his name. He pulled me down to him, crushing me against his chest, shaking with completion.

I lay on top of him in the aftermath, breathing deeply, his skin warm and my body sated.

"We ruined Penny's door-busting moment, do you know that?" I asked, moving to his side and resting my head on his chest.

"I think we did her a favor. Her missteps can be chalked up to distraction. Maybe next time, she'll perform the action with a little more confidence and flair."

"Kicking them in is more my thing, though. You know, because of the strength and temper. It wouldn't really suit her."

"This is true."

"She should make an entrance by opening a door slowly. Like…*really* slowly. Annoyingly slowly. That's more her speed."

I pushed off his chest and propped my head on my hand, my elbow planted on the bed beside him. He was smiling, his eyes a perfect spun honey flecked with green, sparkling with fire and mirth and intelligence. He was an incredibly handsome devil, with his high cheekbones and straight nose, his hair tousled on the pillow and his body perfectly cut with muscle.

His lips fell a little and his eyes turned serious as he studied me. He laid a hand on my cheek and traced my jaw with his thumb. "I have enjoyed our time here, *mon ange*, with just us and our friends. I feel human in an age where being human is sublime. All these years as a supernatural, my mortal life before it—this is the happiest I've ever been. It feels like I am truly *living* for the first time. I am blessed. Truly."

I leaned forward and kissed his lips. "I'm happy, too. I love you."

Despite knowing Penny wanted something and I should really go find out what, I lost myself in Darius again, relishing the peace and serenity of the moment and of this place. Because yes, this life was sublime. Darius made it that way. I could stand living it for a while longer. More than stand it, if he'd be here with me.

A WHILE LATER, with a deep inhale and a slow exhale, I leisurely walked down the halls in a flowing white dress that danced around my ankles. The neckline plunged between my breasts, revealing plenty of cleavage, and even a peek of my stomach when I bent over. The back swooped down low, too, almost to my butt. With the light around me, the thin material revealed what was underneath – a muscular female form, the same thing Penny had recently seen wrapped around Darius's thrusting body.

I stopped and tried to hold back laughter.

To complete the ensemble, I went without shoes and jewelry and left my hair down in a wild halo of sex hair. The goal: embarrass the shit out of Penny. The look would undoubtedly remind her of the big ol' dong that had suddenly appeared in front of her, pointing her way.

I bit my finger to try to hold back the guffaws. Why I found this so funny was anyone's guess, I just knew it was, and poking fun at her was one of life's greatest pleasures.

The dying sun dappled the stamped concrete patio as I came around a large square pillar to the pool area. Cahal stood off to the side next to the bar, his shadows swirling around him as though he didn't want to be seen. He was probably grumpy about something. He had *moods.*

Three people were gathered at the round stone table beyond the bar, sitting in Darius's comfortable wicker chairs. I stopped dead at the sight of the broad back of the one across from me. It stiffened noticeably, and Penny and Emery, seated across from him, looked over his shoulder, finding me.

"What are you doing here?" I blurted, unmoving.

He rose as though uncoiling from an attack-ready crouch, the kind of move powerful shifters excelled at. Pushing the chair out of the way with the scraping of wood feet against stone, he swung around, pecs popping in his overburdened white T-shirt. Good thing cotton was stretchy, though I wasn't sure why he always felt the need to put it to such extreme tests.

Penny and Emery didn't bother moving, and I didn't have the presence of mind to savor the red hue that quickly flooded Penny's cheeks. Roger always spoiled everything.

His dual-colored eyes, one blue, one a faded green, like a beat-up dollar bill, found my face. A crease formed between his brows, and his eyes flicked downward.

Gorgeous. I forgot she was so striking, he thought, and it took everything in my power to keep from mouthing off with a sarcastic comeback.

He didn't know I could pluck thoughts out of someone's cranium, and he *couldn't* know. Very, *very* few creatures could do something like that. Although Roger likely knew—or strongly suspected—that I had demon blood, he didn't know my exact lineage. Much better to keep it that way—which meant I couldn't inform him that he needed to protect his thoughts around me.

I cut off the echoes from his mind, a tactic Cahal had helped me hone.

And while I was thinking about it…

I glanced Cahal's way subtly, acting as if I wanted a drink and was checking out the bar. The druid's magic kept him in people's blind spots, and I didn't want to out the guy if he was trying to be all *seekrit*.

I opened up to his thoughts, and a beat later I heard, *I'm online.*

Apparently he thought he was a computer. Whatever worked.

"You might want to wait to start drinking," Emery said, though I was sure he knew what I was actually doing. That meant he was playing along, just like I'd done with him last night. "Though, given your joke is ruined, I can see why you'd want to start early."

I spat out a laugh despite myself. He knew why I'd dressed this way, it seemed. Penny had chosen well.

"What joke?" Penny asked, her beet-red face making me laugh harder.

...enhances her beauty. Too bad she's with that vamp...

I'd forgotten how forceful Roger's thoughts could be. He was used to broadcasting them to lead his pack, which he'd apparently taken a vacation from to be here. I hadn't realized he thought about the bang-bang train when he looked at me, though. And if I hadn't heard his thoughts, I still wouldn't know—he seemed as annoyed and impassive as ever.

I worked harder to block him out as I started forward again, tossing my hair over my shoulder. I could screw with him as easily as I could screw with Penny. One would have to fight his male reactions, and the other would be embarrassed and probably do weird things in response. Could be worse.

"Darius isn't going to be thrilled you found his hideout," I said nonchalantly as I crossed behind Penny and Emery before taking a seat on Emery's other side, letting those last rays filter through the light cream fabric flowing over my body.

To Roger's credit, his eyes did not waver from my face, and he did not tense even a little. Ironclad self-control, this one. Though I guess it helped that shifters were used to wandering around in the buff. Their animal forms didn't usually have opposable thumbs with which to carry their clothes.

"Hmm, Reagan, what's that scent?" Emery asked as I lowered into the empty seat, nearly flashing Penny as I bent.

"It's called *afternoon delight*. You should try it, Penny," I mused.

Her face practically glowed.

"Roger…" I turned his way, leaning back and clasping my fingers over my stomach. "Did you know that Penny has learned to bust in doors? She's still working up to breaking them down. It'll come."

"Blood-spattered crustaceans," Penny murmured. Through her teeth she said, "Try to be professional, *would you*? I thought you'd be sleeping."

"Don't lie, you wanted to catch us…*dancing*. Tell me, do you like to watch everyone when they *dance*, or just Darius and me?"

Emery coughed laughter into his balled-up fist. "Excuse me."

Get answers before the vampire gets here, Cahal thought.

He had a point. Darius would not be pleased to find one of the world's most powerful shifters in his secret hideout. Given they didn't trust each other at the best of times, and there were hardly any of those, I needed to get some answers before Darius lit a fire under this pile of dried leaves. Penny's torture would have to wait.

I slid my focus to Roger. "So, Roger, to what do we

owe this very dangerous intrusion?"

He cocked his head to one side, his gaze zipping from Emery back to me.

…something is…wrong…

He was cluing in to Cahal, I'd bet, his senses picking up the danger waiting thirty feet behind him.

"Yeah, I don't always wear leather. Surprise," I badgered, bringing his focus back to me. "Want a picture? Unlike the guy who owns this place, I'll show up in photographs."

His brow lowered. That did it. He did not like being on Darius's property, probably especially because it was an island and he wouldn't be able to easily escape if everything went pear-shaped. Which raised the question, why was he putting himself in this situation?

"I'll ask again, why are you here, Roger? I don't really want company out here—or didn't you pick up on that from my disappearing act?"

He glanced at the sky and then the sun, sinking into the horizon like a big, melting tangerine gumdrop. I made a mental note for the next time I trained with Cahal. "The fae sent me. As you know, they have a *Seer* like Karen…"

"Never say those words to my mother," Penny said.

The Red Prophet was a rare breed of…eccentric. Karen would be pissed if she heard anyone comparing her to the fae *Seer*. At least, she would be once she actually met the whacko with fuzzy, unbrushed red hair who sometimes hung from trees like a bat and made owl sounds. That was how I'd first "met" her.

"What about her?" Emery asked, his smile long since wilted.

"I don't want to repeat myself, so I'll wait for Durant," Roger replied, "but she said to make sure to tell you I'm the only one in the supernatural world who's been informed of your whereabouts. She gave me the company to use for the private jet and suggested the best way to bribe them into falsifying the ending point. It's parked next to Durant's jet. She said he would probably want to…speak with the pilots. I assume that means addle their thoughts."

I'll recover them and stash them in the house so they can't escape, Cahal said, and then he was gone, hurrying away from the scene. I knew he'd be back by the time Darius got out here.

"We've had a lot of demons in the Brink, popping up all over," Roger said. His tone was casual, almost conversational, but only a fool would believe it. "I thought demon hunting was kind of your thing. Yet…" He turned and looked back at the enormous residence behind him. "Durant has you living the good life, huh? Hanging up your bounty-hunting hat?"

"Yeah. He needed a pet, and I love wearing collars. A little kink goes a long way in a relationship." I gave some side-eye to Penny. "That'll be the encore. You can come back at dawn for that."

"Seriously, you really need to let that go," she groused. "I had a good reason for barging in." She shook her hand at Roger before mumbling, "I thought you'd be asleep!"

Roger snorted. "Reagan Somerset as a pet. I'd love to see the guy dumb enough to attempt that."

"You can say that again," Emery murmured.

Roger stiffened right before Darius sauntered toward us wearing khakis, a loose white button-up shirt, and loafers, his hair done just so. He looked casual and laid-back, the theme and color combo of his outfit matching mine. This wasn't to mock Penny, though. He was providing a unified front.

"Mr. Nevin." Darius came around to me as Roger rose, pushing the chair back as he had with me. This time, though, his body was all tense lines, his power pulsing and pumping around him. "To what do we owe the pleasure?"

Darius's tone and his stance—body positioned over me, hand lightly touching the back of my chair—clearly communicated a threat. He would defend me with his life and snuff out Roger if the alpha posed any sort of a risk, shifter and fae organizations be damned. He'd always been smoothly aggressive with Roger, but I'd never seen him this outwardly hostile.

I reached back and touched his forearm. "The Red Prophet sent him. Cahal is securing the pilots of the jet as we speak. You can chat with them later."

"Of course." Darius pulled out the chair next to me and gracefully lowered into it. Roger did the same.

"He has been waiting for you before telling us anything," I said as Cahal drifted back into the area, stopping by the bar again. If Roger knew, he showed no sign of it. "I assume Penny didn't want to lead him into the sun-protected areas of the house because she was worried she might find us...*dancing* again."

"That's not why," she murmured, her cheeks firing up again. "The sunset is pretty. I...didn't know how long you'd be..." She popped up. "I'll get drinks."

A smile worked at Emery's lips.

"No staff?" Roger asked in a level tone. He was piecing together the seriousness of the setup.

"As you see," Darius replied. "Now, Mr. Nevin, I assume you didn't come all this way to watch the sunset. Please, how may we assist you?"

Penny placed a pitcher of water on the table, followed by glasses. She avoided looking at me or Darius.

Roger leaned to his right and reached under his butt, pulling out a square of what looked like parchment. He placed it in the center of the table, a cracked red seal on the top.

"How much have you guys heard about what's going on in the Brink?" Roger asked.

"Darius pried a bunch out of me last night," Penny said, sitting down again. She still wouldn't look my way.

"We are well informed," Darius said.

Roger nodded, like he'd assumed that would be the case. "You know, then," he said, "that some very powerful demons have been gaining access."

"It takes some power to tear them down, yes," I replied.

"And you know there have been rumors about a woman and a vampire traversing the Underworld."

Roger's beta had asked me about that in the Realm, and my knee-jerk reaction had been to punch him in the face. It hadn't been brought up since, but clearly Roger knew about it. Roger was too far away to punch, sadly.

"We have heard, yes," Darius said smoothly.

"The rumors started circulating at about the same time Charity was coming into her own. You have probably heard that they stopped her party in the Realm, wanting to take her to the Underworld and ask her some questions."

Roger waited for a reaction and didn't get one. We had heard that, yes. We'd known who the demons were really looking for, obviously. If it had been possible to help, we would've, but by the time we heard the news, the demons were all dead.

"Word clearly never reached the Underworld that Charity was not the person they sought," he said. "They recently sent a few powerful demons to Santa Cruz, looking for her. When they found her, she was…assessed." He paused, his eyes beating into me.

"Look at you," I said with a smirk. "I didn't know you had such dramatic flair. Have you been taking classes at the junior college?"

His eyebrows lowered. "They determined that she was not the person they sought. They must've been able to feel her magic." He paused again.

I see now why you lack patience, Cahal thought, and I felt vindicated.

Roger's gaze flicked to the parchment. "Devon told me the demons didn't even try to fight back. They seemed content to be killed, although it proved a hard enough task, even with an Arcana using hellfire."

I frowned, not sure why the demons wouldn't at least have fought to get back to the Underground.

"Before they were taken down, one of them left that. It was rolled up." Roger gestured at the square.

"Excellent job keeping it in its original shape," I said, reaching for it. I showed Darius the broken seal, but he shook his head, indicating he didn't recognize the design. I wondered if Vlad would have known it. After opening it, I read the short, scratchy words out loud, my heart speeding up. "'The Great Master requests an audience with his heir. Summon her.'"

I showed Darius and then tossed it to the natural dual-mages.

"Does that mean anything to you?" Roger asked, that dual-colored gaze pinning me to the chair.

"Why don't you tell me what you know, and I will tell you what I know," I replied.

His gaze flicked to Darius. "You've been hanging out with him too long."

"Annoying, right? But it gives Penny an outlet to explore her voyeurism, so who am I to say boo?"

Penny's face closed down, her cheeks getting even redder. Teasing her just never got old.

"Obviously the heir it is talking about is Lucifer's," Roger started.

"Obviously," I replied. No sense beating around the bush. It would just eat up time.

"Lucifer had a meeting with the elves shortly after Charity came into her full power. We don't have the exact details, but it seems he was questioning the elves about the disturbance in the Underworld. The elves aren't supposed to go there without approval, just like his people aren't supposed to visit the Realm. The elves were tight-lipped about the situation, and it seems Lucifer got the idea they were trying to hide something."

"In other words, he thought they were guilty," Emery surmised.

"Yes, exactly." Roger adjusted his position. "I think the elves know less than Lucifer, other than that the woman in question isn't Charity. They want to find this other woman, though, and they aim to do it before Lucifer can."

"Why is that?" Penny asked.

"The elves won't want Lucifer meeting his heir. They won't want a possible repeat of the past," Darius said, steepling his fingers, "because this time, they might not win. Unrest in the Realm is at an all-time high. If the vampires join Lucifer, and I'm sure they've gleaned Vlad's interest in such a connection, the elves would be in a poor position."

"Except they have the warrior fae as a fighting force, newly trickling out from the Flush." Emery stared straight ahead. "And they have the shifters."

"Yes." Darius turned his attention back to Roger. "What about the shifters? Will they stand by an increasingly power-hungry and corrupt ruler in order to secure their assets?"

"As opposed to being ruled by a different power-hungry and corrupt ruler, like Vlad?" Roger shot back.

"Both good points, but let's table that for now." I dropped my hand to Darius's knee.

Roger rolled his shoulders. "The vampire does have a point. The warrior fae used to be the peacekeepers of the Realm. They offered fair, impartial judgment on the elves' rulership and prevented them from abusing power. Romulus wants to reestablish that, but he can only do that if he surpasses his mother and becomes the new ruler. He also needs to present Charity to the elf royalty. Hopefully we can re-establish a fair system in the Realm. He did mention, however, upon receiving that note…" Roger's gaze bored into mine again.

"The suspense is absolutely killing me." I lifted a finger. "Wait… No, it's boring me, not killing me."

"He is concerned that if an heir were to step forward, Lucifer's ambition would once again blossom. He also expressed a concern that the elves and vampires might both try to use the heir as a pawn to bring Lucifer to heel. Romulus had to own that the elves might seek to snuff her out to prevent any possible repetition of the past."

I was careful not to move a muscle, but there wasn't much I could do about the sweat suddenly coating my forehead. I'd largely stayed out of the Realm to help keep my magic a secret. I hadn't wanted someone figuring it out and blabbing. I hadn't considered the elves might paint a target on my back, though. Even though I now knew the history with Lucifer and the elves, it hadn't dawned on me that they might want to kill me.

My enemies were multiplying, and they were the

most powerful enemies in all the worlds.

"Did you know about that?" I asked Darius softly.

I considered the possibility, he responded.

"Time to clear the air…" Roger leaned forward onto his elbows, his stare predatory. "You are demon spawn, correct? I'd already surmised that much."

I hesitated. It felt like the future was bearing down on me. Threats were materializing, enemies circling, and I was teetering on the edge of a fate that I'd been hiding from my whole life. Regardless of how bored I'd been here, and how much I wanted to get back to my life, it seemed like an impossible feat to take that step.

Courage is not about the absence of fear, but finding the fortitude to push on in spite of it, Cahal echoed within the walls of my mind. *This is the beginning.*

I will stand by you through everything, mon coeur, Darius thought. *I will let you choose the path you take, and I will step forward with you.*

RIDE OR DIE, BITCHES! Penny thought-screamed at me. She was really good at blocking her thoughts, but communicating with them was another story.

I filled my lungs, held the air for a moment, and then let it out slowly. I met Roger's eyes. "Yep," I replied.

"You are the woman who went into the Underworld," he said. "With Darius. You got him through the fog because of the bond."

"Right again."

"You are Lucifer's daughter—his heir—and Vlad knows it, but Lucifer does not."

"Three for three. What do we have for our winner?" I did a circle in the air with my finger, but I felt anything but mirth.

"Why hasn't Vlad told Lucifer?" Roger asked, leaning back in his chair as though defeated. I had no idea what his deal was. It wasn't like this had anything to do with him. Unless he felt it his duty to deliver me to the elves and thought, correctly, that he'd die before that happened.

"At first, it had to do with me and the bond," Darius replied, curling his fingers around my hand, still resting on his thigh. "He did not want to cross me, because he did not want me to return the favor. Further, it is forbidden to endanger a lawful bond-mate, especially a bond-mate of a vampire in excellent standing, such as myself. To do so would invite scrutiny and punishment. However, if he tries to tantalize my kind with the promise of more freedom and power, of leaving our lair in the Realm behind for the golden castle, the standing of a bond-mate would likely be overlooked. The only thing stopping him at this point, I would wager, is not knowing where she is."

"He can spin the bond-mate thing easily," Emery said, leaning forward, elbows braced on the table. "If he delivers her to Lucifer, he could claim he is protecting her from the elves. He is protecting her from those who would wish her harm. Lucifer would not kill his child, and thus, she would be in no danger from him. Not of death, anyway. He could get away with it."

"Yes. Many vampires would follow him," Darius said. "He is the most powerful in our faction."

"What about Ja?" Penny asked.

Darius squinted a little. "She is physically more powerful, with more experience, and I have no doubt more cunning, but her motives aren't clear. She does not have any kind of standing at the moment. She hasn't properly inserted herself into our hierarchy."

"Where does that leave you?" Roger asked Darius.

He squeezed my hand. "My children are loyal to me. They will follow me."

"And who will you follow?"

"Reagan, naturally."

"And why is that? What play do you have with her? Do you hope to sell her to Lucifer yourself?"

"I do not expect you to understand this, dog," Darius seethed, "but she is my beloved. I have sworn to do everything in my power to protect her. I will keep her from Lucifer and from the elves as long as I am able. I will, for the first time in my very long life, pit myself against my maker."

"Since when do vampires love?" Roger asked, clearly

not buying it.

"Since when do they ejaculate during sex?" I replied, and Roger froze. "Since me. Penny can tell you—she got a peek."

"Really? *Even now?*" Penny demanded.

"Darius does love me, Roger," I said. "I can feel it through the bond, among other ways. He isn't like Vlad and the others, not anymore. Believe me."

"His ability to ejaculate isn't because of you, specifically. The magic of the Underworld allows vampires to procreate," Cahal said, and Roger started out of his shocked daze, jerking his head back to find him. "You are slow, Alpha Shifter." Clearly he'd adopted Romulus's name for Roger. "You need to be better aware of your surroundings. I have been here almost the entire time." He drifted closer. "Traveling through the Underworld would have unlocked Darius's potential to procreate. It will dry up in time if he doesn't head back. Although…maybe that isn't true, with his constant access to the heir's blood. I am not sure. But yes, vampires can be created naturally, like shifters. They can be made through intercourse and born, a process that actually makes them stronger. That's another motivation for the vampires to ally with Lucifer—the elves insisted on shutting them out of the Underworld as a condition of the treaty with Lucifer. They wanted a sort of population control, and Lucifer wasn't in a great position to barter." He glanced at Roger. "The vampires are not the only ones they sought to control. Elves could not stop the shifters' procreation, so they instead withheld the knowledge that shifters can be made in the same way as vampires—but with dragon blood instead of unicorn blood. Again, population control. The elves might hire shifters to police the vampires within the Brink, but had the vampires sworn fealty to the elves, as the shifters had done, I doubt they would have interfered. The elves care nothing for humans and the Brink. The rules are enforced to exert their control, even in places they do not reside. Why no one has questioned that is beyond me. There are a lot of these little maneuverings in the Realm. It is endlessly fascinating."

Penny held up her hand and shook her head. "Wait. Just wait." She rubbed her face. "Let me see if I am up to speed. Vampires can procreate, shifters can turn humans into their kind without procreating, dragons and unicorns are both real, and elves only created rules in the Brink to be asses to vampires?"

"Trying to add to your list of the creatures you want to see fornicating?" I asked her, waggling my eyebrows.

Her shock turned to embarrassed anger, and she balled up her fists.

"We have gotten off track," Darius said, his eyes softening as they beheld me. It seemed as though a question had been answered, and he was now seeing his future span in front of him. A future that involved me, and probably his newfound ability to procreate. A future I couldn't dwell on until I survived the present.

Everyone else stared, dumbstruck. Vampires and shifters were apparently a lot more similar than anyone had given them credit for. That wouldn't go over well.

"How are those secrets?" Penny asked, incredulous. "Like, seriously, how come no one knows all of that?"

"Vampires know about the unicorns, and they usually kill anyone who finds out," I responded, "and demons know about dragons. As for the other…"

"Shifters have short life spans in comparison to other supernatural creatures," Cahal said. "They lose much of their knowledge from one generation to the next. It is why they repeat so many of their mistakes. The life span of vampires is long, but they grow tired of living. Some die in wars, some by others of their own kind, and some let their minds go to sleep. The vampires that *do* know of what I speak, like Ja, who has been around at least as long as I have, keep it to themselves. Knowledge is power, which is likely why the elves are so wary of them."

"And you?" I asked. "Why hasn't your mind gone to sleep? Or did Penny burst in on you, too, and wake you up?"

"I did *not* burst in on Ja when—Oh, you didn't mean it that way." Penny snapped her mouth shut, her face flaming again.

I turned to her slowly, my eyebrows rising. "You dirty dog."

"I said I *didn't*! I heard her through the door, and then I walked away!"

Emery chuckled into his fist, his whole body shaking. "You're busted, Turdswallop." He laughed harder, squeezing his eyes shut.

"And when was this?" I asked, bemused.

"Let's leave poor Penny to relive the memory of her escapades in peace," Darius said in a comforting tone, but he was just roasting her in his own way. Emery doubled over laughing.

My mind will not sleep until I find her, Cahal thought, and the wispy quality gave me the impression he'd forgotten I could hear him. *Until I find my true mate.*

"I think it is time to break," Darius said, leaning forward to stand, cutting off my sight of the stoic druid. "How about some food, and then regroup." He took the demon-scrawled note and stood. "Roger, you will be staying the night. I will show you to a room."

CHAPTER 5

"SO YOU SMELL like Lucifer?" Roger asked me, shaved and showered and changed, though only into a cleaner version of his white shirt and blue jeans combo. I couldn't fault the guy—he looked good in it.

He'd met me outside by the pool, where I was soaking up the starlight and waiting for dinner. There would be no training tonight. We needed to figure out what came next, which would be easier once we had a chance to get over Cahal's truth bombs. He'd leveled the place with those.

"I don't know. I'm sure I smell similar," I replied, closing my eyes and enjoying the cool breeze on my lids.

I heard rustling and assumed he was getting comfortable. "I knew there was something about you. Not just the smell, but the sheer power you displayed at the Mages' Guild. I thought you were bred from a powerful demon. I had no idea you could be *Lucifer's* heir. Not until the Red Prophet sought me out."

"Yep."

"Unicorns? They're in the Underworld?"

"No, but I won't say more. Like I said, it's a secret the vampires will kill to protect. There are dragons in the Underworld, though. I had to fight one, and let me tell you, that was not a good time. I would advise against it. I want one, though. If I get trapped in the Underworld someday, my first order of business will be to get a dragon. Might as well make the best of it, you know?"

"You aren't going to get trapped in the Underworld," Roger growled, and I peeled an eye open.

"Oh no? You'd prefer I got kidnapped and killed by the elves, then?"

"That's what I was going to tell you before the druid...got us off track." He ran his fingers through his hair, and I wondered if he was still processing the fact that dragon blood could equip him to turn a human into a shifter. He was being very loose with all his mannerisms and reactions. It wasn't like him. "Before I saw the Red Prophet, Romulus spoke to me about the note and the potential problems of an heir. He's worried the heir—you—could become a pawn, like Charity surely would have been if she'd been allowed to fall into the wrong hands before finding her family. He also believes the heir is a part of Charity's quest." He hesitated. "That's when—"

"I know what her quest is. The fae are positive a war

is coming, and that she will stand against Vlad and Lucifer."

"Well, now…things have changed. Her most recent vision showed her standing against the elves and their army."

I frowned at him. "It flipped?"

"Twice now. The Red Prophet didn't seem surprised. She said Charity will stand between the two factions and keep them from destroying each other. Her duty is to bring order back to the Realm."

"Basically, she'll get the warrior fae to do their jobs again. What fun for an Arcana new to magic."

"Can you be serious for a moment?"

"No. Can you tell jokes?"

He sighed. "She saw you in her visions. You and the dual-mages. You stood opposite Durant. The warrior fae think you will need to stand with them for Charity to fulfill this quest. Romulus also thinks you need protection until the battle is decided, and he would like to offer it."

I kept staring at him, a little disbelieving. "He is going to stick his neck out to shield me from the entire Underworld?"

"*We* are, yes. In this, the shifters will partner with the warrior fae, as we once did. As we are trying to do now. We are the peacekeepers in the Brink—" He cut himself off before he could stumble over another of

Cahal's truth bombs. Would he now question the elves' reach into the Brink? Time would tell. He pushed on. "We will help Romulus wherever he needs it."

"And you talked to him about all of this...before you even knew who the heir was?"

"Yes. But I have a feeling they had already pieced it together. You haven't exactly been subtle. And you were pictured in the quest, so..."

"Right, right." I ran my hand over my face. "This is a lot to process. I'm not exactly great at working with people. I can't allow—"

"You will allow it." Cahal walked toward us from the side. "It is clear that the time has come." He sat on the lounge chair next to me. "You must embrace what you are. But I agree that you cannot stand alone."

"I wouldn't be alone, though. I have all my personalities to keep me company." I flicked a thumbs-up, not able to smile. I was feeling a little sick, actually. The enormity of what we were discussing, plans and quests and bodyguards—this wasn't my scene at all. I was a small-scale type of gal, with a bad attitude and a love for running at danger. Like...running directly at it. But I preferred the kind of danger I could actually see. This sort of...cloud of danger was not settling all that well.

"Look, Roger, I'm touched, but how would this even work?" I sat up a little more, preparing for Cahal to argue with me. "The fae are peacekeepers in the Realm.

Great. I get why they would want to head off an uprising and calm the elves down. But why would I want to step into the middle of that? I'm actively trying to stay out of it."

"The way will only become clear once you start walking." Cahal stood again before drifting away.

"I hate when he does that," I said, closing my eyes again.

"I have instructions to seek out the Red Prophet once you agree to leave your seclusion," Roger said. The lounge chair groaned, and I opened my eyes to find him swinging his feet around and facing me. "Listen, Reagan. I can't tell you what to do. You're a loner, and I get that. But I heard that Devon's pack put two and two together pretty damn quickly. They don't for sure know you're the heir, but they all agreed that the signs pointed to you. Darius has done a good job of hiding you so far, but he can't hide you forever. You'll be found out eventually. Wouldn't you prefer to step out of hiding on your own terms?"

I took a deep breath. "Why you? Why would the Red Prophet seek you out? And why would you want to protect me? I do nothing but annoy you."

"The elves are overreaching, and Lucifer will do the same as soon as he finds you. Romulus is right—you're powerful, but against the elves and Lucifer, you aren't strong enough. You're a pawn, and whatever motivation the elves had for giving us a role in the Brink, protecting you from magical overreach fits the job description. We'll stand with the warrior fae. We'll stand with you."

"You're making me all verklempt." I waved at my eyes as though I were trying to keep from crying.

"Now who's the bad actor?" He smirked and nudged my shoulder before getting up. "What's the deal with this island? Is it really deserted except for you guys?"

"Yeah. Darius cleared away the vamp-human orgy or whatever was going on and told everyone he needed to refresh the place. It's a seclusion spot for his children. He updates his stuff more often than is probably healthy, so no one apparently thought to question it. Except for Vlad, but Penny and Emery played with magic to keep him out of our hair."

"That's…more information than I needed." He was clearly about done with the truth bombs. "I won't get ambushed if I walk on the beach? Or change to my wolf and run?"

"I can't speak for the druid, but other than him, no. Have at it. Don't be alarmed if you spot Penny through the trees, though, watching you. She likes that sort of thing."

He huffed, smiled, and off he went.

A few moments later, Penny walked out with two

plates, followed by Emery, also with two plates.

"Speak of the devil," I murmured to myself.

"What's that?" Penny lowered where Roger had just been. "Ohh. It's warm."

"I was just telling Roger that he should watch the trees if he strips down to change because you'll probably be hiding in them, trying to get a peek. Bonus if he has a little…private time, huh? If he dances in the dark, all by himself?"

She lowered the plates at the same speed as her eyebrows. "You know I didn't mean to, right? I honestly didn't."

"Is one of those for me?" I held out my hand, and she passed me a plate topped with a large slice of quiche.

"So what do you think about all this?" Emery asked, putting one of the plates aside. It must've been for Roger.

I told them what Roger had just told me. Penny nodded as she chewed, swinging her feet onto the lounge chair and leaning back. "That's probably your best bet. With the Mages' Guild, the warrior fae, and the shifters on your side, not to mention an elder vampire, you won't be easy pickings."

"You won't be able to blend into the background anymore, though," Emery said. "You'll need to stand on your own to some degree."

"Do you know what I really need to do?" I asked.

"Oh no. I know that look in your eye," Penny said, quiche stored in her cheek like a chipmunk so she could talk. "Don't do whatever it is you're thinking about."

"The second I emerge from here, the game is on anyway, right?" I took a bite and chewed. "Vlad will hit the *go* button. He'll get to choose how and when he spills the beans about me to my dad. But instead of that…"

"No—"

"Maybe I'll simply…answer the summons. You called for me, Dad. Well? Here I am. And I'm not coming to you because of that conniving elder. That'll make Vlad scramble." I grinned. "He'll have to change his strategy at the last minute. It would trip him up for sure."

Emery was nodding while Penny was shaking her head.

"Come on." I hopped up. "Let's get ready. Time to claim my birthright."

CHAPTER 6

CRACKED STREETS AND a wayward barking dog welcomed me back to my neighborhood in the definitely-not-posh part of New Orleans. The sticky-sweet air covered me like a blanket as summer refused to step aside for fall, sweltering and unbearable. I loved it.

A forlorn whistle blew somewhere in the distance as I approached the walls of the cemetery that marked my little corner of the world. Dark clouds gathered over-head in the dying light, the greater New Orleans area currently in the cone of expectation of a tropical storm gaining strength off the coast. Having to evacuate would really put a kink in my plans. Not that I had many of those.

Roger had been quite clear that I should seek the Red Prophet first. Darius had been equally clear that I wasn't to go anywhere without him. The natural dual-mages had been adamant that I head to Callie's, where Karen was supposed to meet us. The druid...well, he helped smuggle me out from under all of their watchful gazes and then said he'd see me around. I didn't know if that was figurative or he would actually meet me later, but I didn't stick around to ask questions. Home was calling.

I meandered lazily, soaking in the sights and feel of my beloved city. I'd traveled all around the world. I'd partaken in scenic and cultural delights, sampled some of the best foods, been pampered beyond compare...but when it really came down to it, my heart was here, in this run-down part of a vibrant and alive city that crawled into your skin and lived in your heart. I couldn't imagine never coming back here. It felt so good to be home.

I turned the corner onto my street, not a worry in the world. Soon that would change, but for now, it was like old times. My thick-soled army boots thudded against the baked concrete. My leather pants hugged my legs and a snug tank top wrapped around my torso. My sword was strapped to my back, a couple of throwing knives on each ankle, my gun in a holster around my right thigh, and a new pouch resting against my left hip. This time, I had actual magic in it. No empty casings for me anymore. In the past, when I was hiding my abilities, I used to smash empty casings against my sword, mutter curse words, and pass them off as spells. No more. I no longer had to pretend to be something I wasn't. This time, if something came at me, I'd use my magic, and blast them with spells if I needed more *oomph*.

A thrill of excitement wound through me. I honestly couldn't wait. It felt like I could finally be myself. If they'd hated me before…

A solitary figure waited on the cemetery side of the street. He was lingering in front of one of the cemetery entrances, directly across from my house.

I stopped dead.

My house…

Confused, I looked back the way I'd come. Then further up the street. Then back at the figure I recognized as Smokey, thin and slightly hunched, old and grizzled, human but keeping watch over the supernatural.

Looking back at my house, I crossed the street, my eyebrows lowered.

No-Good Mikey sat a handful of doors away, using someone's stairs as a seat, clearly unconcerned with how they felt about trespassers. Although he was in his early thirties, his dark face was lined with the stresses of hard living. He wasn't a crook, but he wasn't totally straight, either. Like all of us. He didn't have much, like most of us (*ahem*), but he made the most of it. This wasn't a neighborhood for riches or extravagance. It was a neighborhood where most people lived paycheck to paycheck and hoped they had enough to cover rent.

Obviously Darius had changed my stars, but this life was etched into my bones. I belonged here in a way I would never belong on that beautiful tropical island.

"You're back," he said without preamble. "Been a long time."

"A couple months. What's…" I put my hands on my hips, facing my house. "What's new?"

"Around here? A lot and nothing."

"Yeah. Regarding *a lot*…"

"I take it the rich dude did it behind your back?"

"Like usual, yeah." I rubbed my eyes, shook my head, and turned away. "That fucking vampire."

Mikey stood. "I got used to not hearing shit like that while you were gone."

Mikey was human, knew the supernatural existed because of me, and hated anything to do with it. He'd prefer no one mentioned it. He was uncomfortable often. It was hard to be in even the periphery of my life without getting splashed with any of the weird seeping out.

He fell in beside me, topping my height by half a foot. "Been anywhere I'd be jealous of?" he asked.

"It's not like you to make small talk."

"Yeah. It's boring as shit around here lately. I don't gotta police nothing. It's like some sort of ritzy neighborhood at this point."

I looked around at the weed-choked yards, the peeling paint, the broken-down rocking chairs that wouldn't hold a cat, and the old, dented cars that lined the streets. "Yeah. I see what you mean," I said sarcastically.

"You'll see."

"Super."

Smokey crossed the street as we approached my house, and I veered off the curb to get a better view of it.

My…much larger…house.

My…much taller…house.

"What the fuck?" I breathed, looking up at the two-story structure with brick columns supporting the redone front porch, equipped with four new rocking chairs. The planter boxes at the base of the house, in front of the plush green grass, had been replanted with different colored flowers to match the new paint, a bluish gray with white trim. "Why?"

A figure shambled out of the shadows on the right side, the leaves of the bushes getting caught in her tangled fire-engine-red hair. The reaching branches pulled taut, but she kept walking, ripping the leaves free, now stuck in her huge mop of hair. She paused in the center of my lawn, crouching and stooping and leaning to one side with her head cocked like a crow, staring at me.

"Red Prophet," I said dryly. "How nice to see you again."

"I'd say you picked up some manners off that rich boyfriend of yours," Mikey said, stepping off the curb to join me in the street, away from the Red Prophet, "but it's pretty clear you don't mean it."

"Caught that, did you? I was laying it on pretty thick."

"She's been here for the last week, solid," Mikey said, crossing his arms over his chest.

"Hi, Reagan. Nice to have you back," Smokey said, stopping beside me and nodding.

"Hey, Smokey." I crossed my arms to match Mikey. "I think I know the answer, but you didn't think to remove her?"

"At first, yeah. Pointed a gun at her and everything." Mikey spat to the side. "She started spouting off all this shit that she no way coulda known. No way coulda known. Personal shit, about my past 'n' shit."

"It occurs to me how much I missed punctuating sentences with swearing," I murmured, and this time it wasn't sarcasm. I liked the color Mikey could bring to any conversation. The menace.

"Then she started talking about my future, and I got the fuck outta there." Mikey shook his head and spat again. He clearly had not handled the situation well. "I know I was supposed to look after your place, but fuck, there are limits. She is over that limit."

"She's harmless if you leave her alone," Smokey

said, and a certain gravity rang in his voice.

"What happened?" I asked, back to looking over the completely redone house. It looked like they'd torn down the old one, which had already been completely remodeled, and started over. How the hell had they gotten it done so fast? I'd only been away for two months this time.

"She looks like she escaped an old folks' home and is suffering from dementia," Mikey said. "Add to that the gold she was wearing around her neck, and the bright orange clutch she was carrying, which looked stuffed full, and she was a target to be mugged. Easy pickin's."

"First of all, you know what a clutch is?"

"Yeah. What am I, stupid?"

"I took you for a man who doesn't carry purses, actually, but sure. Stupid works," I said. He huffed out a laugh. "Also, let's rewind. You tried to mug her?"

"Are you out of your fucking mind *did I try to mug her*?" Mikey stepped back and gave me an incredulous look. "No, I did not try to fucking mug her. I tried to scare her off your property, realized she was one of *your type*, and made myself scarce. But I saw her ambling down the street like her back was broken or some shit— it's not, by the way. That question has been answered. Then I saw three guys approach her. I put a little gas in my step, heading down to sort it out—she's a whack job, but that doesn't mean she needs to be harassed in my neighborhood. Those dudes should've known better than that. Easy pickin's or not, this is my spot."

I nodded to show I was following along. Mikey was a sort of self-appointed neighborhood watch, although he relied on vigilantism rather than engaging with the cops.

"One guy took that bright orange clutch and another pushed her back against the wall and tried to get at her necklaces." Mikey shook his head. "It happened fast, so I'm not sure of the details, but fuck. In a split second, she had one guy on the ground, unconscious. Another dude was whirled around in some sort of kung fu move and had his dumb brain busted on the wall. The third dude, with the clutch, had already opened it, and he was just staring down into it like his brain had broken. She watched him, like she'd planned for that. So I stopped, because I did not want to know what was in that clutch. The dude kinda shook himself out of it, dropped the clutch, and then tried to turn and run. That old dame was so fucking fast..." Mikey took a step back even though the Red Prophet, still hunched on my front lawn, hadn't moved forward. "She ran so damn fast. Had that guy on the ground on his back in two shakes. Sat on his chest. Then held him there and started jabbering something at him, I don't know what. I figured she could handle it and got scarce again."

"We have zero crime," Smokey said reverently.

"Zero fucking crime," Mikey agreed. "That old dame has scared everyone off. We don't even get the bad sort of fake witches 'n' shit in the cemetery anymore. She has them scared off, too."

"You know what they say about appearances," the Red Prophet said, her voice musical. "It is a weapon like no other."

"That's not what they say." I sighed and started forward.

"She is truly insightful," Smokey said, keeping step. "I enjoy having her around. She even talked Mikey into borrowing money from me and putting it into the stock market."

"What did I tell you about talking about my business?" Mikey growled.

"One good turn deserves another," the Red Prophet said.

I pointed at her as I passed by. "Cut out the crazy. I'm not in the mood. What's your plan? Are you going to force your way in, or do you plan on loitering?"

"Penny *erected* the spell, among other things—"

"She's dirty, too," Mikey cut in. He still stood on the street, and Smokey had taken up a position on the sidewalk. "I forgot to mention that. She is rough as hell with the sexual innuendos."

"I know all about the ward. I can feel it. Are you

coming in or not?" I stopped at the top of my completely redone porch steps. "Roger said I was supposed to
meet you before coming home. I decided not to."

"Correction—you decided *to*, and chose your preferred location," the Red Prophet replied.

"No." I put out my hand and wasn't surprised when
she clambered up the steps to take it. I pulled her
through the ward. If she left, she'd need my help (or
Penny's or Emery's) to get back in. If I took a blood
offering from her, she'd be able to get in by herself. I did
not want a blood offering.

"Talk to you later." Mikey turned toward the end of
the street as Smokey drifted back toward the cemetery.
"And don't worry if you don't see Mince," Mikey called
over his shoulder. "He's scared of that woman and
admits it freely."

"Well, congratulations," I told her as I opened the
front door. There was no need to lock it with the ward
in place. "You've done what no one else has been able to
do."

"Scare your friend?"

"No. Make the neighborhood crime-free. Maybe I
can go back to parking Darius's cars out front again."
The living room was roomier, longer, and equipped
with more furniture. The kitchen was a different shape,
too, and they'd added a dining room down the hall. A
quick look revealed a huge library had taken the place of

the rooms at the back of the house, and a stairway led up to the second floor, where the bedrooms had presumably been moved.

I stopped at the back door and looked out the window. The house behind me was gone. Darius had clearly bought out the shotgun-toting neighbor and extended the backyard into his lot, equipped with a training area and a lovely little oasis with what looked like a koi pond.

Shaking my head, I backtracked to the stairs and looked up. Then aimed for the kitchen. I wasn't in the mood to see the new addition. That sonuvabitch hadn't mentioned any of this. He hadn't even hinted. He certainly hadn't asked.

"They made it bigger." The Red Prophet put up a gnarled finger from her position by the front door.

"Yeah, no shit."

"You'll need the space."

"Great." I checked my supplies. A little light—the vampires who came every night and stocked my fridge and pantry, not to mention cleaned my house and did my laundry, clearly hadn't expected me back. Still, they'd left me with enough staples to get by.

I grabbed the bottle of whiskey.

"Want a drink?" I asked the Red Prophet.

"Sure. Have any Fireball?"

I paused in taking down glasses, then couldn't help

but grin. "Of course."

After serving us each a generous pour, I brought the glasses over to the same kitchen table I'd had before, some things clearly having survived the rebuild. I fell into one of the chairs, and the Red Prophet sat down opposite me and reached for her glass.

"So," she said.

"So," I repeated. "I was supposed to meet with you."

"Yes. Tomorrow you will finally take me to meet my nemesis. Then we will plan your trip into the Realm."

I drained my glass, then got up, brought the bottle back to the table, and poured myself a generous refill.

"The Realm?" I asked.

"Yes. Your journey will converge with the Third's for a time. You need the Second's help. The Second also needs your help, though he doesn't realize it yet. The Third cannot finish her quest without you, though they don't know that yet. You have always been the catalyst."

"Cool." I leaned back, learning the new look of home. "You're definitely a *Seer,* right?"

"Yes. Definitely. Also, I am becoming something of a 'crackhead,' I am told. As I work through all the drugs this new land has to offer, I have been given that label by the people of this neighborhood, though I didn't much like that strain of cocaine. Still, it's nice to be remembered."

"Sure. And you learn things through your craft that

you don't share with others? Because if you told Romulus and Charity all of this, it would probably help them out."

"I reveal that which needs to be revealed, when it needs to be revealed, so that it will do the most good. If you give away all the answers, no one will learn the lessons of the journey."

"Yet you told Smokey and Mikey to invest in the stock market?"

"That's different. They've learned all they need to about how hard and unfair life is. I figured it was time they got a payoff, and since this world didn't intend to settle the debt, I figured I'd step in. I believe they call that insider trading here."

"No, that's something else, and it isn't magical."

"I learned of this sure bet while checking out some of the backyards in the Garden District. Very pretty, that area of town. It reminds me of a blue version of the Flush. Anyway, someone there will go to prison for the part he has played in tampering with the stock market, but No-Good Mikey and Smokey will just get rich. After a short investigation of their windfall, of course. They'll hardly be affected. The rewards will be plentiful for their brief time of pain."

I stared at her for a moment, then couldn't help laughing. I doubted Mikey would've touched anything to do with the stock market if it meant he'd have the cops up in his business. Lessons of the journey, definitely. Mikey would probably never play the stock market again.

"I have something to do before I hitch a ride on Charity's journey." I finished the second glass of whiskey, thought about a third, and then pushed the bottle away. "I need to answer a summons."

"Ah. Yes, I heard about that. You will answer a summons, all right, though probably not in the way you intended."

"*Ugh!*" I held up my hand. "Don't say any more. I don't want to know. I'm not real keen on your line of work."

"I know. That's what makes you so fun."

"A real hoot, yeah." I put my hands on the table and pushed up to standing. Maybe it would be smart to poke her for details, but if I knew answering the summons, or attempting to, would end with me getting kidnapped by a bunch of demons, I didn't think I'd have the courage to keep trucking. I wasn't interested in the future—I'd deal with it when it became the present. "Tell the natural dual-mages, if they come over, that I am not to be woken up or it will result in some sort of catastrophe."

"Will do."

"See you later."

"Okay."

A good host would've asked her to stay and shown her to an empty room, but that would require an equally good and respectful guest. It was clear this woman beat a drum to her own tune, often interrupting a currently in-progress jam session to do so. She'd figure things out.

I let myself into the master bedroom, which was in the same position it had been, only now on the second floor. The furniture hadn't changed much either, although the space was larger and there was more of it. I breathed a sigh and headed to the shower. That finished, I slipped into something slinky and slid between the covers. Before I closed my eyes, I hesitated, and then reached for the throw-away phone I'd put on the nightstand. A phone Vlad didn't know about and couldn't trace.

He answered on the first ring.

"Reagan." I smiled at the sound of Darius's deep voice.

"Hey. I called to say sweet dreams."

His silence matched the frustration rolling through our bond. He was pissed that I'd left without him. That I was spending the following day on my own. That I had been able to so easily slip out, unnoticed (I was *so* glad that druid was on my side).

For all that, I heard his deep breath as he pushed it aside. "I will miss you today, *mon ange*. Sweet dreams and stay safe. I will see you come the evening."

"Love you."

"I love you. Stay safe."

"Yes. I heard you. I'm inside one of the best wards in the world. I'm good."

"Yes. Stay there."

I rolled my eyes and snuggled in a little more. "I'm going to get back at you for what you did to my house."

"We are even on that score."

"How do you figure?"

"That very expensive desert island you bought with my money, without telling me, has very few benefits."

I grinned. "Touché. Well, if anyone can figure out a way to make it profitable, or useable, it is you."

"Your confidence in me is inspiring," he said dryly.

I laughed and signed off with him. Before sleep pulled me under, I wondered how long it would take for demons to start invading my town again. I hoped not long. I felt like kicking a little ass.

CHAPTER 7

"**H**EY, RED." I dug my thumb into the soft spot at the edge of his jaw and just under his ear. The hard clang of a metal band spilled out of the doorway to my back, and people ambled by in the failing evening light with smiles and staggers, holding clear plastic cups with straws and lids, taking in the musical scene. Late summer in the French Quarter, my kinda jam. "Miss me?"

I'd gone against Darius's wishes and left the ward without him, but at least I had waited until he was *nearly* able to travel outside. I called that quite responsible.

Red, a dog shifter who acted as an informant for Roger's pack, let out a high-pitched squeal before clamping his mouth shut to save a little face.

I marshaled him up to standing and against the wall for no other reason than I was pretty sure he expected it.

"Re-Reagan," he stammered, his lithe frame shaking. "I didn't know you were back."

"And now you do." I let him go. "Fancy a drink?"

"You know I don't drink."

"True. Let me revise. Fancy watching me have a drink?"

"Not really," he said miserably, hunching as I grabbed his upper arm and pulled him down the sidewalk.

"What's new? What's the scuttlebutt around here?"

I stopped in front of the doorway to the shifter bar, smooth jazz flowing out of it, the opening blocked by a large guy with a unibrow and an entrancing mystery he just would not help me solve.

"Hey, Jimmy," I said, glancing at his package. "Knock up any mermaids lately? Or even just bumped uglies with them?" He went out into the gulf every year for a "knock 'em up" situation, along with all the other merfolk in the area, and it drove me mad wondering how they procreated with big fins getting in the way. They were annoyingly mute on the subject.

"Reagan." His dark-eyed gaze flitted to Red and then away. "Been a minute. Who're ya looking for now?"

"No one, actually. I'm the one people are looking for this time. What an amazing new age we live in, huh?"

Jimmy smirked and stepped to the side to admit me. "I hadn't heard you were on the watch list. Must not be

Roger looking for you."

"No, he found me. It's the vampires."

He grunted. "Steve will be happy to hear it."

"Nah. Wrong vampire. I'm still banging that one. Speaking of, when you go on your merman retreats, and you're in the water...what happens then?" I looked at his package again.

"You need to find something new to wonder about." He gestured us in as two giggly girls stopped behind us.

"If you'd just explain the dynamics of merpeople banging to me, I would be glad to find something new to wonder about." I dragged Red inside with me.

"They don't like to talk about what happens at sea," he said, yelling to be heard over the frenzied notes of the piano and short blasts of the trumpet.

"Yeah. That's why I'm obsessed. For a guy who gathers intel, you sure miss the obvious."

I didn't let go of him until we reached a few empty chairs on the far side of the bar. When I settled onto a barstool and rested my elbows on the counter, he grudgingly took a seat beside me. I knew he didn't try to run because he wanted to hear about my drama. Which was exactly why I'd searched him out. I *wanted* word to spread, and he was the best one to make sure it happened.

"Hey, Reagan, long time no see." The bartender, Trixie, stopped in front of me and braced her hands on the edge of the bar. Tattoos crawled across her breast-plate and down her arms. A ring on her left nostril caught the light.

"Hey Trix. Gimme a hurricane, please. Make it a strong one. I can't have that many."

"Oh no?" She turned, reached down, and pulled open a fridge door before extracting a chilled pint glass. "What's the occasion?"

"I'm expecting an attack and don't want to be too drunk to thwart it."

Red perked up, as I'd expected he would.

"You guys seen any demons around this place?" I asked as she started pouring ingredients into a metal shaker.

Red's expression closed down. "I thought you said Roger found you…"

"Yes, Red, I know there have been demons. All kinds. I'm wondering about *lately*. As in the last couple of days." I put up my hands. "I'll be helping this time. I'm not bounty hunting right now."

"They took out a few yesterday," Trixie said before pausing to shake the mixture over her shoulder. "Marcus's pack took them out, no problem."

"So they weren't that strong, then?" I asked.

Trixie loaded the pint glass with ice before pouring in the contents of the shaker. "No. Not like the ones a week ago, right, Red? They couldn't kill those."

"Where were those located?"

Trixie pushed the drink across the bar before knocking on the wood, indicating she'd buy me that one. I pulled out a five for a tip. It was Darius's money—might as well spread the wealth.

"Outside of town a ways," Red said, watching me. "There've been a few high-powered ones. Garden District, a couple of cemeteries, out by your house once. We don't have the resources to really take them down, now that Steve and Cole joined that pack in Santa Cruz. Those demons don't do much, though. Not like the lesser-powered ones. Those cause trouble. Try to kill people."

I nodded and captured the straw between my lips. The alcohol made me grimace. "Good one, Trixie. Strong."

"Drink like a shifter." She winked at me but didn't move away. "What do you want with the demons?"

I sucked down more of my drink. "Nothing much. Kill a few and then send a message back with the rest." Trixie's and Red's faces both creased in confusion. "Only the really powerful ones, though. I mean, I'll help kill the lesser ones, no problem. I need something to do. But I have business with the stronger variety."

"Trixie, I'm dying over here," yelled some guy with a Boston accent.

She pushed away from the bar and then turned and

headed to the waiting patrons on the other side.

"What kind of message?" Red asked, as I'd known he would.

I fished the parchment Roger had given me out of my pouch, my stomach swirling. I was about to conversationally out myself. My whole life I'd been taught to keep this one secret, no matter what. I knew what these words would set in motion. I knew what a big deal this was.

What a big deal *I* was, in the grand scheme of things.

These people all knew me as the poor girl with weird magic who didn't have any friends and had made the terrible mistake of shacking up with a vampire. I'd been an outcast since they'd met me. A troublemaker. A recluse, in some senses. A nut case.

Now I was about to show my hand, and it might wow them, scare them, or make them pity me. I wasn't just a poor bounty hunter, I was a little gold nugget, and the largest powers in the worlds were vying for my attention. No biggie.

I laughed and flung the note at him. Nervousness was for ninnies.

He peeled it open and his eyes widened. "I heard about this," he murmured, his gaze sliding across the short message. He looked up at me, shocked. Then his eyes narrowed. "Where'd you get this?"

"You know where I got it."

"No, I mean, did you steal it?"

"You know that Vlad is looking for me, right?" He didn't comment, but his left eye twitched. He did, and he was connecting that knowledge to the note he held. I nodded. "He's sending demons up to lure me out of hiding." I pointed at the parchment. "That is why. Only, that didn't come from the demons Vlad's been summoning. It came from the demons my old man sent. They aren't looking for Charity, if that's what you heard. They are looking for me." I spread my hands wide and laughed. That wasn't so hard, and the blood draining from his face was totally worth it.

He froze, eyes completely rounded, staring at me.

I plucked the note out of his fingers. "Not everyone can say they got kicked around by Lucifer's daughter, eh? See? And you were so put out. Now it's a story of interest. You can tell people you helped out Lucifer's daughter all those times. Maybe someone will care. Probably not, but you can always hope."

I pushed the five-dollar bill forward and finished off my drink.

"But…wait." Red put out his hand to stop me from getting up. "Wait, wait. So…Roger knows about…this? You?"

"Yes." I spoke slowly so he'd be sure to get it. "Hence. The. Note."

"But—wait, wait." He grabbed my shoulder. "Wait, wait, wait." He squeezed his eyes shut, struggling to process the information.

I changed my mind. Telling everyone would be awesome, and I wanted to do it immediately.

I took his hand off and stood. I'd promised to head over to Callie and Dizzy's house—they were expecting me, and so was the Red Prophet, whom I'd promised to introduce to Karen. And although I'd ignored several calls from an increasingly frantic Penny because it was funny and I was an asshole, I'd texted Emery yesterday and told him to meet us there too.

Darius hadn't phoned. I was pretty sure that meant he was incredibly pissed at me for leaving the ward.

"See ya, Trix—"

"Wait, wait, *wait!*" Red pushed off the stool and stood in my way with his hands out. "Reagan, you have to think about this. You can't send a message down *there*. You can't just let *him* know you're...well, you."

"He's going to find out one way or the other." I stepped around him, then physically moved him out of the way when he stepped with me. "It'll be on my terms."

I stalked forward, pulling out my phone to call a cab. I didn't have the ride-share apps on this burner phone.

"No, but...wait." He trailed behind me like a puppy.

"Let's talk about this. You'll be in incredible danger."

"Aww, Red, that's nice. You care about me."

"Yes, I do, damn it." He grabbed my arm and pulled me around, his eyes wild. "You make my life hell, but I know why you occasionally give me the scoop. You're trying to give me Roger's ear. And it's worked. He relies on me to keep an eye on you, both for our benefit and yours. So yeah, I feel obligated to stop you from throwing yourself into incredible danger. Sue me. This is all much bigger than you, Reagan. Lucifer has beef with the elves. If you out yourself, you'll have beef with the elves. They are the most powerful beings in the worlds, and you're just one person. You need to…" He licked his lips, his eyes darting around. "I don't know. You need to work this out with Roger."

My heart squished a little. It was a weird feeling in this setting. Darius was making me soft. Or maybe I just needed to get used to allowing people into my life for a change. It had been happening slowly for a while, and now it felt like it was happening all at once.

"I am working this out with Roger, Red. It's fine. I'm going to have two *Seers* on my case, and the warrior fae will have my back." I gave him heavy pats on his bony shoulder, making him flinch with each one. "Thanks, though."

I turned toward the door.

"Okay, but…"

I slowed, but not because of him. Framed by the door and backlit by the streetlights, the new night flowing in around him, was the most handsome non-man I'd ever seen in my life. He'd come to collect the goods.

Me.

"Hey, Vlad," I said, and sauntered toward him casually. If he wanted to do this now, we'd do it now.

CHAPTER 8

"**H**ELLO, REAGAN." HE smiled that flawless smile. "So nice to see you again."

"The pleasure is all yours." I stopped in front of him. "What brings you to a shifter bar? Wait, lemme guess. Me?"

"Jimmy," Trixie called, perched at the end of the bar on the counter. Shifters were slowly getting to their feet, eyes on the newcomer.

"I apologize." Vlad glanced at Trixie. "The merman is currently indisposed. He wasn't planning on letting me in." He clucked his tongue. "Very rude. I'm afraid I had to force the issue."

"You realize how incredibly stupid that is, right?" I asked, tucking the parchment into my pouch and pulling out a casing containing a concealing spell. I'd throw it in front of the bar and have a nice little time with this meddling vampire. He no longer scared me, not in the least.

"John, Kim, get the humans out," Trixie barked.

Vlad's smile reminded me of a sharpened blade.

"I've learned some things in the Underworld—"

"You weren't in the Underworld, Vlad," I cut in. "You were loitering around the Edges. You have no idea what it's like down there."

He nodded as confused patrons were shuffled toward the door. "True. Let me rephrase. I've learned some things from the powerful demons that reside in the Underworld. Some defenses. Some offenses…"

He let the threat linger.

I matched his sly smile. This clown had no idea. He hadn't even hit up the more treacherous places along the Edges—the places Darius and I had been forced to go through to get around him. He didn't know what kind of power existed in the airless inner reaches of the kingdom. He *certainly* didn't know what sort of training I'd been doing. Darius was plenty strong, and he'd stopped being able to combat my more robust magic. I was no match for Lucifer yet, but I was more than capable of dealing with an elder vampire of Vlad's caliber.

Something I was about to show him.

I waited for the last of the humans to leave. I didn't miss the sense of anticipation in Vlad's velvety brown peepers. A squat shifter built like a brick house grabbed the door to close it. I closed a fist and let my magic swell. Claws elongated from Vlad's hands.

A hand caught the door. It swung back in with

enough force to make the shifter stagger backward. The smallest of wrinkles marred Vlad's perfect face, but he didn't turn around. I got the feeling he didn't want to take his eyes off me. Wise.

Darius strutted through the door wearing a pristine suit with gold cuff links and shoes polished to a mirror shine, his hair a stylish sort of messy. His broad shoulders swayed with his elegant movements as he passed Vlad and stopped beside me, his gaze roaming my face for just a moment before he turned and slipped his fingers into mine, making me drop the casing. Not the best approach for fighting—

Ah. That was the point. He didn't want me to publicly spank Vlad. How annoying.

"Vlad, good to see you again," Darius said, ever polite.

"Darius." Vlad inclined his head just a little. His gaze flicked to our entwined fingers. "It seems you've made a choice."

Another form came through the door, robust and burly. Roger was on the scene. One of the shifters in the bar sucked in a startled breath, and everyone went unnaturally still. The guy was a celebrity for the shifters.

His gaze lingered on me and then swept the bar as he turned and took up a position on my other side, facing Vlad.

Vlad's eyes narrowed. "Mr. Nevin. How quaint. Tell

me, do you ever take a break from your *honorable* duty?"

"My pack will stand with Reagan Somerset," Roger said, his tone rough and low. "We will stand with Lucifer's heir, against Lucifer himself, if need be. Against you."

More gasps this time. He'd just stolen my thunder, the jerk.

Vlad's eyebrow ticked upward, and his eyes sparkled as his gaze shot back to Darius. "Think very carefully, old friend," he said softly. "You are aligning yourself with shifters...against your faction. It's been a long life, Darius, and you've navigated wars, feuds, and political upheaval. You've always played the odds, just like I taught you. How do you think this choice is going to play out for you? Tensions are high between the elves and Lucifer, just like they were before, only this time the other magical creatures are restless and ready for change. They've been brutalized by the elves for far too long. The time is ripe to step in and create a better play for vampires within the Realm. With Lucifer's help, we can claim control of our destiny. I understand the closeness that comes with a bond, but you must be rational about this. She is not worth your eternal demise. *Think.*"

"The elves have taken too much power for themselves, that is true. The dynamic must be shifted so we can restore balance," Darius said, his tone low so his voice wouldn't carry. I tried not to flinch and stare at him. I had no idea he'd been thinking along those lines. "We do need a better setup within the Realm. But helping Lucifer tear it all down isn't the right way. It won't put us in power, it'll put *him* in power and us at his mercy. Your ambition has blinded you. You are walking a dangerous path, and it will lead to your destruction."

Vlad stepped forward, and now I could barely hear his words. His gaze picked up intensity. "You do not want to stand against me, *old friend.* There are forces in play that you can't even imagine."

"I don't want to stand against you, correct," Darius responded, "but you are wrong. Reagan *is* worth my eternal demise. If that means I must pit myself against my maker, so be it. If it means I must once again join forces with the shifters, fine. I will not lose her—not to Lucifer, not to the elves, and certainly not to death or captivity."

Vlad stared for a very long moment, and although his exterior remained smooth and glossy, his eyes revealed a sort of viciousness that raised my small hairs. Darius held the stare without comment. Moments ticked by.

"I will try to spare you," Vlad finally said. "She will be lost, however. It cannot be helped."

He spun and took off, so fast that it was hard to identify the details. The door slammed behind him.

Darius turned to me, anger burning just below the surface. I had every suspicion it was because I had left the ward without telling him.

"I would ask that you do not engage any vampires." His tone was even and calm, but he didn't fool me. "I need you to let me handle them."

"So…if they threaten me…" I lifted my eyebrows.

"Play defense, do not kill, and extract yourself from the situation. That is within your power."

I squinted at him. That was no fun. I could finally reveal my power, and now I wasn't supposed to use it?

If you wish to fight me on this, you will do it away from the shifters, Darius thought. *The vampires and shifters will not want to work together again. The conflict between us is old and bitter, even if it was begun by the elves. You and I will need to play mediators, and for that, I need you to withstand your desire for violence.*

He made good points, and it didn't improve my mood.

"Fine," I ground out.

A few of Roger's wayward thoughts surfaced in my mind. Cahal had taught him how to shield his thoughts when we were out on the island, and I was also suppressing them, but the enormity of the situation was bearing down on him. I felt his urgent need to get his people moving.

"So…" I pulled my hand from Darius's. "What's next?"

"Karen is waiting for us at the Bankses' house," Roger said, stepping further away. "Romulus and Charity are en route. Their plane landed, and they've all been picked up. They should get there soon after we do."

"You're really teaming up with vampires?" someone at the back of the bar asked.

Roger turned and speared the skinny guy with terrible taste in fashion with a commanding stare. *Shut up.*

That thought came through loud and clear, to both me and the kid. Everyone around Skinny Guy edged away from him, actively trying not to catch any of his *stupid*, leaving him standing there in the middle of an empty bubble of space.

"The Red Prophet was originally supposed to meet us there," Roger said, jerking his head. Darius put out his hand, and I took it, taking his hint that we should be walking and talking. The three of us headed out the door. "She's gone missing again."

"Oh, she has?" I asked, seeing Darius's black town car waiting by the curb. Jimmy sat off to the side, leaning against the building wall, a couple of people attending him. Vlad hadn't killed him, thank God. "She slept at my place last night, and she was there when I left. She's probably just out terrorizing the neighborhood."

"Romulus suspects she is on hallucinogens." Roger stopped at the curb as Darius opened my door for me.

A middle-aged woman passing by caught sight of Roger, swayed into her friend, cackled, and said, "Well, hell-*ooo*, Mr. Muscle Man." Her friend shushed her. "He's hot, though, right? I'd jump on." They both cackled this time, ambling away. The hurricanes had clearly gotten on top of them.

Roger continued as if he hadn't heard her. He probably got that a lot. "She apparently likes acid a great deal. It seems to help with her *Sight*, more so than the hallucinogens in the Flush. They think it's the chemical nature of it. They don't have anything like it in the Flush. Don't worry, though. It doesn't affect her like it does humans."

"Uh…" I put up my finger. "Are you sure about that? Have you seen how she carries on?"

A slight squinting of Roger's eyes was the only indication he gave me that he agreed.

"She'll make it there," I said. "She wants to meet her nemesis."

"Yes." The word rode Roger's sigh. "You're probably right. We've heard a lot about the nemesis situation."

"We'll meet you there." Darius ushered me into the

car and then slid in beside me.

"You're not going to offer him a ride?" I asked as Moss glanced at us in the rearview mirror. Assured we were in and ready, with a second to spare to flash me a routine scowl, he got underway.

"Our relationship will always be fragile, at best," Darius said. "He would not accept a ride from me, just as I would not accept one from him."

Silence drifted over us, filled with expectation.

"You're mad, aren't you?" I asked in a small voice, because I did love making his life hell, but I preferred to stop just shy of making him angry. Given he was incredibly hard to piss off, and often took my crazy in stride, that usually wasn't too hard.

"I had hoped you would wait for me within the ward so Vlad wouldn't see an opportunity to act." His even voice didn't fool me, especially since I could feel the rolling anger through the bond. "I had hoped to continue making plans without expressly relaying my intentions to the vampires. Challenging him like I did—in front of shifters, no less—will make things…complicated. Our various positions are no longer a gray area. However…" He clasped his hands in his lap. "I would be foolish to assume you would suddenly take your situation seriously when you never have before. Wishful thinking on my part. My anger, such as it is, is not justified."

We'd still have hard, angry sex later on, immediately followed by sweet, loving make-up sex. They were both equally amazing.

A shiver rolled over me, and I slipped my hand onto his upper thigh, then pushed it further up until I felt the hard bulge. He was thinking along the same lines.

"I like when you talk yourself around," I said, my voice husky.

"Hmm." He moved his hands and let me rub, making no move to reciprocate. "The only salvageable outcome…is that you didn't reveal how far you've come with your…magic…"

His eyes fluttered closed, and he opened his knees just a little, allowing me more access. He sighed as I sped up, completely unconcerned that there was someone else in the car. Vampires did not care, at all, about expressing their passions or desires in the presence of others. They had parties where they shared blood sources, sometimes at the same time. They turned people in groups. Sometimes they collected in a room, got naked, and just went for it. It was wild. I obviously wasn't into that level of shenanigans—Darius and I had a different situation—but I'd learned that I was not bashful in the least. Clearly.

"We also made a statement in front of the…shifters…" He tensed, his breathing coming fast now. "Roger trusts that I will handle…the vampire aspect…of our situation. He knows me well…enough to—" He tensed, and then shuddered. Vampires could also handle business when they were in the throes of passion. That I didn't love so much. He continued, "He knows me well enough to realize I'm the best hope we have."

"And you think the elves need a *come to Jesus* moment?" I asked as we stopped in front of Callie and Dizzy's house. "You actually want a war?"

"I would like to discuss the matter more thoroughly with Romulus, but from what I've seen, a war is inevitable. I don't think the elves will take kindly to the warrior fae resuming their policing duties. Their power is currently mostly unchecked, and if they need to answer to the fae, they will lose a lot of their…less-than-reputable freedoms. The current ruling party will suppress anyone who tries to make that happen." He pushed the car door open and got out, reaching for me. "I think so, at any rate."

"Okay, but"—I scooted across the seat and got out of his way—"if you think the elves need to be overthrown, you're talking about siding with Lucifer and Vlad."

He gave me a look. "I think Lucifer's main goal concerns finding the woman he saw in the Underworld. If he thinks the elves have played him false, and actually did have a role with her, he will rise up, I have no doubt.

If he wins, I can see him turning the kingdom over to Vlad, but not as an equal. He will set the parameters, and he will maintain the guidelines. Vlad will be nothing but his steward. He is a fool for thinking otherwise."

"Or maybe he thinks he can sit on the throne, or whatever, and weasel out from under Lucifer once he's established."

"As I said, a fool. Lucifer has been a ruler for a long time, and Vlad only *thinks* he rules our vampire faction. His ambition has grown too big. They are unevenly matched, and Vlad will be on the losing side. *Vampires* will be on the losing side, just like they clearly are with the elves."

"So then…" I shook my head at him. I hated when he got going. His strategizing got dizzying. "How are we going to knock the elves down a peg while also keeping me from Lucifer while *also* protecting us from Vlad's efforts?"

Darius paused at Callie and Dizzy's door. "While also freeing up the Underworld so that vampires can relinquish their dependence on unicorns and humans and procreate naturally?"

"Yes. That too."

A loud rumble vibrated up the street, and a souped-up blue Mustang pulled up to the curb. After a moment, the door opened and Roger stood. Alder, his beta, got out of the passenger side.

"The answer, I believe, lies in Miss Taylor's quest. She sees herself, and the fae and the shifters, standing between two different armies. The images flip-flop. Vlad and Lucifer opposed her first, and then the elves. It seems she is in the middle. She is tasked with leading the army to instill order."

"The fae and shifters against two huge armies?"

Roger slowed as he neared the porch steps, Alder behind him. He was clearly listening in, and given Darius didn't start thinking his comments at me, he was fine with that. It was actually nice when they worked together, since it saved me from being stuck in the middle, but it was definitely weird.

"At first glance, yes, that would seem to be the case. But Vlad was correct when he spoke of the unrest in the Realm. I wonder how hard the elves' forces will fight if they think there is a reasonable chance someone will, in essence, rescue them."

"Not hard, probably. They'll probably just get lost."

"Precisely."

"That's not the situation with Lucifer and the vampires, though."

"I will halve the vampire forces. I must. We all know we must keep our numbers up, so we will not rush to kill each other. If we block the other vampires—if I block Vlad—that will take him out of the equation. That leaves the demon forces." He held my gaze for a long moment.

"I don't have a merry band of demons at my back. I can't take on all their forces."

"You have Penny, and Penny has the mages. And you have the type of power demons are used to following, not fighting. That will cause confusion, which might be enough to give the mages an opening."

"Right. Except Lucifer."

He stared at me for another long, silent moment.

"I'm sensing I won't like the answer to this riddle," I said softly.

"*You* will handle Lucifer."

I laughed to stop from throwing up. Then shook my head and opened the door. "You need to get a new plan, bub, because that one isn't going to work. I'm a novice, he's a master, and you're an idiot. There's no way I can go up against my dad and win."

CHAPTER 9

PENNY SAT AT a round table in Callie's living room with Emery, across from her mother's intense scowl. A couple of days ago, her mother had gotten a reading she didn't much like. It came down to this: she couldn't do the job herself. She would need help. Presumably help from the Red Prophet. Since then, she'd pulled out all the stops, taking to her crystal ball, cards, you name it, trying to get a different reading. *Any* other reading. No go.

"I just don't see what sort of help I could possibly need," Karen said, crossing her arms over her chest.

Callie and Dizzy walked amongst the other tables, identical to the one in front of Penny, usually pulled out for mage meetings or cards. This time, though, they were planning stations. It was generally agreed upon that tonight would be the meeting of the minds, and tomorrow they'd do whatever the *Seers* worked out.

The warrior fae had shown up ten minutes or so ago, along with Devon and his pack, and they were just waiting for Reagan and the Red Prophet.

"Nice setup you got here, Missus Banks," Steve said, stretching back in his folding chair with his hands clasped behind his head and his elbows flared out to the sides. "The mage business pays well."

"Beauty pays well. The mage business pays in the form of ulcers," she replied, pouring wine for Romulus.

"She's got that right," Karen murmured.

Reagan burst into the room with a hard scowl, leather pants ending in thick-soled boots, and weapons strapped all over her person. Darius strutted in behind her, followed by Roger and Alder. The shifters in the room straightened up immediately. Romulus looked around with interest.

"By all means, come on in," Callie groused. "Why bother knocking?"

"Like a bunch of barnyard animals," Karen intoned.

"Oh, great, they're joining forces in their bad moods," Penny murmured.

"Still no sign of the Red Prophet," Roger told Romulus as he took the few stairs down into the room. Roger sat in the empty chair in the corner, his back to the wall, facing the room.

"She'll turn up." Romulus crossed an ankle over his knee and leaned back. "This is her way. Though you might want to have someone do a sweep of the yard. It's possible she tucked herself into a tight spot and can't get out."

"The Red Prophet." Karen huffed. "Anyone that needs to use a stage name isn't the real deal."

"Mother, *shh*," Penny hissed. "You're embarrassing me."

"Penny Bristol, how can I possibly be embarrassing you?" She turned a little to shoot her glare at Penny head-on. "*I* am not the one suspected of wandering the yard like a lunatic, calling myself ridiculous names—Oh Lord, what on God's green earth…"

The Red Prophet stood halfway up the stairs to the second floor. Given Callie and Dizzy's jumps, they hadn't known she was in the house.

Her fire-red hair frizzed around her head like some sort of tumbleweed in motion, wilder than if she'd stuck her finger in an electrical socket. She wore a long plaid coat tied at her waist with a dirty rope she'd clearly found on the street at some point. Or a construction yard. A brown suede skirt dusted her shins, and worn black snow boots covered her feet. She held a bright orange clutch that looked empty, and she was staring down at Penny's mother.

"You…" she said, followed by raising a gnarled finger.

"Oh, you have *got* to be kidding." Karen turned in her seat and reached for her tea.

"Red Prophet, meet your nemesis, Karen Bristol," Reagan said, a grin on her lips as she moved through the tables. She chose an empty seat at Roger's table rather than one of the two open spots next to Penny. She probably knew Penny was going to yell at her for sneaking away, unprotected.

"Yes, fantastic," Romulus said. "Let us begin, shall we?"

He uncrossed his leg and leaned forward into the suddenly quiet room. That was, until Karen said, "Isn't someone going to make the nutter on the stairs sit down?"

"Oh, I don't think any of us want to try to wrangle someone like that," Dizzy said with a calming smile. Karen harrumphed.

"I have some new information to share," Darius said, sitting near the door in the last seat at the table hosting Devon's pack. Rod, the big kid a little younger than Penny, gave him a confused look. It was clearly a day for strange occurrences.

The room listened as Darius laid out the chat he'd had with Vlad not that long ago, and though he didn't show it, Penny got the distinct impression he was irritated with Reagan. Maybe *that* was why she'd taken a seat across the room. Romulus spoke of Charity's quest changing again. She'd had another vision, apparently, and this time she'd found herself looking at Vlad and Lucifer again.

"I think our next steps are clear," Romulus said

when Darius was finished. "We need to go to the Flush to take care of some business." It was clear he didn't want to openly discuss what business. But then, no one liked airing family-related dirty laundry, and the issues he was having with his mother were just that—Penny had been there to witness. "After, we have to present Charity to the elf royalty. The presentation and following meetings will help us figure out how best to proceed. Until then, we have no idea whether the elves will be amenable to us aggressively resuming our roles in the Realm."

"Shall we consult the oracle?" Darius asked. "I was given to understand that was a chief function of this meetup."

"Yes, of course." Romulus smiled pleasantly at the Red Prophet, who had not moved an inch, including her outstretched, pointing finger.

"Oh, for heaven's sakes," Karen said under her breath after a glance that way. "I'll take up my post in the formal dining room. My supplies are already laid out."

Now the Red Prophet did descend the stairs, much faster than a human could've. At the hall landing, she jumped the last couple of steps down into the living room and said, "Hah!"

"It appears she is at her most dramatic this evening," Romulus intoned. "It can be trying, but this is when she does her best work, I assure you. Granted, I am usually not on hand to actually witness her readings, but…well, hopefully it won't take too long."

A grin tickled Emery's lips.

"What?" Penny whispered.

"I'll tell you what," her mom butted in, pushing up from the table. "The last thing he wants to do is be subjected to this…this…*nutcase* and her crazy antics. *Most dramatic*," she grumbled. "Batshit crazy, that's what he ought to say."

"You've *Seen* me," the Red Prophet said, crouching down to walk and waving her hands over her head like a chimpanzee. "You know."

"Bah. I don't know anything." Karen batted it away, walking ahead with a stiff back. "I've been wrong before. There was this pizza episode…"

CHARITY WATCHED IN utter fascination from the edge of the dining room as Karen started shuffling her tarot cards. The fog in the crystal ball rolled and boiled, lights sparking within it. By Karen's glances at it, her brow furrowed, that obviously wasn't normal or expected. The Red Prophet sat on the actual table like some sort of centerpiece, looking on. Karen was doing her best to ignore the situation as she worked, but it couldn't have been easy. Charity was having a hard time concentrating with it herself.

"Why does she...turn on the dramatics?" Charity whispered to her dad, who was standing next to her, watching. Darius, Roger, and Emery stood in the room with them, wanting the information as it came. Reagan had flat-out refused to attend. She didn't much like *Seers*, it seemed. So Penny had stayed with her in the outer room, and Charity got the idea it was to keep her from taking off. Reagan was as bad as the Red Prophet, she gathered.

"She is very old," Romulus answered. "And she has done a lot of mind-altering substances. She—"

"That's not why," the Red Prophet interrupted, her gaze drifting toward the ceiling. She stuck out her tongue and placed a little white square onto it. "Your mother is why. She is a very exacting woman, and she likes to have her way. I am something she cannot control, not even with her magic. I remind her of it, often, which is why she keeps me...apart."

Charity tried to keep from stiffening. Though her dad wouldn't admit it, he was having a lot of anxiety about what would happen with Grandmama's situation. The First had kept her people hidden away for years. She'd divided them, essentially forcing those who didn't want to remain idle to leave. She'd torn Romulus from Charity's mom in the Brink, and created a hostile situation for the visiting shifters. She had a lot to answer for, but she was also family. She was the matriarch of their people, and had been for a long time. Calling her down would be a terrible burden on them all.

"Can I have a little quiet, please?" Karen asked.

"You don't need quiet—you need to stop being so stubborn," the Red Prophet replied. "You have a block for a head."

"Says the drug addict."

"I am not an addict. I am a crackhead."

Karen blinked a few times, then minutely shook her head. "We're not going to get along, you and I."

"Correct. I look forward to our arguments. It'll create all the energy we could possibly need." The Red Prophet looked behind her, at a spot on the wall. She nodded.

"Right but...you're here now, and Grandmama isn't," Charity said to the Red Prophet. "There's no need for any kind of ruse."

"True. Old habits, as they say. Though...these Brink mind alternants seem to promote exaggerated behavior. It's best just to go along with it, I think."

"Only a hack needs drugs to use her *Sight*," Karen murmured, placing the cards as the crystal ball cleared for one solid moment. Energy rolled over Charity's skin. From Romulus's shiver, he clearly felt it too.

The Red Prophet jumped down from the table. "I

will go and enter—"

"You need to go to the Flush," Karen told Charity and Romulus, "that's true enough."

The Red Prophet hissed, straightened up, and faced Karen. "We must record our findings in private, so we can reflect on them before we speak with the others. That is how it is done. Then we must—"

"We have a job to do," Karen spat back, "and that job does not entail making everyone wait while you dream up more *dramatics*." With a closed-down expression, she looked at Romulus. "When you get to the Flush—"

"No. That is not to be revealed," the Red Prophet said, and climbed back onto the table.

"I know very well what *is*, and is *not*, to be revealed, thank you very much. Or didn't you know that I foresaw Charity's journey into the Flush?"

"You are too rash, but even still, we make an excellent, powerful team," the Red Prophet said, now smiling. "We are the best in the world when we work together. We will hate it immensely."

"Good God," Karen said. "Anyway, Romulus, you must take care of your business in the Flush, then make your journey to the elves as planned. That much is very clear. With you, to both of those destinations, must travel the Triangle of Power."

"Yes. I *Saw* that, as well," the Red Prophet said, and

Charity noticed her sudden gravity. "The Triangle of Power is very important to this journey. But what is it?"

Karen straightened up just a little, her chin lifting. She clearly liked knowing something the Red Prophet didn't. "I *Saw* this in the past, as well. It's not a new grouping." She looked at Darius, then Emery.

"Reagan, Penny, and I," Emery said, dipping his hands into his jeans pockets.

"They were the driving forces behind the victory against the Mages' Guild," Roger added.

"Yes, the three of them working together are incredibly powerful," Darius said. "But they are not leaders, per se. The ladies are...largely unpredictable."

Emery chuckled. "Reagan or Penny, when working alone, are unpredictable. Together they're in another league. They're a natural disaster. They can't even be led, never mind doing the leading. They have to be corralled, at best."

Charity noticed Roger nodding. Charity wished she'd been there for the mages' battle to see all this in action.

"This is why they must stay with the fae," Karen said. "He and Charity, with their people, will guide the powerful trio. They will stabilize their might. It is essential."

"You will need your wits about you, boy," the Red Prophet said to Romulus, and it wasn't often someone talked to him like that and called him a boy. Charity was pretty sure the Red Prophet didn't notice. "You have been sheltered for a long time, and the world is not as you've imagined it. Working with the shifters will be your greatest strength. Hold on to that asset. Trust in the Alpha Shifter's morality, but do not always trust in what you see. Or feel."

Karen shot Darius a grave look. "You will have to leave your people behind. For a while, at least. The Pyramid of Power is important, but so is the team you've created with Reagan. She will need her most loyal supporters by her side to start this journey—to keep her on the right path. It is necessary. You can…corral her like no other." Charity stifled a grin. She didn't know Karen well, but it was clear the woman knew how to control a space, and using the right language in times like these was clearly important in that, especially with a vampire. "You must start this journey with her if you hope to end it with her. But then what you dread will come to pass. When it comes time to visit the elves, you will need to let her go, come what may. She will take more risks and charge into the unknown, as is her strength. You will strategize and plan. Manipulate and enlighten, sometimes with lies, sometimes with truths, always with an agenda. You need to be the reason people should never trust vampires. Only if you are in your element, and Reagan is in hers, will your pieces of the puzzle work toward the greater good. And they must."

"Seek the one you once sought," the Red Prophet said, looking skyward. "The most dangerous will prove the safest. The newly awoken will be your ace in the hole. Use her, and allow her to use you. It is in this partnership that a new path shall be forged. Beware the trickster, for he will ruin you."

Karen turned in her seat and looked at the Red Prophet. "I didn't get that in the reading."

"You will not *get* everything. Just as I will not *get* everything. It is foretold."

"By who?"

"By *whom...*"

"Jesus Chri—" Karen turned toward the others again, her face red and her tolerance for the Red Prophet completely dried up, if she'd had any in the first place.

"If Reagan travels with the vampire, it'll be immediately clear it was they who went into the Underworld," Romulus said. "Especially if Charity is traveling with them."

"Correct," the Red Prophet said. "And if she travels without the vampire, it'll be *almost* immediately clear who she is. The dam has burst. She has been unknowingly waiting for this moment since she was born. It is time she spreads her wings and challenges the lord of the Underworld."

"Buckle up," Roger said. Darius nodded grimly.

"Will you be going?" Romulus asked her.

"No. I must stay behind for now. Thankfully. I've had about all I can take of the Flush. What a boring waste of time."

"What joy is mine," Karen said sarcastically, looking over her tarot. She glanced back up at Darius and said, "It isn't clear to me what is in store after you make it to the elves."

"That journey is not yet written," the Red Prophet said.

"I am not doubting you ladies, since I have seen your—at least one of your—merit in real time." Darius slipped a hand into his pocket. "But you heard about my exchange with Vlad earlier. If I leave him un-checked, even for a few days, the damage he could do…"

"You must," the Red Prophet said.

"Leaving him will do more good than harm." Karen tapped a card. "I am in agreement with the nutter. You must. It is the only way to protect the heir. Otherwise she'll never make it to the elves, and that would be the end. She must make it to the last battle."

"She must," the Red Prophet added. Karen rolled her eyes.

Darius shifted his weight in frustration, but he did

not argue. Although Charity hadn't been in the magical world for long, she knew a *Seer*'s reading was like a cheat sheet for a final. These *Seers* agreed on the path forward, even though they hated each other, which inspired plenty of trust.

Still, Charity worried about what would come. It was pretty clear from all her dad had said that there would be a trial. That Grandmama would be judged and might even be asked to step down. Tensions would be high. Charity hadn't assimilated very well in the Flush, and she'd been actively trying. From what she'd seen of Reagan, she assumed Reagan wouldn't try at all. That would drive Grandmama crazy, which would add even more complication to an already complicated situation.

"You must leave behind a small force to protect the back door, Romulus," Karen said.

"The Brink being the back door, of course," the Red Prophet added.

"The power players must take the heir into the Realm…" Karen wiped her brow and shook her head. "That is all that has been revealed at this time. There are a lot of moving parts. After a break, I'll try to look again and get more details. For now, however, we'll have to go with the bigger picture."

"All of this is about what we'd deduced," Romulus said, and Roger nodded. "It gives us confidence. I thank you for that. You relay your findings…quite clearly."

"I'll try not to take offense," the Red Prophet said, and cackled.

Romulus ignored her. "I do wonder, however. What is our end game?"

"The shifters have shown you what duty means," the Red Prophet said, and jumped off the table like a cat. She straightened up and swiped at her hair. "You must do your duty, regardless of the outcome." She sobered and her eyes cleared. She met Charity's gaze. "Your quest is incredibly important—not just to the Realm, but to all the worlds. Your task is to restore order. It is to find balance. You have all the pieces. Now they will be set in motion. At the end of this, you will either have righted the wrong, or you will die, and your family and friends with you."

Adrenaline spiked through Charity's blood and shivers washed over her. She'd gone from a lonely, poor kid to all of this in a matter of months. She couldn't believe anyone would go along with her role in all of this, but there was no question that they were.

"No pressure," she mumbled, and the Red Prophet cackled again.

CHAPTER 10

THE NEXT DAY, in the dead of night, I put my hands on my hips and sighed in annoyance as we waited in front of a jagged line cutting through the sky, marking a gateway into the Realm. Everyone in this group had more than enough magic to step through without even a twinge of pain or fatigue, but they had stopped to assess the situation all the same. I got the feeling they were worried about what was on the other side.

I hadn't progressed that far yet. I'd purposely sat out of the *Seer* readings, so I didn't know what to expect. When you pretty much only had downhill to go, hearing your fate seemed like overkill.

"I wanted to send an answering message down with a demon," I grumbled. "It doesn't seem right that my journey should be hijacked by a bunch of fae."

"That's the sort of thinking that is going to get everyone in trouble," Penny replied, chewing on her lip and staring at the gateway.

"How do you figure?"

Emery stalked back from the group of planners like

a fighter getting ready to enter the octagon. Darius stayed in the cluster, speaking to Romulus as Roger, Charity, and Devon listened in. Everyone else waited nearby, Steve leaning against a tree and a sour-faced woman whose name I didn't remember standing guard ten feet away, looking out at the empty field.

We'd chosen a gate about a hundred miles outside of New Orleans. There were reasons for it, but I honestly hadn't paid attention to any of them. There didn't need to be one more boss in this outfit, and I didn't like planning anyway. Give me a castle to storm, and I was in. Chatting about what waited beyond the keep? Yawn.

"Because you're going to get bored and cause trouble," Penny replied.

"I beg your pardon," I said indignantly. "I do not *cause trouble*. I create mayhem. It sounds much cooler. And yeah, probably. But still. I should be sending a message to my father through a demon, then...like..."

"See?" Penny pointed at my face. I slapped her hand away. She pointed again. "You don't know what comes next." She nodded like I'd answered a question. "This is the right way."

"This is the only way." Emery stopped next to Penny and looked out over the field. "Lucifer showed up at the castle demanding answers, and left unhappy. Those elves weren't being coy to protect their secrets—they didn't have answers. They'll be as stirred up as an anthill after a kid comes through with a stick. What we saw last time will be nothing, I guarantee it."

"Did you hammer that home to Mr. Magical Policeman?" I pointed at Romulus. "He still tends to think the best of people for some reason."

Emery's lips pressed together tightly. He gave a curt nod.

"Ah." I shook out my hands and faced the field as well. What else did I have to look at? "The all-powerful and important Second seems to think his position will protect us all."

"He seems to think so, yes." Emery lowered his voice. "He's been gone a long time. He's going to get a rude awakening."

As someone who'd been hunted for years, Emery would know. He'd seen the underbelly of the Realm and all the problems caused by the people in charge.

This situation was starting to look up.

"Who is...?" Penny squinted through the darkness and then put a hand up to block an absent sun. "Do you see that?"

"We got something," the sour-faced woman barked, planting her feet shoulder distance apart.

Darius, one of two who could see in the dark, turned and peered into the night. I followed suit, pulling Penny's hand out of the air to keep her from looking ridiculous. That's what friends were for.

Two shapes moved through the night, tramping over the weeds, one of them jerking as though it had tripped.

The sky lit up, accompanied by a bug-zapper-type sound. Charity's magical sun.

Darius shrank away, and I sent a peal of air to punch Charity in the face. Her head snapped back before she dropped like a sack of bricks. Devon bristled, turning toward me with his arms pushed away from his sides and murder in his eyes. The sun clicked off.

"'At ease, disease,'" I quoted, and wondered if anyone would get the G.I. Joe reference. "We have a vampire in our midst. Watch what magic you use."

I sent a blanket of fire crawling through the sky. Flickering light sifted down to illuminate the two forms doggedly coming our way. I groaned.

"What are they doing here?" Penny asked.

"They never seem to understand 'you can't come' applies to them." I let the fire crackle above Callie and Dizzy as they neared, sweat beading on their brows from exertion and heat, each of them carrying a backpack and a satchel. Callie wore a lime-green sweat suit with two stars on the chest. I was pretty sure those stars were supposed to be in the nipple region of someone whose breasts weren't yet on a downward trajectory.

"Why did you choose a gate way out here?" Callie demanded, breathing heavily.

"You have to go back," Penny said, shaking her head. "This is going to be incredibly dangerous—"

"Wrong approach," I murmured.

"We're going to be walking for days. Maybe running," Penny amended.

I nodded. That was the better deterrent. The dual-mages were in their sixties. They could hold up their end of the bargain when it came to magic, but they weren't big into hardcore exercising. Or any exercising.

"I have a duty to that girl's mother." Callie pointed at me, and I knew better than to slap her hand out of my face. "Amorette gave up everything so her only daughter could have a chance. She might be gone, but Dizzy and I have picked up the torch. Besides…" Callie took a deep breath and adjusted the straps of her backpack. "Someone has to fix her up if she blows off her eyebrows. She can't go meeting the elves looking like a Q-tip."

"She does have a point." I nodded. I had a horrible habit of burning off my eyebrows. It wasn't exactly a good look.

"Missus Banks, Mister Banks, so nice to see you." Romulus gave them a pleasant smile. "Do you need a rest before we continue?"

Callie waved him away. "I don't need any special treatment."

"Fantastic." He looked over the group as everyone

clustered together, Darius returning to my side. We'd worked out his anger issues the day before, and now he slipped his arm around my waist. I felt nervousness swirling through the bond we shared. He clearly shared Emery's skepticism about our likely reception. "Charity and I will step through the gate first. After that, those strongest in power will follow. The weakest will go last, followed by Roger, as is the shifter way." His gaze hit me. "You will walk through with Darius and Halvor, in the middle." Romulus flicked his hand, indicating the assassin-looking guy he called his assistant. "This is both to—"

I waved him away. "Sounds good. Let's get to it."

Given the political situation, the gate will almost certainly be guarded. All of them will be. Try not to use your magic, Darius thought at me as everyone geared up. *Let Romulus handle things. Let him do the talking.*

"That'll last until the guards decide he's a nuisance."

Yes.

"And then?"

At that point, I doubt you'll be still long enough for a plan.

Good point. I didn't plan to stand idly by as elves rushed us.

Fire rolled over me, and the heat felt damn good.

The first few people went through.

"I've always wanted to see the Flush," Dizzy said,

pushed up behind me. Apparently they'd be traveling in the middle as well. "I've heard it is absolutely beautiful."

"I feel like a donkey, carrying all of this stuff." Callie pulled at the backpack straps again.

"Here." The big dude, Rod, stepped up and put out his hand. "I can take that for you, Missus Banks."

"Oh." She smiled at him sheepishly. "Well, thank you, young man."

Penny and I exchanged a look, our eyebrows hiked up. *Young man?* It wasn't like her to play the old biddy. Then again, if it took the load off…

"Did you really come for me, or because you didn't want to be left behind?" I asked as we stepped forward, like waiting in line at Disneyland. These people were much too cautious.

"I'd be lying if I said I savored the prospect of waiting in the house," Dizzy said, "doing nothing, listening to the two *Seers* bicker."

Callie elbowed him.

"What?" he hollered at her. "She's not a dummy. She knows we hate taking the safe approach."

Callie scowled at Dizzy. "We wouldn't have bothered if it hadn't been you and Penny in the mix."

"I'm just coming along because of Reagan," Penny said. "The Flush"—she reduced to a whisper—"was not very fun."

"Why is that?" I stepped up again as the rest of the

fae ducked through the gate. "You never said. I mean…you didn't give me a reason I actually believed. Boredom and hunting for weird stones has never been a problem for you."

"Why didn't you pester her about it, then?" Callie demanded. "It's a little late now, with curious ears listening in."

"We're the only ones with curious ears, hon," Dizzy said. "Everyone else has been there."

"I didn't badger her about it before 'cause Charity's story was more interesting, and then I just forgot."

Penny was still whispering. "I didn't want to…speak badly. But… Well, you'll see. They aren't exactly welcoming to strangers."

"Oh, that's okay." I shrugged. "I'm rarely welcome anywhere. This will be no different."

"It might be a little different," Emery said, and started laughing. That was promising.

We finally stepped up to the gate. Darius put out his hand to stop us.

Halvor, a hard-eyed man with impeccable posture and an air of unspeakable violence, stepped up to my side. All of the mages took a step back.

"'ello, guvna," I said in a terrible English accent.

He didn't respond. Not real chatty, that fae.

Here we go, Darius thought.

Like prickles lightly sliding across my skin, the magic of the gate washed over me. The dark sky became orange with little gold filaments floating around us. The path turned to cobbles, flanked by sweet-smelling flowerbeds laden with magic and trees with perfectly manicured branches. The whole thing looked like a children's picture book, down to the little bench under a green light pole off to the side.

Romulus stood near that bench, speaking to two tall and swishy elves, their hair flowing in the lack of breeze, their red and orange tunics draped down their slight bodies *just so*, and their hands flared to the sides just a little, like they were about to dance forward and frolic in the flowers.

It was all an act.

All of it. After my stint in the Underworld, I knew in my blood this was a magical construction painted over the natural habitat.

To that end, I looked upward, wondering if it was like earth, and the universe waited beyond, or if it was like the Underworld, and we were actually inside an enormous cave or something. And if the former was true, were we in a different universe than the one that existed on the Brink side, or was it somehow the same?

Darius moved us forward, Halvor still at my side, forcing us to stay within a protective bubble of fae. I let them shepherd me, looking back at the gate, wondering if the worlds weren't separate at all. Maybe we all existed together—the magical people and the humans—and the magical people sectioned themselves off into these pockets in time and space. Maybe we actually stood on Brink soil.

"Oh no," I murmured, grabbing my head. "This place is just as much of a mindfuck as the Underworld."

Do not mention that here, Darius thought, his hand tightening on my wrist.

"Can the elves hear as well as you?" I whispered, no longer able to see them through the thicket of fae surrounding us. "As well as the shifters?"

Nearly.

I nodded and tried to ignore the urge to explore the magic stitching this place together. Maybe my magic couldn't crack the Realm open like it could the Underworld. Then again, with Lucifer so suspicious of the elves, and the elves so distrustful of him…

It seemed logical that the two could be very detrimental to each other's setups. I bet I *could* crack this place like an egg. Dang it, I really wanted to try.

"Come forward. You, there."

The elf's musical voice wasn't nearly as pleasing as Vlad's. It was like he was trying too hard. Or not made for seduction.

Halvor pushed in a little closer to me. "You do not have to go forward unless the Second wishes it."

"And not even then, since he's not my Second." I

peered through the spaces between the various heads and necks and caught both elves looking my way. Shifters stepped through the gate, Andy and Sour Face, my buddy the yeti, and Yasmine, who was a serious looker. Charity already stood up front with Romulus, and they had not turned. Apparently he didn't wish it.

Let this escalate, Darius thought. *Let them see how the elves handle not getting what they want. It is a lesson the Second must learn.*

I felt Penny tight to my back. Emery was right there too, content to hide with us.

I hated hiding.

"Nope," Penny said, and grabbed the back of my tank top. She'd probably felt me tense. "We don't need this to kick off, Reagan. Just stand back."

"They think they own the world, do they?" Callie asked with a huff. "Since when do people need a pass to enter the magical world?"

"That's part of the problem," Darius murmured.

"Step aside." The elf put out his hand, ready to move Romulus away.

"There is a vampire," the other elf said.

Magic condensed around the area. It grew heady and heavy, pushing down on us. Squeezing us.

"Weird magic," I murmured, splaying out a tiny bit of fire to eat through it. Like oil on water, it flicked over it. "Hmm."

"Vampires are permitted in this part of the Realm, are they not?" Romulus said, raising his voice.

Roger finally stepped through the gate, brawny and ready for action. He evaluated the situation and immediately strutted to Romulus's side.

"Bring them forth," commanded the elf clad in red.

"Good luck, dipshit," I murmured.

The one in orange took in the largish cluster of powerful magical people. The fae surrounding us. The shifters filing in. Roger staring them down. Romulus losing his patience. He looked back at his buddy.

"Leave them," the one in red said a moment later. "For now."

"Yes, good choice." Romulus bowed. "We will present to the castle as soon as we are able. I know that you are eager to officially meet the Third."

The elves didn't stay to chat. They started jogging out of the area, and any idiot could tell they were going to get backup.

"Time to go," I called out, and did a circle with my finger. "I don't think we want to be here when they get back."

"I agree," Romulus said softly, and turned toward the path.

I could feel Darius's approval, and suddenly the *Seers'* insistence that he come with us made all kinds of sense. He was needed to steer the fae. They had to know the real state of affairs, and through subtlety and suggestion, he would help show them just that. He would do what Vlad had been trying to do for months.

It wouldn't be Vlad who ultimately gained their favor, though.

"Those sneaky littles witches," I said with a grin, pushing Halvor further away.

"Who?" Penny asked, still pushed against me.

"No offense, bub," I told Halvor, whose expression darkened as soon as I addressed him. "But I don't know you well enough to wear you as a skin suit."

"Ew," Penny mumbled.

Working just a little bit of magic to pick at the setup around me, I answered Penny, "The *Seers*. They got it right. Never trust a vampire."

CHAPTER 11

"INCOMING."

Charity looked to the left as Devon hung back a little, none of the shifters having shifted yet. Based on what she saw coming toward them, that might change in the next few minutes.

A group of five elves in various shades of *bright* sauntered along the path, almost like they were skipping. Behind them trudged what could only be described as a magical horde, made up of various thick-bodied and heavily armed magical creatures. One had a bludgeon, another a cudgel, some were equipped with daggers, and one with a boomerang, of all things, laden with spikes.

Romulus slowed as they reached an intersection with the fast track, a path that magically sped up travel time. They'd only been traveling for half a day—the journey would take at least another two—and already the elves were coming in numbers. Darius had assured them that this would happen. Emery had agreed with the vampire and told Romulus to be ready. But even though Romulus had gotten a taste for how the elves handled things on his way out of the Realm, he hadn't thought the situation would escalate. He'd hoped his rebuff, plus his intention to reinstate the warrior fae's traditional duty in the Realm, would grant him a pass. And it probably would've. But it did not grant his party a pass, that was clear.

The elves at the gate had spied the young blond woman traveling with a vampire. They suspected, correctly, they'd found the woman Lucifer was looking for. The one who was causing all sorts of problems for the kingdom. They would want to capture her at all costs, warrior fae be damned.

"Darius was right," Charity said to her father, because that truth had to be acknowledged and acted upon. It would change the way Romulus had planned this travel. It had to.

His movement was incredibly slight, and Charity read it as two things. One, he agreed. And two, he very much hated being wrong. He was probably a reformed sore loser.

He angled his body, silently giving the signal, and their people formed into their usual battle cluster, locking Darius and Reagan in the middle and forcing the mages to the outside.

"Shift," Roger commanded, and puffs of green preceded skin and hair boiling into animal forms.

"Let me out," Reagan hollered.

"She doesn't know how to fight this way," Charity told her dad as they positioned themselves on the path, moving head-on toward the slowing elves. The elves could read the signals—this wouldn't go smoothly.

"I do not wish to advertise what is in our midst," he responded.

"The vampire has it under control," Kairi said, always with Charity in battle and now at her back. "Though from his posturing, he doesn't seem confident she'll hold back for long."

"I'm surprised she's holding back at all." Charity quickly loosened her sword and then let her hands fall to her sides, like her father was doing. The song of battle rose through her. The feel of Devon's wolf urged her on.

"Greetings," Romulus said as the elves drew within speaking range. They stopped on the path, facing the warrior fae. A soft breeze flowed through them. Fragrant flowers bloomed all around. "It seems you have a battle party ready. Please, what is the disturbance? I did not see anything along the way."

The warrior fae had certain ways of handling things, and arrogance and posturing were two of the favored tactics.

The lead elf stepped forward, and the slight tightening of Romulus's shoulders suggested the creature was dangerous. Powerful, in other words, by rank or magic or both. Probably both.

"Second, so good to see you," the elf said, and its cadence, words, and politeness made Charity ten times warier than the brutish creatures at its back. It suggested someone higher up in the ranks, and she'd learned through her life that those types of people always had the upper hand. In the Brink, that meant money and power. Here, that would also mean fighting prowess.

"Yes, hello. I apologize, I do not know your name and rank…" Romulus smiled and bowed slightly.

"That won't be necessary." The elf flicked a finger, and the others fanned out, preparing for what came next. Romulus's arms tensed. This would be bad. "It has come to our attention that you are traveling with someone the elf royalty wishes to speak with. You and your party are to come with us immediately. Full quarter will be given to those who come peacefully."

"Are they all one sex?" Reagan asked softly, her voice carrying in the sudden quiet. "I can't tell. They're all trying a little too hard to appear jolly, obviously, and they kind of look like clones."

"*Ssshhh*," someone said, and it was probably Penny.

"Full quarter…" Romulus smiled while squinting, showing the humor he found in those words. "You are attempting to treat peacekeepers like war criminals."

"I'm glad you see it our way. Now, if you'll step forward, one at a time, we'll apply the necessary restraints."

"I see." Romulus put his hands behind his back. "And what infractions did we commit?"

The elves fanned out more on the path. The creatures waiting behind them shuffled forward a little, anxious to fight.

The lead elf said, "Before you left the Realm, you killed members of the kingdom. You—"

"We are all members of the kingdom. There is no law against defending oneself."

The elf hesitated, and it was clear its patience was running out. "You killed members of the elfin royal throne, and for that—"

"Nonsense." Romulus waved the thought away. "We killed foot soldiers, nothing more. They were too stupid to be in your employ. That is something I must bring up to the royal family. Having those types of drooling simpletons working for your kind brings all of you down. It's an embarrassment. No, I did you a favor. What else?"

The lead elf—possibly a female—blinked and popped out a hip before regaining control of itself. "You refused to hand over the mage sentenced to death. For that—"

"You see?" Romulus said. "That is the problem with employing idiots. I already explained the details of young Emery's inclusion in our group, something I will also take up with the royal family. It is above your pay grade, I'm afraid, and given the way you're carrying on, I'm starting to assume it is also above your comprehension ability. What has happened to the royal guard? Is your goal to become a laughingstock? Because I must say, madam, you are well on your way."

"Oh my God, I like him so much," Reagan whispered.

The lead elf straightened indignantly. "Second, it is in your best interest to come quietly. We do not wish to harm you. It is the mage, the woman, and the vampire that we want. The rest of you will simply be questioned."

"*Simply* be questioned?" Romulus laughed. "Oh my, no. No, that will not do. We will not turn ourselves over to you, we will not be questioned, and we will not stand for you wasting our time any longer. Either disperse now, or we will kill you all. Those are your options."

The elf's voice turned sharp. "With respect, Second, you've been gone a long time. Things are done differently now. It would be best if you educated yourself on those changes rather than make an error that you cannot unmake."

"There has been no respect here, just wasted breath." Romulus centered his weight and let his arms drift to his sides again. That was his cue that he planned to fight.

The elf clearly saw it. Her hair stilled, no longer

waving in the absence of a breeze. "This is your final chance, Second. We take no pleasure in shedding your blood."

"Ridiculous." He drew his blade in a swift, practiced movement full of grace and power. Charity was right behind him, and she knew from the way the elves moved, and the speed with which Halvor leapt out from within the group of fae, that this battle would be a challenge.

Before she could even start forward, however, the orange bled from the sky and the flowers and trees along the path melted into fire and brimstone, with a few random candy gumdrops stuck in. Large carrion birds swooped down, screaming curse words. And then, in a blink, the scene was all gone. All of it. And only flat desert remained.

CHAPTER 12

"**I** KNEW IT!" I pushed out through the pack of fae, using the hole Halvor had just made. Magic swirled around me, tearing down the elves' construction just like it had my father's, but this was so much easier because of all the practicing I'd been doing.

The elves stood on the path, stunned, looking around at the desert landscape in confusion. Black sky stretched overhead with stars punched through, just like in the Brink. Barren dirt ran underfoot, smooth and flat, no rocks or debris in sight. It must've been cleared away long ago to create the alternate reality that had been there a moment before. A pale moon hung in the sky, its light dappling the ground. It was bright enough for most to basically see, but would hinder those without the advantage of vampire night vision.

"Mind fuckery," I said, running with my sword in hand. I knew better than to hang out and admire my handiwork. Cahal had been an excellent teacher.

Halvor reached the lead elf first. His sword cut through the air and then the elf's neck. I reached the elf beside it, dodging the falling head. It startled at my sudden appearance, having been lost to its surroundings a moment before. I stabbed it through, bowling it over, and kept going. As it fell, I yanked my sword free and rammed into some sort of troll-looking dude with a small head and enormous arms.

A roar shook the ground from Steve's lion form, followed by Cole's yeti bleat. I took those sounds, deep and primal and consuming, and magically echoed them. Using just my sword to hack at the (still confused and obviously very stupid) creature horde, which was second nature to me, I used my magic to fashion more beings on the periphery, hiding in the darkness. Working quickly, I duplicated, tweaked, and animated.

A spell bloomed in the air and then splintered, corrosive and volatile. Also, not well directed.

"Jesus, Penny, some of us are working in here," I yelled, and dived to the side. I didn't want to disrupt the nasty-ass spell. That thing would kill very painfully.

"Then turn on the lights," she yelled. The stress was getting to her.

I lit up the area in fire, circling our new friends, who had (mostly) come out of their shocked stupor and started to fight back. My magical creatures stomped through it, their legs moving too slow for their speed, but the horde didn't seem to notice.

I ran to the front of the shindig, where an elf's

curved blade was slicing through the air at a pace that made me just a little jealous. It slashed at Devon, the big black wolf, and then made a move on Charity, who fought alongside him.

I stabbed it in the back.

"All's fair in illegal magical battles!" I ducked under another elf's blade, rolled, and chopped at its ankle. It hopped out of the way and met the yeti's big paw. Cole slapped the face off that elf, and it was very, very gross. "Don't look, Penny!"

The lesser-powered fae and shifters worked around my fire, taking swings at the cowering horde, which was now focused on the magical creatures closing in on them. I still hadn't figured out how to make my creations solid, but the elves' pets were too stupid and scared to catch on.

I pushed the fire out and ran down the middle of the horde, spraying hellfire as I did so. I'd been so good for so long. I needed to let off some steam. "Here's Johnny!"

Skin and limbs and magical parts burned away. There wasn't much that could withstand hellfire, and I did not look forward to eventually meeting the creatures that could. Spoiler alert: it was my dad and his upper-tier minions.

I stabbed into a chest and then hacked at a neck, not nearly as graceful and elegant as the fae, and not caring in the least. A wolf took down a sorta blob-looking thing, and I wondered if it was a dybbuk—a disembodied soul. I didn't even know how one of those killed. Not like it mattered. The wolf solved that problem by killing it first.

Turning, I went to slash, only to lose the mark to Yasmine, her white wolf form just as lovely as her human form. Some women had all the luck. On the other side, an elf met a grisly end in a combined attack from Steve and Kairi, and the wolf of Sour Face took down a cute little sprite that apparently spat acid. Yikes.

Before I could find a new target, I found myself standing in flickering firelight amid a bunch of bodies and panting good guys. Or, at least, "guys and gals with sometimes questionable ethics, who were currently not in the wrong."

"Dang it, that was too fast," I said, let down.

I cleaned my blade as Romulus worked his way closer, a smear of blood on his cheek and a sparkle in his eyes. He stopped beside me and looked from my still-flickering fire to the darkened sky.

"Here." I fished another cloth out of my pouch.

"Thank you." He took it and applied it to his blade. "That is a very handy…"

"Pouch," I supplied.

"Yes. I saw some in the Brink. None so plain as that, but I like it all the more for it."

"I'm not after the fashion element of it."

"I wish no one was after the fashion element of it," Emery groused as he wandered by.

"What'd you do, one spell?" I asked him.

"Half of a spell. I'm *that* good."

"Lazy."

"Ungrateful."

I smirked and bent, stuffing the dirty cloth into a dead creature's pocket. It wasn't technically littering that way.

Romulus was still standing there. He was clearly trying to tell me something, but these guys seemed to prefer charades to words, and if it didn't involve a weapon, I didn't read body language.

"Hi," I said, just to break the ice.

"Use your words, Dad," Charity called, stowing her sword and then looking at the sky.

Taking the hint, I said, "Oh right, yeah. I'll put the Realm back." I grimaced and got to work. Not too many people made me nervous, but this guy did. It wasn't that I feared for my life—I didn't—but I felt the discomfort of being the crude chick among rich and polished people. It was the same nervousness I got when trekking into Darius's French Quarter house, with its cream-colored rug and decor. This feeling had once prompted me to take off my shoes to eat dinner in his house, only to try to hide my shoeless feet when the very posh Marie joined me. In other words, it made me an even bigger shitshow.

"Use my words, yes." Romulus chuckled quietly to himself, staring out at nothing. "Charity's mother always used to say that to me. I do miss her. I wonder if the longing will ever go away…"

"Yeah…I'm not really…sure what to say to that."

"Of course, yes." He paused for a moment, and I wondered if something was expected of me. Where was Darius when you needed him? "I must say," he finally went on, "you are effective."

I gave a little smile and nodded, but something caught me up short. It sounded like a compliment, but his tone wasn't all that different from the one he'd used to make a fool of that elf earlier. I didn't want to be the person who preened when they were actually the butt of the joke.

I was going to end up embarrassing myself with him. It was inevitable.

"Until this moment, I had no actual proof that you were Lucifer's heir," Romulus continued. "Now, there can be no doubt, of course." Romulus gestured around him as I reset the orange sky. The cold breeze still blew across us, though, so that wasn't right. It should be a gentle, warm breeze with a hint of spicy fragrance. Except the fragrance and temperature of that breeze were supposed to be tailored to each person, something

I didn't know how to do. "You have been in the Brink all this time, within the magical community, and no one was the wiser. Amazing."

"Kinda the same with your daughter, though, right?"

"No."

He and Penny should get along well. They both had the radical honesty thing down pat.

I set the yellow-orange glow of the faux-sun, only then remembering it was actually nighttime. So I took the sun out, but then I didn't really know how it was supposed to rise in the daytime. Did I, like, put it on a timer or something? Could I do that?

"I probably shouldn't have torn this down," I murmured. "This'll be a dead giveaway that I came through."

"Yes, most likely."

"Good, yeah. Honesty. Very refreshing," I said dryly, stitching the flowers back in and laying the cobblestone path.

"You clearly don't have a mastery of the intricacies of your magic, but your fighting prowess is exceptional."

"Thanks. I have a lot of experience."

"It seems so, yes. The colors of the trees and flowers are completely wrong, by the way. The type of cobblestone is not accurate either. This color scheme will never work."

"What do you mean? The flowers were purple, red, and yellow. That was the color scheme. And how many types of cobblestone are there? It's brown. Wasn't the other stuff brown? Or was it gray? Crap, I can't remember."

"The flowers were heliotrope purple, carnelian, and butter yellow. These are—"

"Whoa, whoa...wait." I tried to pore over the words he'd used for colors. "So...deeper purple...maybe?" I changed those out.

"Now you are using majorelle blue."

"Blue?" I dropped my hands. "What are you seeing? I'm seeing purple."

"No."

I gave an exasperated sigh. "Well, hell, I don't know. Obviously this is not going to work. I don't know colors."

"It is not your specialty. There is nothing wrong with that. In the Realm, a master gardener usually works with a magical structuralist to create the designs, and then lesser structuralists to maintain them. Your imagination is very vivid, but your gardening..."

I left the flowers as they were. Hopefully no master gardeners would be wandering through anytime soon. The trees were easy enough, even though Romulus's *tsking* when I added the leaves indicated they were the wrong green. The gold filaments came next, and since those were annoying and I had no idea why they were here in the first place, I didn't bother. Maybe they'd get the hint.

"I do wonder, if you were fae, what your contribution to the community would be," he wondered aloud.

How did you politely tell someone they were starting to get annoying?

"Demolition. I'd give all your masters something to do." I finished up and surveyed my handiwork. "The colors look kind of like a circus."

"Yes. It is quite hideous. I think you should pass it off as making fun of the elves. It's the only way to avoid public ridicule."

"Wow. Don't pull any punches, huh?"

"You don't seem like the type of person who would appreciate it if I did."

"You're not reading me very well." I put my hands on my hips as Darius sauntered over, just as freshly pressed as ever, with his suit jacket buttoned and a hand in a trouser pocket. He didn't believe in dressing down for the occasion. How he was comfortable traveling—or fighting—in a suit, I did not know.

"They are going to know someone messed with their scheme," he said.

"We've established that, thanks. Maybe get on my team for a moment."

"What I mean to say is, if you can't join them, beat them. Make your father proud."

I studied his handsome face for a moment, seeing the glitter of mirth in his eyes. This was a plot of some kind. It was part of his strategy, the one he'd probably just developed after the elves showed their cards.

Given it sounded like an amazing idea, I didn't question him. I just tore the illusion down again.

"Can we help?" Emery walked over. "If you're going to mess with them, let's really mess with them. I have some experience with that."

He certainly did. It was why they were so eager to hang him. Grinning, I nodded at him.

"Are you sure we should be doing this?" Penny asked, standing behind us. "Won't we get in more trouble?"

"What *more trouble* can I get into?" Emery asked. "What are they going to do, hang me twice?"

"They're not going to hang you," Penny said with grit in her tone. "My mother would not send us to the elves to be hanged."

"You, no. Me…" Emery let his words hang.

"They will not hang you, Mr. Westbrook. Their bounty on you is a gross miscarriage of justice. We will rectify the issue," Romulus said, and his arrogance was on par with that of any vampire.

It didn't seem like he'd learned much from the

meet-and-greet we'd just had with the elves. Thankfully, he clearly had no problem with extreme violence when things didn't go his way. I assumed it would be no different at the castle. Our best bet was to believe the *Seers* and stick together. Otherwise they could pick us off one by one.

CHAPTER 13

"Home." Romulus heaved a sigh of relief as we dragged our weary butts along the path and into gorgeous lands filled with real flowers, lush, green, *natural* trees, soft, springy grass, and dusky stone slabs. A sweet perfume filled the air, but it wasn't magically generated like the perfumed air in most of the Realm. The scent was from the actual plant life around us.

"I just do not get it," I murmured, veering off to the side and bending to touch a bush with waxy, deep green leaves. Romulus could probably tell me the exact shade of green, not that it would matter. I couldn't be bothered to remember it.

I peeled a little of the magical construction away from the ground and found the exact same fertile earth. It was like someone had taken the real scenic elements and painted over them with magic.

Darius knelt down beside me, and Penny and Emery stepped off the path, Penny's eyes on the ground, probably looking for rocks. She'd found a whole bunch so far, and Emery was now making her choose a select few from her bounty. The decisions were not quickly made.

"These paths need more benches along them," Callie said, stopping on the path and not bothering to get out of anyone's way. She looked ahead with longing. She was clearly happy to be done with the journey, or at least to have halted for a little while.

The fae pushed on, speeding up now that they were within sight of home, a natural preserve that reminded me of a greener version of Seattle, but without the clouds and rain. And cold.

The shifters followed, a couple of them in human form to carry packs, and the rest in animal form. We'd run into a few more kidnapping parties, a couple of them more robust than the first. Romulus had tried to talk the first two around, but by the time the third showed up, he just offered them a warning, very polite and lovely, and then gave the directive to kill them all.

That guy did not fuck around. I was on the right team. There was no question.

"How are these multiple worlds working?" I rubbed my head as I looked beneath the layer of magic around us, seeing down to the bones. I'd gotten good at doing that without affecting the magic too much. If I accidentally delved a little too deep, then the image would sag, sure, but that hardly ever happened anymore, and it wasn't noticeable unless you were looking. Kinda.

"These are all earth-type settings. This one is lush and fertile. There was the desert, those huge tracks of dirt that were probably fields at one time, and the hills with the scraggly bushes made into weird shapes. Like…is this an alternate universe? Or a parallel universe and the gateways are where the two universes kiss, or what? It's bending my brain."

"You read too much fiction," Penny said.

"And you think rocks have personalities. You're the last person I'll be listening to. Because there is no way this world could fit into nooks and crannies in the Brink."

"Not even with magic?" Emery asked.

"I mean…" I threw up my hands and stood. "I don't know. Maybe."

"What I'd like to know is why they cover every inch with magic," Penny said, then gasped in delight and bent behind a bush. She came back with a beaming smile and an ugly gray rock.

"They don't. A lot of these trees and plants are actually real. But the ground is covered in magic. I think that is necessary to keep the integrity of the whole thing intact. Like…if you build a house without a foundation, it's weak. But anchor it to a solid foundation, and the whole thing will be stronger."

"It's something you can take away from here," Darius murmured, studying a pine tree.

"I'll be taking a lot away from here." I started after the others. "Including any gold nuggets I find lying around."

"Why would this place have gold nuggets just lying around on the ground?" Penny asked as she followed.

"Who knows? Stranger things have happened."

We made our way through a flowered wooden archway, to a flowered square packed with people welcoming the returning fae. The shifters stood removed in a cluster, most having changed to human and a couple, like Cole and Sour Face, staying in their animal forms. Which seemed a bit rude.

"Right." I stopped before the crowd, the others stopping with me. We didn't have anyone to greet, and I wasn't in the mood to start a fight with the shifters, which might happen if I ventured too close. They were a very touchy bunch. "Now what? I assume we just wait around for Romulus and Charity to sort out their family drama with the First?"

"That would be the gist of it." Emery nodded and glanced right. In the distance, behind a wall of trees, I could just make out some construction going on.

A woman stepped through the crowd, wearing a weird, long robe-like thing decorated with sequins and beads and stitching. Her wheat-colored hair was pulled up into a bun, and she didn't smile as she approached. Given her smooth face and her stiff walk, she was more of an errand girl than anyone with experience or clout. Her arrogance wasn't on par with someone like Romulus, and she wasn't old enough for something like a council position, if these people had them.

"Welcome," she said.

"Don't bullshit a bullshitter," I replied, because she wasn't even trying to make that greeting hospitable.

Her deadpan stare said that she wanted a punch in the mouth. I refrained, of course. We were outnumbered.

"Follow me." She led the way, heading in the direction Emery had glanced. Quaint bungalows overlooked a fragrant garden boasting benches and a fountain. It felt a little like overkill. Half of the area was still under construction, as I'd noticed, but the other half seemed fine and dandy for a little R&R.

"Oh good, a bench. *Finally.*" Callie hurried to sit down. Dizzy followed, tromping through the flowers. I smirked.

"These are nicer than the last ones," Penny said as the woman stopped in front of the finished section.

"Yes," the woman replied, turning away from them. And us. "It was thought…by *some* that the guest quarters should be a little roomier."

"Why have guest quarters if you don't actually want guests?" I asked, honestly confused. I mean, I had a spare room back home—three now—but they'd come with the house (or the unasked-for remodel).

"If you should need to order food, the order form is in there." She lazily gestured to the side instead of turning. "If you need anything else, I believe the Third is your point of contact."

"Dang it," I murmured as she left. "If Charity held a grudge for that one time I killed her mark and then beat her up, this would be the perfect time for her to get even."

"She's not the type to hold a grudge," Penny replied as the shifters approached, Charity and a strange dude in the lead.

"*I* would hold a grudge," I said.

"That's because you're an asshole."

"Touché."

Charity's gaze took in the construction and then the completed bungalows.

"After all that," she said to the man, and I noticed Kairi was following close behind them, "you still put them way out here?"

"It was decided that this would be a good location for guests wanting a little privacy," the man said.

Charity huffed, marching straight past Penny and up the couple of steps into the closest bungalow. Both Kairi and the warrior fae dude followed. I could hear their quick-fire exchange of words but not what they were actually saying. A moment later, Charity came back out, her face screwed up with anger.

"I will take this up with Grandmama," she said, stopping in front of everyone. "Roger, forgive us. It seems we don't have the capacity to house you as you housed us. Rest assured, I will take it up with the governing body immediately."

"Don't trouble yourself," Roger replied, holding a folded-up garment, his backpack, and standing nude. He'd stayed in animal form in the rear for most of the journey, ready to be the first line of defense turned offense. The last two of the three groups foolish enough to approach us had been dispatched by him before everyone else caught on. "We'll be fine here."

"I just hope the beds are actually off the ground this time," the surfer guy—Andy, I thought his name was—said miserably.

Charity nodded, gave Devon a poignant look, and then stalked away. Devon glanced at Roger.

"Go," he urged.

Devon nodded and jogged after Charity. He'd be staying with her.

"Okay." I looked at Roger. "Any rhyme or reason to where we stay?"

"We'll be protected here," Emery responded. "The elves won't risk approaching these lands with the intent to do violence. They know Romulus plans to visit them, and bring us with him, so they'll start planning for that."

"Awesome. We're giving them a head start *and* home advantage, all on a couple of *Seers*' say-so." Even though I'd tried to ignore talk of what the *Seers* had said, I'd picked up on that much.

"Yup," Roger murmured, which was surprising, given he didn't usually voice things like that. But like everyone else, he didn't seem inclined to do anything about it. Maybe he just didn't know what else to do. I couldn't say I did either. So instead, I turned toward the first bungalow.

The one I chose had two bedrooms, a smallish kitchen without an oven, a menu that I would absolutely be ordering from—though, without a phone, I wasn't sure how—and a table in the living room. I fell onto the couch, which was plush and comfortable.

"Better than a hotel room," I said, wishing there was something to prop my feet up on. The coffee table would have to do. "Nearly as big as my first house. You know the one, Darius, before you came in and expanded it so much that people now feel comfortable camping out in my living room."

Darius checked out the kitchen then disappeared through another door that presumably led to the bathroom. "Rudimentary," he said.

Penny and Emery poked their heads in. "I guess we'll be sharing," Emery said. "There's just one place with a solo living space, and the older dual-mages have claimed it. There isn't enough room for everyone to have their own spot."

"It's not much smaller than that cottage in Ireland, remember?" I put my hands behind my head.

Penny stood in front of me for a moment and stared.

"What?" I asked.

"You don't care that they were rude to you?"

"Who was? The welcome chick?" Penny continued to stare. I took that as a yes and shrugged. "A lot of people are rude to me. In fact, *most* people are rude to me. Have you met Moss? That guy still hasn't warmed up. I'd be wary if she were too nice."

"And this…" Penny held out her hands. "This is cool?"

I frowned at her. "What's with you? You hangry?" I let a smile slowly drift up my cheeks. "Oh, I get it. You're worried that, with a place this small, you won't be able to help yourself from barging into my room at suspiciously inopportune moments."

She rolled her eyes and headed to one of the bedrooms.

"I'm on to you, dirty girl. I've got your number," I called after her.

"These are much nicer than the last…bungalows that were here," Emery said, taking a chair from the table and placing it by the square window. He settled in and looked out.

"What happened to those?" I asked.

"Charity blew them up. I'd tell you the story of why, but I don't want to ruin the surprise. We'll just say the welcome chick was nothing compared to the others around here, and your patience is a lot shallower than the shifters'."

CHAPTER 14

CHARITY LEFT HER new bedroom the next morning with trepidation swimming in her gut. Given she had an accepted place in the leadership of these people, they'd moved her from a temporary house, which was large, to a house near her father, which was too large. What was she going to do with five bedrooms, two living rooms, and a library? Especially because these people were getting ready to move out of here.

She hoped.

Butterflies filled her belly as she forced herself into the living room, where her father waited. Kairi, Hallen, and Devon stood outside, allowing for a little privacy. Charity and her dad needed to discuss family business.

"Good morning. Did you sleep well?" Romulus asked with a smile, sitting on the flowered couch that wasn't exactly to her taste. Or maybe she was just used to all of Devon's leather.

"Yes, thank you."

"And your new accommodations, they suit you?"

She didn't voice her complaints. They wouldn't do

any good. Though she did want to mention one thing that she hadn't gotten a chance to last night.

"Mine were fine, yes, but the guest quarters…"

He held up a hand as she sat. "Yes. I know your displeasure. We will amend that issue. It seems Mother didn't quite understand your…critique as to the original problem with the accommodations. I assure you, I understand completely, especially after Roger was so hospitable to us. I will speak to her."

It wouldn't do any good; Charity knew that in her bones. Her grandmama was kind and pleasant to those she deemed worthy, which was her people. That was about where it stopped. Charity didn't think the older woman would change her ways, not after all these years.

Which led the conversation to the sticky future.

Romulus bowed his head, as he'd clearly read her thoughts, advertised through the positioning and movements of her body.

"You don't think she can be brought around," he said.

She turned up her palms and shrugged, letting down her defenses in his company—she didn't have to try so hard to fit in to the ways of the people with him. "I don't know her that well. Or that long, you know? I don't know what she will or won't do. But she had an opportunity to change, and she didn't. Yeah, the…accommodations are a little bigger, and the beds are at least actual beds, but that's it. She didn't make an effort. Not a real one. She clearly thought a sort of patch would help. So that makes me wonder how willing she will be to do all that obviously needs to be done in the Realm. Can you talk her around?"

Romulus entwined his fingers. "The honest answer is that I don't know. She has a good heart. She wants the best for her people. In time, I am sure we could convince her that the best place for us is among the people of the Realm. It is with the shifters, who are our counterparts in every way."

"In time…"

He tilted his head slightly, approving of her picking up on that little nuance.

"We don't have that kind of time," she surmised, seeing in his body that this was killing him. He had nothing but respect for Grandmama—to face these hard truths was wearing on him. To face the role she played in his own heartache. Charity wondered if he'd been mostly avoiding thinking about it since he'd learned of it, right before they'd decided to leave the Flush for the Brink. He certainly hadn't spoken about it. Now he would have to pick at the scar, open the wound, and allow himself to fully heal.

To do that, he had to officially accuse his mother of wrongdoing. They all did.

"With Lucifer's heir revealing herself, and with the

unrest in the Realm, and the elves...no," he said softly. "We do not have that kind of time. And from what I am gathering, the village wouldn't allow us to try, anyway. Not without a reckoning of some kind. She and some of the elders have been holding people here without their consent. Without their knowledge. She has been breaking our rules. They must voice their displeasure. They have to, in order to heal."

"They want a trial."

"Yes." He took a deep breath. "We thought they might, but..."

"You hoped maybe we could just talk it out."

"I do not want to see my mother's name dragged through the mud. She meant well, I believe that. She wanted to do what was best for her people."

"That will come out in the trial." Charity hoped her shallow words weren't coming through her movements. She wasn't sure if Grandmama felt even the least bit sorry for what she'd done, and even if she had originally meant well, now she seemed hellbent on maintaining her control. She didn't know how easily the people would forgive her. Or maybe that was just her own anger talking.

"We must meet with everyone shortly to set a trial date and time. We'll have to do it quickly. I fear the elves will get restless if we don't take Reagan to them quickly."

"And Emery?"

"Emery is a grudge match, nothing more. He showed his power and caught them unaware. They want to make an example of him, that is all. That should be easy enough to talk around. Lucifer's heir, though…" His shoulders tensed, and she didn't know what that meant. "That is another matter."

"Will you allow Roger to sit in on the trial? Or Reagan?"

"No. And certainly not the vampire. No, this is a private matter. Roger needs to know who is in charge. He does not need to know the why. After the trial, we should have a better idea. Once that happens, we can move swiftly, I think. Hopefully."

That was all they really had right now: a bunch of dirty laundry, danger, and a long list of hopefullies.

CHAPTER 15

THE DAY HAD been unpardonably dull so far, and given we were sliding into early evening, it didn't seem like it would get much better. The soggy toast soaked in what tasted like sugar and honey and spices for breakfast had been decent, but the egg-like things served with them had been a little gross. I couldn't put my finger on why, though. Maybe because it was an unidentified type of animal, and I tended to like knowing what was going into my mouth. What if they'd stolen those bad boys, and now we'd have a pissed-off magical creature after us? It would be a good hazing situation.

Wandering around, looking for more of Penny's rocks, had only been fun because she tromped into people's yards and they pretended not to notice. That was a green light for me to peer into their windows to see how far they'd go before saying anything. Turned out, it was really far. Sometimes they didn't even glance over in annoyance. Didn't even flick their eyes my way! It was a lesson in self-restraint that had me really admiring these people. I never could've pulled it off.

The cucumber-like sandwiches for lunch were gross. I didn't know what they were attempting with those, but whatever it was, it had failed. I ate them, because I was hungry, but told Darius in no uncertain terms that he'd better start cooking or we'd have a problem. I didn't know how he was going to manage without an oven, but I had faith he'd figure something out.

Now, early evening, kind of dreading dinner, Penny, Emery, Darius, and I had been wandering around aimlessly, but we were running out of things to do. Per Charity's request, we were giving her people time to sort themselves out. But man, this place boasted some horrible hobbies to pass the time. I didn't want to do any of them. Painting? *I suck at it, thanks.* Cross-stitch? *Why bother?* Table making? *Good Lord, where is the alcohol...*

Callie and Dizzy, tired from the traveling, were taking time to lounge. If only I was tired enough to do the same thing.

"What's this...like a fighting thing?" I asked, at the edge of a large expanse of spongy grass filled with organized groups moving in a dance-like way. One guy flipped over a woman and then landed on his back. She swung her wooden sword down and stopped at his neck.

"What was your first clue?" Emery said with a smirk.

But it didn't look like any kind of fighting I'd ever known. They were almost civil with each other, stopping the moment it might get dirty, swinging their silly practice swords and ignoring their other body parts, like elbows, feet, or foreheads. What a waste of time. When, in the real world, *weren't* things dirty?

It took me a moment to spot the shifters out there, because they were all in human form, Roger's muscular body standing out among the lithe, graceful forms of the fae flitting around him.

I spotted Devon next, his bare back shining in the faux-sunlight, his movements nearly as quick as Roger's. He'd be a serious alpha one day. I hoped he headed up to some other country, though. He seemed much too stuffy.

Even Cole had taken to the fields in human form, and that guy liked to show off his yeti.

"How dumb." I started forward because…well, why not?

"Hey, pretty lady, fancy a fuck?"

Aaaaand my trajectory was altered immediately.

Steve lay within the shade of some big tree that I was sure had a long name, utterly relaxed with his dong hanging down. He caught sight of Darius trailing us, taking everything in.

"What's up, bud?" I crouched down near his head.

"Oh, pity, you have that neck sucker with you."

"He doesn't just suck necks, if you know what I mean." I waggled my eyebrows at him. "You're all battled out?"

"Didn't bother. I got plenty to do in this place."

"Oh yeah? Is it hanging your dick in people's windows and seeing if they'll notice? If I had one, I'd absolutely try that. I bet they wouldn't even look."

"The women would. All the little fae come running when this big lion shows up in town."

"And yet…" I looked around us. "You are alone. That bad in bed, huh?"

His smile was lazy. "Just taking a break. Also, I think they are getting ready to put the First on trial. The fae are all distracted by that."

Darius stilled, looking down at Steve for the first time. "Emery," he said, "can you hide me from view in this place? I've never heard that fae can sense spells."

"No, they can't. Yeah, sure."

"Fantastic. I intend to witness it, though it might be wise to ascertain when it will be held and scope out the location beforehand."

"Should you do that, though?" Penny asked in a small voice. "What if they catch you listening in on private matters? They aren't really cool with strangers."

"Understatement," Steve murmured.

"Reagan," Darius said. "Can you distract the village so no one is bored enough to look for me?"

Steve started laughing. "Livin' the dream, huh, Reagan? Causing mayhem."

He had that right. Another green light to act against social norms? Yes, please. "Yup."

"Don't get us kicked out," Penny said, grabbing Emery's arm. "We can't afford to be kicked out. We need their protection."

"We have Lucifer's heir." Emery wrapped a comforting arm around her. I rolled my eyes on reflex. "They won't kick us anywhere."

"So good to be needed." I grinned at Penny. Her expression darkened.

Steve pointed at the practice field. "You headed in?"

"What's the deal with the shifters being in human form?" I asked.

"Ah…" Steve sighed and then scratched his chest. "These people are taking a while to warm up to us. The ones that were more receptive are either in the Brink watching the back door, or are busy with Romulus and Charity. These cats out here are still a bit iffy. They like fighting with us but aren't sure yet about the animal form. Roger decided it was best just to fight in human form."

"Huh."

"You gonna go make them uncomfortable?"

If you can draw people here somehow, it would help Emery and me, Darius thought. *I would like to get more information about their inner workings—their politics—but I need to get closer. They mistrust vampires.*

"And for good reason, given you plan to skulk around and eavesdrop."

"The first sign you're cracking up is answering out loud questions that you asked yourself in your head," Steve drawled.

"Only the first sign? Man, I'm way ahead of the curve." I glanced at Darius. "How long do you need?"

You have a shelf life before people run screaming. Try to draw that out as long as possible.

Yeah, that might be hard.

Ever determined, I started forward.

"No, you're going with her," Emery said, and Penny had the look of someone who'd just realized she'd pulled the short end of the stick.

The soft breeze felt a little cooler here than it did elsewhere in the Realm. I wondered if the warrior fae had requested that of the elves, since it was a practice yard. The sun hung up there in the orange sky innocuously, and I really wanted to see how that whole thing worked, but I didn't dare tear it away. The real sun would be up now, and Darius wouldn't do so well in its rays.

"I don't want any part of this," Penny said, catching

up to me.

"Then you should get more comfortable hanging out on your own. Co-dependency is a real issue for some, Penny."

"Oh." I could tell she nearly hesitated. "Is hanging out by myself an option?"

"No. Come on. It'll be fun."

"It almost never is!"

No one noticed me as I approached the weapons area on the side of the yard. There was a stack of wood and a chest filled with…balls? Hard rubber tennis balls, they seemed like. How odd.

I picked one up. Kind of heavy. *Let's see if it hurts.*

I turned, aimed at Cole, and fired it off. He'd probably be the least forgiving of anyone in this whole practice yard. At least with me. We had beef. I planned to reignite old flames. Literally, since our first altercation had ended in me lighting his fur on fire.

The ball just barely missed his big melon.

"You throw weird," Penny said, pushing me out of the way.

"I'm used to throwing knives. I never did get around to learning baseball."

"Here, I'll show you." She grabbed another ball. "If you point with your other hand, and follow through with the throwing arm…" She turned and rocketed off a shot. It flew straight and true. "I had to learn baseball so

I wasn't made fun of. Then I *was* made fun of because baseball is apparently for boys, and I thought softball was just plain stupid. We have smaller hands—why should *we* get the bigger ball?"

The ball clunked off Cole's head, knocking him to the side and giving his opponent a clear shot to stab him with a wooden sword. The dulled point obviously wouldn't kill him, but it would definitely hurt.

"Do you know what you just did?" I asked with a grin as Cole cradled the side of his head. He shook his head, then snapped it back in our direction, looking at me. I pointed at Penny. "He gets real mad. He moves slowly, though. You'll be okay."

I grabbed a couple of the smaller practice swords.

"Wait…" Penny's face turned bleach white, her hands now hanging loose at her sides. Sometimes she was so determined to show me up that she forgot what was at stake. I considered it my duty to remind her. "No." She pointed at me, but her guilt was etched clearly on her face.

I laughed, picking out Roger's tree-trunk frame amidst the reeds. "Good luck. Light his fur on fire. He hates that."

"I'm not associated with her," Penny yelled, and waved her hand. She shook her head for good measure, then pointed at me again. "I was forced into this friendship. If you knew me, you'd know that is entirely plausible."

"He does know you. He's not fooled," I called back.

Cole started toward her.

"Tom Hanks's doppelganger! I don't want to fight! I'm not the fighting sort!" Penny started backing away, but I could already feel the spells stuffing the air. She was absolutely amazing under pressure, and given she had sneaky magic that allowed her to borrow the gifts of the people around her, she could use my magic to defend herself. Poor Cole. He'd learn to pick on someone his own size, and save the small, mousy types for the power hitters.

Roger took a wooden sword to his side on purpose, making the opponent commit, turning and lifting his arm so it would hit him in the thick slab of lateral muscle. That wasn't the place you went for with a shifter like him. It wouldn't hurt him with a practice sword, and it wouldn't kill him with a blade. He was pure strength and power. He'd spent his life building that up just so he could withstand basic attacks. His brawn alone would make him a solid predator, but paired with his superior intellect and uncanny ability to read his opponents, it made him nearly unstoppable. It was why he was the alpha of the North American pack, generally heralded as one of the best alphas in the world. It was also why I always got a little nervous around him. But if Vlad didn't give me pause, Roger sure shouldn't either. I just had to rip off the Band-Aid.

"Hey, little doggy." I whistled like I was calling him.

His focus snapped to me, and he took a jab to the shoulder without flinching. Boy did he hate when I riled him up.

"Here, little doggy, come to your master." I whistled again, and then used air to push the fae he was fighting out of the way.

I needed to get the shifters really fighting. If these people were wary of them, all the more reason to show them what the shifters could do. Respect might come from that wariness. Or at least a hasty truce. I was no master negotiator.

Roger turned to me slowly, and a sheen of green magic flowed around his body. Good. I considered that progress.

"Don't make me do it again!" Penny screeched right before a yeti's pain-filled roar rolled across the field. "Sasquatch-shedding sonuva donkey! That throw was Reagan's idea!"

She'd be fine. She was still stuck in the phase of blaming everything on me.

Roger rolled his shoulders. "This isn't the time for this," he said as I stopped twenty feet from him. I wanted a running start.

"Two thises don't make a right." I hefted the practice sword. "It's a practice field. It's the perfect time for this. And look." I tossed it up, grabbed the blade end, and threw it like a knife. It did a lazy half-turn, right for him. He stepped to the side, and it flew past him. "That would've hit you. See? I have aim."

"I commanded the shifters to stay in human form. You undermined that command."

I furrowed my brow, then gestured to Penny, who looked pretty funny jogging backward and wagging her fingers, her hands raised in front of her body. I couldn't feel the spell from the distance, but given she was still facing the (quite slow) lumbering beast rather than blindly running in the other direction, she was handling everything pretty well. The spell wouldn't be that nasty. It would just really hurt. "I didn't do anything. She did it. Punish her."

"Do you think I'm stupid?" Roger asked.

"Do you really want me to answer that in front of all these people? It wouldn't be a good look." His stare made my bowels a little watery. So I gave him a little spur to get things moving. "Big, dumb doggy."

The green, swirling magic intensified. He was trying to keep control. The guy was hard to crack.

"Isn't it a rule that shifters can defy a command when their life is in danger?" I asked, going about this a different way. I didn't want to keep belittling him, or he might hold a grudge. Or more grudges. But I did need him to change, so as to allow his people to change.

Romulus said that shifters and fae fought incredibly well together—they loved the pairing—and these particular fae would never see that unless the shifters were in animal form. Roger needed to make that command, and to do so, he needed to give in to his beast.

But also, trying to get him to lose control was a little bit of fun, and I was doing insanely well on my job of turning everyone's attention our way. This whole situation checked all the boxes. As long as Roger didn't hate me forever because of it, obviously.

"Cole's life was not in danger," he growled.

"I suppose not, though Penny could certainly take him on. But I was talking about you."

"We're on the same team, Reagan Somerset."

He'd used my full name. He knew what was coming.

I grinned. "I know. You're welcome."

I slapped him with air. Then I ran at him, catching up as he tumbled ass over head across the ground, and *thwapped* him in the head with the wooden sword, something that required perfect timing. I only got it wrong a couple of times—slapping his face—before getting it right. The instant he completely stopped, his legs flopping everywhere, I jabbed him between the butt cheeks. Strangely, he didn't jolt as I would've. Then again, he probably hadn't occasionally gotten prodded in the wrong hole during an intimate moment. That kind of thing made a person jumpy.

He jumped up as if on springs, so I punched him in the face. He jolted backward. I kicked him in the balls. Would nothing break this guy and force him into his wolf form?

"Enough, Reagan," he commanded, and a stray thought curled around me. *Or I'll make you beg for mercy.*

"Oh, kinky." I jabbed at his jugular, expecting him to dodge—which he did—and roundhouse-kicked him in the face. He staggered back. You couldn't increase face muscle like body muscle. It left him wide open to people who knew what they were doing. Or to those who were crazy enough to try.

"Here, doggy." I whistled again, back-pedaling a little. Hunching over, he wiped the back of his hand across his mouth. A sliver of red interrupted the line of his lips. "Does the itty-bitty-widdle doggy want a treat?"

"You sound ridiculous."

"You look ridiculous. Your mom said so, and that's saying something."

"Two saids don't make a right." He ran at me.

"Different tense! Doesn't count! Don't steal my jokes—" I dodged his punch, felt his other hand press against my side, and knew I'd screwed up. "And don't steal my moves!"

His other hand touched down on my ribs, and just

like that, I was airborne, his strength easily that of an elder vampire.

I wrapped my magic around me and slowed my flight, then stopped, hovering in the air. His eyes widened.

"Yep. This bitch can hover. And you are starting to annoy me. Your life is officially in danger, Roger. Give in. Fight me how you were meant to fight me. Show these little fae what an alpha shifter can really do. *Fight me!*"

I lit him on fire. First his clothes, then his hair, definitely his eyebrows. Callie was on hand, after all. She could fix him right up.

He took a running leap at me, ignoring the pain. Ignoring the burns. He would heal, and he knew it. He also knew I wouldn't actually kill him.

He did not know, however, how far I was willing to go to press the issue.

I pushed up higher into the air so he couldn't reach me, then encased him in a bonfire. The heat was reduced, so it wouldn't kill him nearly as quickly as real fire, but it would hurt more than the beejeebus.

He screeched, and I called that a huge win. I wished I'd recorded it. I had *never* heard that sound from his mouth.

A moment later, a wolf on fire jumped from the flames, big, burly, and mad as hell.

"Now." I lowered to the ground as he rolled around to douse the flames. I sent a shower of ice to put them out and ease the pain while he healed. I took off my pouch and tossed it aside, then took off my throwing knives, daggers, sword—all of it. It would be his wolf, and Lucifer's heir. These fae would get a taste for what real fighting was. If they planned on lasting any time at all in a war, they'd need to up their game. Or at least start to fight dirty. Roger and I would set the bar quite high. It would help us all.

"Wait." A familiar voice rang out across the practice field.

"Dang it," I murmured as Roger got to his paws, his head a little lowered, his eyes on me. He wanted blood. I cocked my head, my focus sliding back toward him. "Come at me, bro."

"Wait, please," Romulus said, and clearly the trial wasn't happening right now. Pity.

I clenched my jaw. I did not need Romulus's politeness to distract me.

"Alpha." Romulus put a hand on his heart as he stepped to the side, making a triangle out of our group with lots of space between the points. "Your control is incredible. We are all amazed. Very few could resist going against their word under such conditions."

A thick line of fae stood at the edge of the grass, watching. Everyone had stopped what they were doing to look our way. Cole lay on his back some ways off, his arms and legs spread wide, making a star with his body. Penny and someone else crouched beside him, probably trying to patch him up.

"I must side with Reagan on this, however." Romulus bowed. "You should be fighting in your animal forms. Had I known you'd decided against it, I would have raised the issue myself. Fighting beside shifters in their animal form is a joy few here have experienced. I would ask that you give them a taste. A *real* taste. Stage a battle with your shifters against these *custodes*." I knew *custodes* meant warrior fae. It was what they called themselves. I had no idea why. "Seeing your pack work together will open a few eyes."

Roger lowered his head just a bit, but he didn't change back into his human form. Given his fur was still smoking in places, it was probably because he wanted to use all his energy to heal.

"Now." Romulus turned to me. And bowed.

"Hi," I said awkwardly. "Nice to see you again. Kinda."

"I realize I am interrupting a practice session, but I wonder if Roger would do me the great honor of stepping aside so that I might try my hand at Lucifer's heir?"

I took a deep breath. "I'd really rather not. Do you heal quickly? No, I'd rather not."

Though I kind of did, if only so I could punch him in the mouth for always making me feel so freaking socially defunct. Vampires might be equally debonair and polite, but most of them were morally bankrupt, and they all changed into horrible monsters. That evened the scales a little. This fae was just…lovely. Attractive, pleasant without being sickly sweet, polite, and morally sound—he was really tough to be around, if I was being honest. Total goody two shoes.

"Please, come. We will make a show of it." He motioned behind him. "Half the village has assembled to watch your fighting. They've already heard rumors of you from our journey here. They wish to see what you can do."

"I'll gladly show them…with Roger. He has it coming."

"Yes, of course. Only"—he smiled—"he does not have the capability to use hellfire."

I turned my head to the side and squinted one eye just a little, thinking, trying to confuse him with my body movements. If I didn't know what it meant, he surely wouldn't, yet he'd think he was missing something.

"Yeah, but that doesn't actually work on me," I said.

"Correct. And I'd like everyone to see it." He clasped his hands behind his back. "In case they doubt."

So there were doubters. I honestly didn't care, but

had the feeling he'd keep pushing for this.

I glanced behind him at the crowd again, not because I felt pressured to perform for them, but because it was a good showing. Fighting the boss would probably bring out a few more, thus emptying out the village and giving Darius ample room to skulk around.

"Yeah, sure, why not." I pointed at Roger. "This is postponed. I will make you do doggy tricks before we leave this place, just you wait."

He backed away slowly and then turned toward Cole, who was still lying in the grass. Baby.

Penny had left him and sidled closer to the practice field, picking at her nail, watching me. If I could find a way to get her involved, I would, but Romulus was talking about hellfire, and that was one sandbox she couldn't play in.

It was a sandbox Romulus shouldn't be playing in either. Not with me, anyway. Some of my reactions were built in from years and years of practice. If he triggered one, I would fire back. And I didn't think he could withstand hellfire like I could. I really didn't want to kill the Second Arcana.

CHAPTER 16

"As far as weapons"—Romulus glanced at everything I'd set aside already—"I see you did not plan to use them."

"I was going to fight my magic against his. He doesn't use weapons."

"I do, however."

"Right. Well, go for it. I can't really stick you full of throwing knives, anyway. Right? That might kill you?"

"I do heal quickly, but that might kill me, yes. Would it not kill you?" He kinda…*slunk* down a little, and a shiver rolled across my skin. He was preparing to fight. It made me feel like hovering for some reason, though it would have been pretty pointless to try. I couldn't go very fast in the air. I didn't even know why Lucifer had that sort of magic. What was it good for, besides negating a ladder?

"They wouldn't reach me. Unless they did, and then…probably. I also heal quickly."

"Then no throwing knives. But I assume—"

"Oh my God, just use whatever you want and I'll

make it work. I miss Cahal. He rarely spoke. And he certainly wasn't polite when he did."

"Fantastic."

"That was a put-down, and still you sound so nice. I really hate that," I grumbled.

He unslung something from his back, and I realized it was a bow, of all things.

"Wait…"

He held it out in front of him and reached back with the other hand, pulling out an arrow. He nocked an arrow, pulled back, and paused for a moment.

"Dude, what the fuck—since when do you people use—"

He released. The arrow flew right for my heart. I should have thrown up a shield of air, but in that split second, only one idea came to mind—sword!

I had an air sword in my hand immediately and swung, clanging against the wood arrow and knocking it away. Another came, and another. Romulus nocked an arrow, released. Nocked an arrow, released. So fast his arm became a blur. But he was only shooting center mass. He didn't vary the shots.

He definitely didn't have the type of battle knowledge I did. His skills were the kind you learned from practice, not from evading a mark intent on killing you. He'd gained some experience in the field, but clearly he hadn't been pushed to the limits. Not like I had. Not like Roger.

Intending to give Darius as much time as I could, I swung my air blade, cutting down or deflecting the arrows, one after the other, almost bored with it. Out of arrows, he dropped the bow. His hands came together, and I knew what would happen next.

I released the air sword as a jet of hellfire spewed toward me, blistering in heat, half the size of my wrist. It would get the job done with most creatures, including most demons. I covered my hair and clothes with ice, so they wouldn't burn away, and let it wash over me. The heat felt like a comforting caress.

My turn.

"Stay put or this will kill you," I yelled.

I sent jets of hellfire out of my palms, each bigger than his, although the heat was the same. They sped toward him, and I noticed his assistant start off across the grass, afraid for his boss.

"Halvor would've been too late." I bent the fire at the last moment and wrapped it around him, cocooning him with air so the heat wouldn't harm him. I rose a sheet of regular fire in front of Halvor. He came out the other side hairless but determined to get to his master. "Jesus. That guy is intense. I hope Callie brought enough hair stuff."

The hellfire wore away, and Romulus just stood there for a moment, his face slack and his eyes wide, breathing heavily. The guy had thought I was going to kill him.

"You don't trust me, huh?" I walked toward him, letting him get his bearings. "It makes me like you a little more. Though..." I finally punched him in the kisser.

Halvor was on us a moment later, his sword out, his decision-making a little off. I tossed him away with a burst of air. He really should've expected it.

"That was...enlightening," Romulus said in a shaky voice, patting his lip and coming away with a spot of blood.

"Don't try hellfire on Lucifer."

"No. Shall we continue?"

"Always with the freaking politeness," I said, exasperated, backing off a little. "I just scared the hell out of you on purpose."

He pulled the sword from his back in one smooth, fast motion. His moves were good; mine were better. His people wouldn't get to see that, though, because I'd put my weapons in the grass with the other stuff. I now regretted that.

He thrust with his sword, hit my air sword, pulled back. He spun and swung. Dodging the blow, I fast-stepped toward his body. I rammed my forearm across his jaw, then brought it back and slammed my elbow against his cheek. As I turned, I followed through with my other fist, clocking him a good one. Dancing back out, I prepared to air-club him, since the sword would leave a rather large hole I didn't know if he could come back from.

Lightning rained down around us, all the strikes missing him but crashing down on various points of me. I could withstand the heat, no problem. The freaking jabs of electricity were not pleasant, though. Like, really not pleasant. I hated it.

"Charity, how lovely of you to join us," I said, sarcasm ringing through my faux-politeness.

Without even looking in her direction, I shoved Romulus away with a burst of air. Doing that was as fun as kicking in doors. He went tumbling across the ground. These people clearly did not realize that their magic could cut through it if they applied enough force and pressure. Or at least lessen the impact. I thought they might've learned it battling demons in the Brink. Clearly they hadn't been paying enough attention. I didn't plan to enlighten them until right before they needed to use it against an enemy.

The crowd of people now stretched halfway around the practice field, everyone trying to get a good vantage point. Most of the village had to be out here. The shifters were all with Roger, including Cole, who was sitting at the side. Penny had really done a number on him.

And Darius thought I had an expiration date on my ability to keep people distracted?

I finally swiveled to look at Charity. She stood about a hundred feet away, her hair high on her head in a ponytail, her sword sheathed, and the loose fabric of her top, tied around her middle with multiple bands, lightly moving in the breeze.

"You look hot," I called. "Like a warrior princess. Oh, wait…you are, right? A princess of the *practice yard*?"

Even from the distance, I could tell she narrowed her eyes at me. Vampire vision from the bond—it was amazing.

"I didn't grow up practicing. I grew up surviving." She turned a little and bowed to Romulus.

"Oh no, not you too. I was actually starting to like you. We were on our way to being friends."

"Hardly."

"Yeah. Penny said that too. And now look. Besties."

"No," Penny barked. "It's like a…captive situation."

"Yeah." I shrugged. "Whatever works. I bonded a vampire, after all. My decision-making is questionable."

"Father, may I take this fight?" Charity asked.

Romulus bowed back. "But of course. I will take this time to consult the shifters about—"

"Oh no, no." I waggled my finger at him, then pointed at Penny. "She just took out a yeti. Try your hand with her. She can borrow magic, remember? That means mine. You want to see what a mage wielding Lucifer's magic can do? She's your best bet."

"You know what?" Penny said, and I could tell she'd reached her threshold. "Yeah, sure. You want to fight, let's fight."

"Be careful," Cole called out.

I didn't wait to see what happened. I started running straight for Charity, air sword in hand.

Lightning rained down around me, striking my shoulders and head, vibrating down through my body. I threw up an air shield, and that helped diffuse it, but bolts still made it through.

"That *can* be used on Lucifer," I said as she started forward, charging toward me as I ran at her. She knew my fighting style.

We clashed in the middle, and demons spun up around us, the really gross kind, distorted in the way they'd probably looked to her on her last journey through the Realm, when she'd had to face them while fighting magical poisoning. Insects crawled across their flesh and poked up through their skin. They belched fire and hobbled.

Her eyes widened for a moment, long enough for me to jab her in the stomach with a dull air blade. It didn't pierce flesh.

"You're supposed to lead the battle," I said as she

bent over, losing her breath. "If I don't make it to the end, someone is going to have to take on Lucifer. It'll likely be you. You can't get distracted."

The demons still moved around us as she straightened up. I stitched in a big black wolf, like Devon, figuring it might help anchor her. The detail in the image was great, but I couldn't get it to move.

Charity barely spared it a glance. She learned fast; I had to give her that.

She slashed her sword, and I blocked the move and sidestepped to sweep her legs. She jumped over my leg and turned, her blade coming down. I swiveled and threw a punch at her face. She jerked to the side, barely missing the impact, and stepped in the direction she'd turned. I created my sword as her thrust came at me. I blocked it, then shoved at her with air.

She wasn't like the others. She thought two steps ahead. She'd already seen me use this trick and had clearly been thinking about how to work around it.

She swung her blade in figure eights, chopping through the air, pushing back rather than going down and rolling. Clearly she *had* been paying attention when fighting demons in the Brink.

"*Shh*," I said, even though she wasn't speaking, and slammed air down on top of her. I wasn't ready for the other fae to know they could fight my power like that. It would steal all my fun. She bent under the weight, and her electricity started up again, reducing my magic. Which was fine, because it didn't seem like the other fae had that in their arsenal.

"Where's your hellfire?" I asked as she pushed her way to standing, sweat beading on her brow. I let her.

"I don't have the power."

"Bullshit. You have plenty of power."

She sent a buzzing ball of light at me. I braced myself, because it would probably be electricity and would hurt something fierce. In a moment, though, it bloomed into fire before enveloping me. I'd already protected my hair and eyebrows from a possible attack, so I ran with it. Literally. I bore down on her covered in flames. It was probably really freaky.

"To make hellfire…" I said, pooling the fire onto the outside of my air blade, letting flames shed as I swung it through the air. She danced away when one of the embers landed on her, burning. "You need a little bit of love…"

I thrust forward. She barely dodged. I was faster than her, but not by much.

"A little bit of lust…"

I kicked out. She blocked with her shin, then danced forward and side-kicked at my chest. I ducked under the attempted kick and spun around, at her back and hacking, catching the edge of her shoulder before she could face me. She let out a gasp. That smarted.

"A little bit of hate..."

Demons descended on the wolf, ripping and tearing. She didn't so much as flick her eyes in that direction.

"And a little bit of violence. You need them all, in equal doses. You need the balance. The desire and the pain. The love and the loss."

She danced backward, and I wasn't expecting it, so I stood there like an idiot for a moment.

Her eyebrows lowered over her intelligent red-brown eyes, and silence descended on the practice field. Bodies crowded in, more than before. It had to be nearly the whole village.

It is good that she has this knowledge, Darius thought, clearly in the area now. I'd been too busy trying not to get skewered to notice his proximity increasing. *I half hoped it would come after I was out of these lands, however. You are magnificent, by the way. Your power is unequaled in this village. It is giving them a lot to think about.*

Skulking and eavesdropping. Doing what a vampire did.

"Are we breaking? What are we doing?" I asked as Charity put her sword away. "I'm not winded. Are you? Or are you passing me off to Penny?"

"No," Penny called from somewhere behind me.

"She really does like me, you know."

Charity leaned forward, thrusting her hands out. A very thin stream of hellfire blasted forth, and I let it wash over me so she'd get a little joy out of it.

"Good," I commented after it diminished. She panted as though she'd run a mile. "It'll get easier and your stream will get bigger."

"I have a lot of anger," she said after a moment. "A lot of violence." She paused. "Until Devon, I'd forgotten how to love with my whole heart. How to lust with my whole body. I've never merged those two halves of myself. Part of me, I think, was afraid of all that anger."

I grimaced and then worried the grass with my foot. "Yeah, I'm a little uncomfortable with emotional revelations. Your people seem to just hand that stuff out willy-nilly."

"My father has tried to explain how to make hellfire. My grandmama. They said it comes from within. That I would grow into it with time."

"It does, typically. Living here, it would take a long time, I imagine. What sort of hate do you have in this place? It's too nice. The violence is all for show. Like...look. Watch this."

I rose into the air, above her head, swelled my power, and blasted it out at the people gawking on the sidelines. The air rolled over the ground, gaining speed as I pumped more power into it. It slammed into them like a tidal wave, knocking them down and on top of one another, sending them rolling. I smiled as I watched. It really was a good time.

"And not one of them will get pissed enough to come after me." I lowered back down. "It would take these people years to accumulate enough anger here to really harness it, I think."

"Not for long, hopefully," she murmured, and then bowed to me. "Thank you for teaching me. For joining me. For giving me status."

I grimaced again and started edging away. "I think we're good here."

"You will make it to the last battle. We will make sure of it."

These people were so positive. They clearly had no foothold in reality.

"Okay, well…"

Darius walked across the grass to meet me, and I had a feeling he was doing it to show his face. To put forth a show of having been there the whole time.

Let's head out of the public eye, he thought as he neared, looking behind me. *They have a lot to unpack.*

Penny was getting a bow from a bloodied Romulus.

"Did she win?" I asked as she reciprocated the bow awkwardly and then walked toward us, storm clouds on her face. I was going to get yelled at.

I only saw the last portion of the fight, but yes. She threw a spell over her shoulder as she ran away from him.

"Oh yeah, that's her signature move. It means in-credible pain if you let that spell land."

He did. He watched your fight with Charity lying down. Tomorrow, while I get into position, I'd ask that you fight Penny out here. Let them see how you can negate her spell weaving. They saw her take down the Second and the yeti, so it'll have a big impact.

"You'll have to ask her yourself. She's done with me."

"Yes, I am," Penny said as she stomped by. "I will be spending the evening in my room, thank you very much. Darius, you're cooking. I need edible food. Charity taught them to make good food the last time she was here, but clearly they didn't keep it up."

I want Callie and Dizzy here, as well. Hopefully that'll distract people from realizing Emery and I are away. They are speaking in hushed tones, even amongst themselves, and have organized a closed trial with sentinels. They are wary of strangers in their midst. I was able to glean that people are angry with the First. They want their say. Even still, I do not know if they'll tear her off her post.

"You're taking Emery with you tomorrow? Can't you just use a spell casing to hide?"

I could, yes. But he doesn't trust me to relay the information I gather.

"Wise."

He is absolutely correct, yes, and his knowing that is...frustrating.

I laughed as I collected my weapons and we made our way off the field. Fae were returning to the practice field, giving me a wide berth but facing off with the shifters, now in their animal forms.

"The thing is, though, I might be more valuable to you if I wander around the village and maybe just...kinda...insert myself into the proceedings? I can make a show of Penny anytime, but if I'm fighting, I can't very well listen to the melons, if you know what I mean."

Listening to thoughts...yes. How stupid of me to forget. I will still need a distraction so I can slip away undetected, but after that, slip into the trial and find out whatever you can.

Another green light to behave badly. And even though I was a real asshole, I'd still lent Charity status! I was with Steve—this place was amazing!

I wondered if I could get anyone to lose their temper with me...

Tomorrow I would find out.

CHAPTER 17

"THIS IS MAKING me uncomfortable. I want to leave, except there's a castle full of elves out there who want to capture you and kill Emery, so now my stomach is in knots and there is nothing I can do about it." Penny wrung her hands beside Reagan, pressed against the wall and trying not to crush the flowers.

"What is the difference between doing this and rummaging around in people's yards for pet rocks?" Reagan asked as she stood in someone's window, watching the occupants eat a late breakfast.

"I was inconspicuous. You are not."

"You were not. You mutter to yourself constantly. If they didn't see you, they certainly heard you."

"What are you girls up to?" Steve asked from the edge of the garden. He had clothes on, thank goodness.

"Just trying to make people uncomfortable," Reagan said, finally peeling away and allowing Penny a sigh of relief. "It's working, I think, but damn, they're really good at ignoring things. Which you know, obviously.

Why you guys are bent out of shape about it, I don't know. Look what fun I'm having."

Steve laughed. "I don't think normal people get a kick out of being ignored."

"It's not being ignored so much as the effort behind it. Like…" She tromped through the flowers. A glance back saw no reaction from the people whose garden she was ruining. "They are conveying the message that we don't belong in the most passive-aggressive way possible. Doesn't that tickle your funny bone? Why didn't you guys just randomly trip people or something when you were here last time? Or barge into their houses and just take a bed if you didn't like your setup?"

"We were trying to play nice for Charity's sake. Still are, actually, though Romulus is trying to pave the way for Roger to gain more status. They are defrosting to us a little. Given your…lineage, I would expect they'd do the same for you."

"Meh." Batting a hand through the air, she stepped away from the crushed flowers and started down the little pathway further into town. Steve walked with her, and Penny followed, resisting the urge to apologize. "I couldn't be bothered. I've never fit in before. Why should I try now? It's much more fun trying to pick fights. They will crack first, believe me. Someone will punch me by the end of the day."

"It'll be me," Penny said, lagging behind just a little,

hunching for all she was worth. She was so annoyed that Emery was the political one between them. While he got to be invisible and attend the hearing of the First—the warrior fae called it something different, but she couldn't remember the term—she was stuck following Reagan around, a party to crazy antics that were so against the social norms of this place. "I'll be the one punching her in the face."

Reagan nodded with her lips turned down in a duck bill. "Quite possibly."

"You gave ol' Cole a good wallop yesterday," Steve said, falling back just a little so he could talk to Penny.

She shrugged. She'd tried to explain that she hadn't actually meant the ball-to-his-head situation as an insult, merely as a way to show Reagan up. She'd figured he might understand that. But he'd persisted until it got dangerous, and then she'd had to react. Everyone knew she went overboard when she was reacting. She didn't know what he was expecting.

"And then you rang the Second's bell. I don't think he expected that. He had you on the run." Steve smiled with a twinkle in his deep blue eyes.

She shrugged again.

"Never get Penny on the run," Reagan said as she waved at someone coming from the opposite direction. "Your fly is down." The man didn't glance over. "Hey, bro, your dick is hanging out." He looked straight ahead, realizing, of course, that his robe thing lacked a fly (if he even knew what that was) and his dangly bits wouldn't hang out if he tried. Which Steve probably had at some point. "Here, I'll get it."

Reagan darted toward the fae, bent, and reached between his legs.

That did it.

He jumped back, looked her way with wide eyes, and covered his junk all in one harried movement.

"Ha!" She pointed at him, her finger inches from his face. He blinked under her crazy stare. "Got you. Try harder, bub. Your countrymen are better at this than you."

He let out a wavering breath and stepped away gingerly, working around her.

"Low," Steve said with a smile. "Going for a guy's junk is low."

"I kicked Roger in the nuts. You think I really care about the rules of polite warfare?"

"This is true." They kept sauntering along the path as though it were a pleasant stroll and Reagan *wasn't* trying to cause havoc and turn the place upside down. The terrifying part was that she hadn't really gotten going yet. She was supposed to take it easy for a while, then turn up the pressure, then pop into the proceedings and learn what she could from people's thoughts.

Penny missed the days when they could just go

home after Reagan caused a scene. She'd never complain about those instances again.

"Ah, there's Callie and Dizzy." Reagan pointed up ahead.

The dual-mages stood in the center of one of four gardens that made up the corners of a small square. In the middle was large shrubbery fashioned after a fountain. It was cool but weird, and it fit this place perfectly.

"Roger was fuming after that fight," Steve said as Reagan veered toward them, cutting across the path of two people who stopped and looked straight ahead.

She touched one of their noses. "Boop."

The woman's eyebrows sank low, and fire lit in her eyes.

Reagan smiled at her. "Oh. Where are you headed? You'll break, I can see it."

"Reagan, stop pestering the townsfolk and come here." Callie pointed down at a grouping of flowers. "Look how lovely this is. Do you think these exist in the Brink?"

"He would've come for blood," Reagan said, responding to Steve as she walked toward the older dual-mages. "Romulus got in the way, though."

"It worked out to everyone's benefit," Steve replied. "The fae got to see what they'd be protecting—or fighting beside, at least. Romulus got to show his might with the hellfire, Charity got to show off her prestige in battle, and, after you left, Roger got to pour his anger and pain into *crushing* the fae. We did a mock battle, and we stomped all over them. Too bad you weren't there. Speaking of…"

Steve paused long enough for Callie to show Reagan the flowers.

"I must ask Romulus if we can plant these in my garden," she said, moving on to look at another grouping.

"Where was your vampire when all that was going on?" Steve gave Reagan a sly smile. "And"—he looked around dramatically—"he seems to be missing again. Along with a very powerful mage. Hmm." He tapped his chin.

"Messing around in a vampire's affairs is not a wise pastime, young man," Callie said, turning to the back corner. The word "moneymaker" was scrawled across the butt of her bright pink velvet sweatpants in silver cursive.

"Yes, ma'am," Steve replied, pretending to be chastised.

"Reagan, what are your plans for causing mischief?" Dizzy asked, sidling closer. His left boot crunched down on a tuft of violet flowers with spears of yellow inside them. He didn't seem to notice. "How about if I set my T-Rex running through the center of the village?" He patted the satchel hanging at his hip. "That would be good, right? It shocks whenever it bites down on someone."

"Yeah, definitely set that one loose." Reagan squinted and looked upward. "Maybe even a few things. They don't really have specific guards in this place, but more people have been lingering around now that we're here. We'll need to pull them away so I don't have to actually get violent."

"Okay." Callie walked back over, apparently having had her fill of the flowers. "Let's get to it. We have a couple of hours, right?"

Penny sagged. It would be a long couple of hours.

I FOLLOWED CLOSELY behind a woman with a bedazzled robe, my feet catching her heels again and again. Penny skulked behind me. It was nearly time for the hearing to start, and this woman was heading over to watch. The dual-mages were in the village center, readying their magic. I'd opened my mind to others' thoughts, and given these people didn't know to guard their gourds, I was bombarded with unsolicited feedback on my actions, mannerisms, and appearance. These people definitely knew I was in their vicinity, and they were curious, but they seemed compelled to ignore me at all costs. Except it didn't seem totally natural, like they were under some kind of compulsion. It severely reduced my joy in how far out of their way they were going to pretend I wasn't annoying the crap out of them.

I leaned forward so my mouth was closer to her ear. "Did you hear the one about the walrus?" I yelled.

What does she want with me? the woman thought, her robe swishing around her feet.

"Are you trying to look like a wizard?" I asked, and then sent some air buffers to hassle two people walking on either side of the road, giving me plenty of room in the middle. I pushed them into the hedge.

She is so powerful. She will bring great status to who-ever is in her inner circle, the one on the right, a woman with a slight frame and short brown hair, thought. The man on the left had his mind in the gutter.

"*Turn around*," I sang to the woman I was follow-ing. "*Every now and then I get a little bit sad that you won't just turn around. Turn around…*"

"Those aren't the words," Penny said.

Not a great singing voice.

"Killjoys." I stepped out from behind her, right into the path of a tall man with a slight frame and lean muscle tone. He stopped suddenly, and I heard a mental sigh of relief from the woman I'd been following.

Maybe if I just looked now… But the woman's

thoughts trailed away, and her bearing tensed as if she were fighting the urge.

The man's gaze skittered off me and to the side. He stepped to the right to get by me. I did the same to keep even with him.

So powerful, so fierce, so beautiful. What would it be like to... The man's thoughts trailed off. He took another step to the right to get around me. *Desperate for my attention. Taboo... One night...*

I had a feeling he was imagining things. I was a forbidden attraction, like the shifters at first, only now Romulus was trying to assimilate the shifters and normalize their presence. But he hadn't interfered with my fun. I might just like the guy more because of it.

After listening to everyone's thoughts, though, that joy was bleeding away slowly.

"I would rock your world so hard," I told the man, and that brought his peepers to mine in a hurry.

Thoughts crowded in too fast for me to process them. Levitating and gyrating and, wow, this guy wanted a messier life. He was cooped up here, I could tell. Normal people didn't pine after the exotic this hard.

"You know what?" I turned around and faced Penny, done with that guy.

What just happened... Why did she... His thoughts about me kept drifting away now that they weren't solely fueled by lust.

"You said the First is in trouble for manipulating people, right?" I asked her.

"Yeah." She watched the man I'd been harassing pass on by, his gaze focused straight ahead again. "She magically affects her people's moods and desires, I think. Makes them happy to stay here, want to return if they leave, stuff like that."

"So she could definitely keep them from wanting strangers in her midst, right?" I was walking before the words stopped falling.

"Yes," she said. "Which…makes all kinds of sense, actually. She's been hiding people away, trying to protect them, so she wouldn't want strangers coming in. And if they did, she wouldn't want them staying, because that might entice some of her people to leave. Or…more of her people to leave, I guess. I heard that some did get out."

"Yeah." A roar blasted out over the village. The T-Rex had been let loose. "Do you think they know that?"

She thought for a second, catching up. "Probably not," she said. I took a left and cut through someone's yard. "But would it really matter? They know she's doing something she shouldn't be."

"It might make a difference in how they feel about the shifters. Romulus is trying to bridge the gap between them, but people are still weirded out. They need to be tight with each other if they're going to work together against the elves, and the memories they create here will stick with them. Any tension between them will be easier for them to overcome if both sides know the warrior fae were duped. See what I mean?"

"You're really smart when you want to be."

"Nah. Everyone gets lucky some of the time."

I hopped a fence and emerged on a little lane surrounded by flowers—this whole freaking place was flowers and gardens, it seemed like, and because they were all real and natural, instead of elf creations, it made the area incredibly cute and picturesque and a huge nuisance. I much preferred the Underworld, which had plenty that was weird and unsavory to balance out the lovely and beautiful. It was a startling realization.

Across a carefully tended plot of grass surrounded by more plants and flowers stood a wooden gate painted white, a man and woman to either side of it, swords on their backs and eyes hard. A chest-high fence stretched away, a tended hedge rising to head height behind it, blocking the view in a beautiful way. A voice rose from within the space, and it seemed that I was a bit late for the proceedings, or they had started early.

Not to worry. I had a plan. One I'd created a split second before.

"What's up, dickweeds?" I strutted up to the guards,

and their gazes landed on me without hesitation. They had been excused from the emotional sabotage the others were plagued with. Unless I was wrong and this was a huge mistake…

I pressed on. Might as well.

"Miss Somerset, please forgive our rudeness, but we—"

I sped up so they couldn't step in front of me, reached the gate at a blinding speed, and kicked it, right in the middle. The satisfying *crack* made me smile, followed by the *bang* of the doors flying open and hitting whatever was on the inside.

"Reinforced steel," I said as they lunged for me. I shoved them away with my magic. "Reinforced steel makes it harder to kick in doors. Or gates. And now you know."

"Sorry," Penny said as she trailed behind, using my magic to create a sort of barrier.

"Good idea." I nodded. She might resist it, but she was made for a life of mayhem.

Stones dotted the grass walkway, flanked on both sides by the tall hedge. The space opened up near the end. People in those bedazzled white robes sat in rows upon rows of white wooden chairs facing a stage. Charity and Romulus sat on one side of the stage with flat expressions, and a regal woman with graying hair and very few laugh lines sat on the other side, her hands in her lap and her hard scowl on me. A woman stood at a little podium, no longer speaking, her face turned my way in confusion.

Magic thrummed to my right, a concealment spell. Obviously no one was the wiser to the vampire and natural mage listening intently within their midst.

You're late, Darius thought, and it was a wonder I could even hear him amidst all the thoughts suddenly crowding me.

Heir.

…what a strange dress code…

I can't believe Lucifer sired another child.

What is that sack around her hips?

She can levitate—only demons can levitate. Does she change into—

"Hey," I said, cutting out the thoughts for a moment. I'd wait until I dropped my news before listening in again. "So sorry to interrupt, but your gate was basically inviting the whole neighborhood to kick it in. I couldn't resist. Anyway, while I'm here—"

"Reagan Somerset, yes." Romulus stood, his hands clasped in front of him.

He is incredibly annoyed, Darius thought, and it occurred to me that I always had our channels open, even when I was blocking everyone else out. *I'm sure you have a point, and you had better make it quickly.*

"If you don't mind me saying—" Romulus went on.

I held up my hand. "This concerns this meeting. Darius will kill me for giving this away, but I have Lucifer's magic."

"Yes, we know. We all saw that rousing display of your powers—"

"Yes, yes, yesterday. I meant *all* of his magic. Including the ability to read minds."

I opened back up really quickly, getting slammed with surprise, outrage, fear, and an attempt to think nothing at all. People didn't realize that usually backfired, leading to an out-of-control thought spiral.

"I very rarely use it," I said over the din, except it was actually quiet, and I was just yelling over the noise in my head. "I was taught to tune it out. People mostly think irrelevant garbage, and I have enough garbage in my own head—I don't need anyone else's. But…" I held up a finger. "But something was deeply troubling to me about this place. About the way you all ignore strangers."

"Yes, that is something I meant to—"

"Romulus, please, if I may," I said, as polite as I was capable of being. "You were hoodwinked by your mother for…how many years? You are clearly blind to the very obvious. I am not so blind. What I have to say is relevant to these proceedings. Let me—very quickly— throw it into the ring, and I'll leave you to discuss everything."

He stilled for a moment, and I heard, *She should've been barred from the Realm. She does not belong here.*

I pointed at the regal lady, whose pinched expression and hostile thoughts marked her as the First Arcana.

"I am magical, from both parents. I belong in the magical world just as much as you do," I responded, and she couldn't stop her eyes from widening. "Thought I was lying about the mind reading, huh?"

Insufferable dirty demon...

"Sticks and stones, lady. Anyway, I was mostly delighted by your people ignoring me. I am not as fragile as the shifters. I don't need to be liked." This was where I had to hedge a little. "After a few...experiments on how far people would go to ignore me..."

"Yes, you really did push the limits," Romulus mentioned.

He apparently finds your colorful personality humorous, Darius thought, and I knew he was reading some subtle changes in the Second's body language, because I hadn't gotten that at all.

"Yes, I did. Because it was crazy to me that a"—I did bunny ears with my fingers—"'warrior race' didn't get pissed that I was throwing them around. Or standing in their way. Or just being an ass for no reason. So I used my magic and peeked into their craniums to at least see if I was having an effect."

"That is a violation of privacy," the First said, outraged.

"Yeah, you should talk. Why do you think you're up there? I'm about to add to your list of crimes, too."

"Mother, please. I would like to hear what Reagan Somerset has to say." And now Romulus's gaze was keen. "If she has new insights to offer, we need to hear them."

"How can we possibly trust a creature that listens in—"

"I agree with the Second." An older man stood up from the audience, his long white beard ridiculous and his robe quite plain.

"As do I."

"Yes."

I took advantage of the opening. "I discovered some interesting things. For one, your people are extremely interested in the exotic. You think of it as sexually taboo, which is…off-putting, but also just crazy. The Realm is host to a multitude of creatures. Even the most isolated groups, like the vampires, mingle. To be so closed off that you think someone different is taboo is just fucking crazy. What's wrong with you people? The other thing I noticed is that people *couldn't* think about me for long. Their thoughts would drift away, as though they'd lost the thread of consciousness. They weren't keeping themselves from noticing me; they were unraveled from noticing me. It seemed like manipulation of some kind, and honestly, it just took the fun out of the whole thing. Given the First's magic, my guess is that she's not just keeping you put—she is injecting the desire to ignore strangers. To ostracize them. To keep them apart. So that ain't good.

"But here's the real issue. The only one among you that can really fight—*really* fight—is Charity. Why? Because she knows how to survive. My fighting prowess isn't magical, by the way. It was learned out of necessity. When I fought Romulus, it was clear he had spent most of his life on that practice yard. Charity saw it, and that's why she intervened. If you go up against a bunch of vampires, you're going to get a rude awakening. A force of stronger demons would ring your bell. Those buggers fight dirty. Hell, you went up against the shifters yesterday, right? They didn't beat you because they were better, but because they have more real-life battle experience. A *lot* more. The longer you stay in this God-awful natural hideaway, the weaker you will inevitably become, until someone comes in and gets you. I was expecting to find a bunch of people like Charity here, but instead I found a bunch of softies that are going to need my protection, not the other way around. So you all better get your shit together, or you'll lose the battle that is coming, and it'll be your death sentence."

Silence descended, everyone staring at me. Waiting for more. It occurred to me that I probably should've stormed out after that last bit to end on a dramatic note. Now I just looked like the doofus who didn't know when to leave the party.

Take the concealing spell away, Darius thought.

"What?" I asked, barely stopping myself from turning and looking in his direction.

"You were just saying—"

I held my hand up to Romulus. "Sorry, I was just listening to Penny communicate with me. I can read thoughts, but I can't inject them in others, sadly."

"I didn't—" Penny started. I threw a kick to shut her up, and she dodged the blow. "Stop trying to kick me."

Our teamwork was impressive.

Take the magic away with a flourish and expose us. We have what we need. Your new information will be the nail in the coffin. Outing us will show them just how sheltered they really are.

"Oh, and one more thing," I said, a little louder than was strictly necessary.

I ignited fire over the spell, realizing belatedly that the spell was a whole lot more powerful than I'd expected, and then quickly slapped up an air shield before the whole thing exploded outward. Fire and ice ballooned against my air shield. The back row of the audience jumped out of their seats, turning to look or struggling over each other to get out of the way.

"We've been experimenting with inverting the power so spells don't read as powerful to other mages," Penny murmured. "And you, I guess."

"Yeah. Might've been nice to mention that before I blew everyone up," I groused, tearing down the air wall.

Darius stood as though he'd expected that shitshow, and Emery slowly uncurled his hands from over his head.

"The explosion happens outward like we planned," Penny said. "That's good news. We didn't have time to test it."

I shook my head, turning back to Romulus. Definitely impressive teamwork.

"I don't think I have to point out how naïve you all are when it comes to the magical world, right?" I hooked a thumb at Emery coming out of his crouch. "It's pretty obvious?"

"I would say that you have made your point," Romulus said, pressing his lips tightly together.

I pointed at Darius, who came to stand beside me. "He's not even sorry. He was caught, and he's not sorry. So...take a hint."

He got that hint, loud and clear. Darius rested his hand on my hip. *Let's head back to our...very cozy hovel and keep our heads down for the rest of today. We'll be leaving soon, and then we must part.*

"Wait, what?" I let him nudge me toward the battered gates. He gave an apology he didn't mean to Romulus, which I was sure Romulus didn't accept, and then we were walking back to our bungalow.

"We have to part, *mon ange*," Darius said. "I am not meant to go with you to the elf castle. They do not like my kind."

"Which is a problem, since you should have equal representation there, just like everyone else."

"A chat for a later day, perhaps."

"And two, that can't be right. We're a team. We do dangerous things together. And paying a visit to the elves is very dangerous. This crowd isn't going to provide me with much backup. I'm starting to really think we shouldn't go at all."

"The *Seers* both agreed."

"And you tell me this now? No way they're right about this. The Red Prophet takes hallucinogens and terrorizes neighborhoods. She likes that better than she likes it here. She's probably just pretending so she can stay in the Brink."

"Karen *saw* it, too, and we both know how effective she is."

For the first time, worry lodged in my gut. Darius and I had been through the absolute worst together. We'd overcome incredible odds and combated incredibly dangerous situations…as a *team*. I didn't know how this was going to go without him. I hadn't been entirely honest a moment ago—the fae were excellent fighters from what I'd seen, but they definitely lacked battle experience. They lacked the ability to improvise on the fly. They'd be outgunned if we faced a large force of vicious fighters, and both the elves and Lucifer had numbers. They hadn't thrown them at us yet, but they had them. It was only a matter of time.

"This is right, *mon coeur.*" He opened the door and let me into our bungalow. "I must head to the lair and drum up support. The *Seers*' direction to come here first has proven fruitful. We need to trust in them. They are our best advantage."

I blew out a breath, planning on stopping and falling onto the couch, and was instead ushered into our bedroom.

"Let's give Penny a reason to bust in," he whispered before dropping his lips to mine. His tongue urged my lips to open and then swept through as he lowered his fingers to the clasp of my pouch. It fell away and then he was moving at inhuman speed, removing my weapons and my leather pants.

I pushed his jacket off his muscular shoulders and then undid his shirt buttons.

You excel when you're out of your element, he thought as he stripped off my shirt and fastened a hot mouth to my nipple. I moaned, stilling as he ran his fingers over my panties before dipping in. *Yesterday, you captivated. Today, you took control of a people. Tomorrow, you will help lead them. You are a wonder, and I cannot believe I have been so lucky as to have secured your good affection.*

He dropped to his knees and peeled my panties away before pushing my knee onto his shoulder and leaning in, running his mouth along my sex. I fluttered my eyes closed, delighting in his fingers entering me, then his mouth and digits working together, winding me tighter.

"I can't wait." He rose in a rush and pushed me back onto the smallish bed, perfect for cuddling. Or one person on top. He was out of his pants in a flash, his tip pressed against my opening. "You are incredible, my love. As surprising as you are powerful. I love that there is never a dull moment."

He thrust, pushing all the breath out of my lungs. I pulled his neck, lowering his lips to mine, and savored his taste. The feel of him.

"I don't want you to go," I murmured, tightening my hold, wrapping my legs around his hips.

"It'll only be for a short time. I have eyes near the castle. I will get constant reports on what is happening. Have no worries—even if they capture you, they will not kill you. Not right away. If the worst should happen, just hang on until I get there."

Feeling my heart swell, I kissed him harder, so grateful that my journey had led me to him. Not just because I did trust that he would come for me if something happened, but because this feeling for him was so powerful that it felt like it might crack me in half. It almost couldn't be contained within me, stretching my skin and filling me to bursting.

"I love you," I murmured against his lips, holding on for dear life, scared to death that something would happen to one of us, and we wouldn't be able to live out forever. "Will you marry me?"

He chuckled. "No. I am old-fashioned. When I propose, it will be an event."

I smiled, because of course he'd say something like that. But at least he knew where I stood. I'd resisted the idea, but now, on the cusp of more danger than I'd ever faced before, it seemed like a good time to embrace the things that made me the happiest. He was one of them.

His rhythm sped up, and I lost myself to it, letting everything else go. The sensation wound me so tight that it was almost unbearable. I dug my fingers into his back, squeezing my eyes shut, and then I exploded, pleasure blistering through my body.

I called his name. Or maybe a profanity. The bliss was so overpowering that I couldn't be sure. He shuddered above me, moaning against my lips.

In the aftermath, as we came down, he asked softly,

"Do you want children?" I could hear the vulnerability in his voice, the slight hesitation.

"If I wasn't being hunted, and we knew we could keep them safe…"

He pulled back a little, his beautiful hazel eyes opening all the way down to his soul. "We'd wondered, but what Cahal said…" He swallowed. "I've always wanted children. I'd thought that option was denied to me. After we visited the Underworld, I started hoping. And now…"

I pulled him down and kissed him. "And now, if we can survive all this, we'll figure out a future and have a really weird family."

He started moving again, and I knew it would be a long, pleasant night of painful goodbyes.

CHAPTER 18

A KNOCK SOUNDED at the door. I opened my groggy eyes, heat coating my back and a muscular arm draped around me. Darius stirred before squeezing me tighter.

"We've got movement." Emery's voice was muffled through the door.

"Your sermon yesterday spurred them on like I thought it would," Darius said, the low rumble of his voice vibrating through his chest.

"Plus the way you hid among them while they discussed a very private matter. That's a quick way to help them realize how naïve they are." I turned around and burrowed into his warmth. "How far will you walk with us?"

"It depends on the route they take, but likely halfway. After our paths…diverge, I'll go to the lair." He kissed my temple. "We won't be separated long."

"Famous last words. What will you do for blood?" I squeezed my eyes shut as a blast of jealousy tore through me.

He squeezed me a little tighter. "Given my age and the amount of blood I took last night, I'll be good for months. Your proximity makes me crave it. That is why I take so much from you on a normal basis. It isn't necessary when we aren't together."

"I really don't want you to be with another woman. We're clear on that, correct?"

He kissed me languidly. "And I don't want you to be with anyone else, either. We're clear on that. I will wait for you for more blood. If the very worst should happen, I will have an assistant draw blood and offer it in a glass or thermos. It's not ideal, but it will keep me functioning."

"A thermos—Oh, to stay warm." I shuddered. "I'm glad I didn't get the vampire card."

"I'm glad I did. It allowed me to stay alive long enough to meet my soul mate."

I grinned and kissed him again. I usually wasn't the soul mate/hearts-and-flowers kind of girl, but this guy had really burrowed down deep into my heart and taken up residence. He'd turned me into a total sap.

"I do not want to kick down this door," Penny yelled through the wood. "But I will."

"It's a sturdier door than the one on the island," I murmured, reaching down and wrapping my fingers around his fun factory. "She'll never get through it. How about a quickie?"

His lush lips curled into a smile, and he rolled on top of me, settling between my thighs. His kiss was hungry as he slowly slid into me.

"I'm sure they have packing to do," he murmured against my lips. "They'll wait."

I squeezed his middle with my legs and gyrated up to meet him. Although I'd gotten very little sleep last night and was still sore, it was not dampening my fun even a little. He slammed against me, fast and glorious. My body wound up, the pleasure overbearing. It crashed over me suddenly, and I groaned, squeezing my eyes shut as the orgasm took me. He shuddered against my body.

"I warned you!" The door blasted open, tearing off the hinges and coming right for us. I threw up a shield of air as Penny stepped in. She got a glimpse and quickly turned away. "Are you serious? *Again*? I warned you I was coming in!"

"Just had to see us naked again, huh? Can't get enough." I laughed, wrapping my arms around Darius for one more squeeze before allowing him to roll off. "You cheated, though. Magic to bust in a door?"

"Ew. Just get dressed." She stomped away.

"Where are they?" came Callie's voice. It sounded like she was just coming into the bungalow.

After dressing and quickly tossing all my things into my backpack, I strapped on the last of my weapons and met them out front. Darius had made it out there before me.

"Hey." Charity walked up to us, her expression hard and eyes bloodshot. It didn't look like she'd gotten much sleep last night. Kairi and Hallen trailed her. "I have news."

"We're leaving today," I finished for her as Dizzy watched an orderly line of fae march past. It was the first time I'd seen that sort of theatrics. "How many are going?"

Charity turned to follow my gaze. "Ahead of us? Two couriers. They are alerting the elves that we will present ourselves to them."

"And us with you?" Emery asked.

She glanced at Emery, then me. "Yes."

"And going with us?" I asked.

"A force of about two dozen, plus you guys and the shifters. That's apparently a normal force for visiting the castle. Roger has sent Barbara to get more shifters. He's confident she can sneak past any trouble to get to the Brink."

Barbara had to be the sour-faced woman. The name rang a very small and hard-to-hear bell. Even if she was awfully sneaky, it seemed like a mistake to send just one person out in this pressurized climate.

"So…you all know that the Realm isn't exactly normal right now, right?" I hedged, not wanting to insult her intelligence. "It's really intense and shifters won't get a pass?"

"Yes." She, thankfully, didn't sound offended, and she didn't linger on the issue. "As Emery probably told you, my grandmama has...stepped down from her duties as First. My father has taken over her role."

"I didn't, actually," Emery said, standing off to the side with his hands in his pockets. He didn't fool me with that relaxed, uninterested pose. The wheels in his cranium were turning. He was preparing for a sticky situation ahead. "They were busy."

"Penny knows. She probably checked in a few times when we weren't looking." I winked at her, and she glared back, her cheeks red. "Congratulations on being the Second, though."

Charity shifted uncomfortably. She offered me a curt nod. "By the way, thanks for telling everyone about the way Grandmama was manipulating our people to react to strangers," she said. "The shifters will never admit it, but they're grateful. It isn't fun being made to feel like an outsider."

"I have zero problem with it," I replied.

"Well..." Her brow furrowed. "Right. Except for you, I guess. Anyway, Grandmama pulled away her...influence. She stopped using her magic to control people. At least, she says she did."

"She will never fully stop using her magic," Darius

said. "It is ingrained in her now. You are simply forcing her to be much more discreet."

Charity nodded. "My dad figured as much. Which is the other thing I was going to tell you guys. The *custodes* are officially leaving the Flush. This will be a sanctuary for the old or wounded, or those who do not wish to fight. Everyone who wishes to fulfill their duty to restore order will leave with us. We hope to find the rest of our people who left over the years and organize our forces. Representatives will be posted throughout the Realm. The goal is to eventually enforce the rules that have long been set. For everyone. But we'll make a plan after we meet with the elves."

"You mean after the big battle, right?" I lifted my eyebrows. "You must know the elves won't just give up their advantages because a bunch of freedom fighters decided to show up to work after a long hiatus."

"Yes, though we're not talking about it in those terms. Romulus wants to give the elves the benefit of the doubt."

"And get killed for his efforts," Emery murmured.

Charity studied Emery for a long moment before turning to look at the shifters gathered down the way, Roger in loose sweats with a backpack full of clothes. He probably wasn't planning on carrying it long. At the first sign of trouble, he'd hand off his things to someone who'd stay human, and then shift.

"Oh." Charity put up a finger. "We're bringing carts. You guys can put all your stuff in that. We're assembling at the practice yard. Grab everything you need and head that way. We'll be leaving at dusk, but Romulus figured you'd want to gather early so you can talk and ask questions."

I looked at Darius. "I guess you're not going to handle everything for me this time, huh? I actually have to participate?"

He rubbed my back. "Sadly, yes. You'll have to pull your weight."

"Dang it." I smiled at the jest and shot a glance at Emery. "Shall we?"

"I never thought I'd go to the castle again," Emery said, sounding uncomfortable.

"It'll be fine." Penny rubbed his arm. "We'll get it sorted out."

But I wasn't so sure that was true. The elves didn't seem to want to let his infractions go. By now they probably had a list of grievances about me too, including stirring up drama in the Realm. We likely wouldn't get opposed on our way to the castle, but once we got there...I had a feeling we'd be staring down a butcher's bill, and the fae and shifters wouldn't be enough to pay the tab.

CHAPTER 19

S URE ENOUGH, THE journey to the castle was quiet.
Too quiet.

"My feet are killing me," Callie murmured as we finished the last leg.

Romulus hadn't plotted a path directly there, and it wasn't because he was worried about meeting elves. We'd seen a few, watching us from a distance. Getting out of our way. They weren't idiots—they knew we'd kill them if they tried to apprehend us. And why bother? They knew we would be personally delivering ourselves to them. All they had to do was wait. And prepare.

I filled my lungs, held the oxygen in, and then let it out slowly, ignoring my increased heart rate and the adrenaline soaking into my blood. This felt so wrong it was ridiculous. Charging into danger was one thing, but strolling in, asking which dish they'd like to see our heads on, and then showing up for our own slaughter? That was not the way I did things. Not at all.

Those *Seers* were the only reason this was happening. They didn't even know what would come afterward! We were blindly following them and hoping for the best.

A fool's hope, I was certain.

We'd taken a long, winding journey rather than the direct route because Romulus was advertising his presence in the Realm and dropping off some of his people in various old-timey strongholds. Which would undoubtedly go over about as well as lead boots in a swimming pool with the elves. They might not have stopped him, yet, but they couldn't be happy about the situation.

The only good news was that people were legitimately happy to see the *custodes*. They smiled and waved, offering up food, drink, and lodging. One creature even offered her baby for a kiss. The *custodes* had been isolated for a long time, but they had not been forgotten.

We'd ventured close to the vampire lair, an area mostly ignored by the elves. The vampires obviously preferred it that way, but Romulus didn't think it was right. Changes were coming, and I was pretty sure the vampires would hinder some of them. Then again, get in line. No one seemed to deal with change exceptionally well.

Reaching the lair had meant something else, too. I had kissed Darius goodbye, swallowed my heart, which had climbed into my throat, and tried to put on a brave face as I turned and walked away. My vampire crutch had been taken away. I sure hoped Emery was half as good at strategy.

That had been a while ago now, though, and we didn't have much time before the battle or the ambush or whatever was going to happen when we reached the castle.

"Is it your bunions?" Dizzy asked Callie. They were walking behind me with the mages, while Halvor stoically kept pace with me. A circle of fae surrounded us, taking up the whole path, and for the life of me, I could not convince them to let me out. I had even offered to walk with the shifters. No dice.

"I haven't had bunions a day in my life," Callie replied.

He tried again: "Is it your secret bunions that you pretend not to have?"

"You know very well I don't have bunions. Old people get bunions. I'm not old."

"Not just old people have—"

I threw Penny a glare to shut her up. This wasn't a conversation she needed to get involved in.

"I agree about the walking," I said, watching as the landscape gradually became more floral. The trees looked too cultivated, like a kid had stuck a bunch of perfectly round green lollipops into the ground. Unlike in the Flush, there was no floral scent to accompany the rows of bright, multicolored flowers lining the gold-cobbled path. No lush feeling of foliage chilled the air.

"Is that real gold?" I scuffed the ground with my toe, not wanting to mess with the magic in case I screwed it up. This close to the elves' home, they'd be sure to find out about it sooner rather than later, and it would be considered a serious offense. I didn't want to add that to their list of grievances.

"Yes," the woman to my right said, looking off into the distance at the spires of the castle. "They like to make a statement about the wealth of the Realm. They always have."

I slowed and scuffed at the ground again. "Does anyone steal it?"

"Why would they need to? Everyone in the Realm is provided for," she replied.

"Number one, that's not true and never has been," Emery said. "Number two, they most certainly do not steal it, no. The elves would hang you for that infraction. Or kill you in some other way, probably on display."

"Stealing is a crime," the woman said, and lifted her chin a little.

"Sure, if you get caught," I muttered, watching my boots tread on the gleaming gold. "What a waste. I could make great use of one of those gold stones."

"You have all the money you could possibly need," Penny said.

"No, *Darius* has all the money she could possibly need," Callie replied. "Reagan needs to get her own money."

Dizzy scoffed. "I can't see a blasted thing around all these bodies. But I'm sure you could take one or two and get away with it, Reagan. If you wait until there's no one around, how would they know?"

"They'd do an inquiry, which is a very hostile way of asking questions until they find someone to blame it on," Emery said.

"You're familiar with how the elves do business, Emery?" Romulus called back.

"Very, which is why I am not overly enthused about heading to their castle. If I didn't think this was the only way to clear my name, I wouldn't go anywhere near this place."

"Clear your name and help out a friend, I think you meant to say." I glanced back at him with an eyebrow cocked.

"Are we friends?" A grin pulled at the corners of his lips. He watched the side, peering out between the press of bodies. "Penny seems to think you only tolerate me because of her."

"Well, isn't that a little self-centered, Penny?" I glanced at her this time. "You think my life revolves around you, do you?"

"It's not like you have a friend factory you routinely visit," she replied. "I doubt you'd give Emery the time of day if he didn't hang around because of me. And he'd definitely keep you at an arm's length. Admit it, I'm the reason you guys are in each other's lives."

"Wow. What a big head." I clucked my tongue. "She seems so quiet and kind, and then she opens her mouth and everyone learns what she's really about. Quite the ego."

"You know it's true," she said. "Don't try to make me the bad guy! I'm just being honest."

"Honestly self-absorbed, yeah." I shook my head, seeing a cluster of elves standing to one side of the path, watching us as we passed, carefully avoiding the flowers. I was tempted to unravel the magic then and there. "Very enlightening, Penny. Should we expect you to tell the elves that you taught me everything I know? That you hooked me up with Darius and found me a place to live? I mean, is there no end to the things you'll take credit for?"

"You have been absolutely unreasonable since I *accidentally* barged in on you and Darius on the island. You really have, Reagan Somerset." I could tell she was crossing her arms over her chest. "This is going to come back to you tenfold, just you wait. Stop laughing, Emery! This isn't funny!"

My grin faltered as the castle came more fully into view. Unlike castles in the Brink, which were built for defense, this one did not have an outer wall, a draw-bridge, or a moat. In fact, it looked more like an incredibly fancy hotel made to look like a castle, with a wide, gleaming path leading through an expanse of grass, with lines of flowers to a large arch with a red double door nestled inside. The spires on the roof were made out of gold, or at least covered in it, and windows dotted the front of the three-story structure, much larger than arrow slits. I didn't sense any magic shield-ing the place from attackers. They were confident in their safety.

Several elves were outside, tending to grass or flow-ers, one chiseling part of a fountain, the water gurgling as it ran out of a fawn's mouth and splashed into the basin below. None of them ignored us—they all stopped what they were doing and stared. Clearly they hadn't gotten the memo that we were on the way. They weren't important enough to hear the news.

How easy it would be to get them to rebel?

"They do their own landscaping, huh?" I asked, connecting eyes with one of the gardeners. The onlook-er's brows pinched together, its eyes rounding in surprise. I had a feeling it suspected who I was and why we were here. "They don't hire out to other creatures?"

No one responded to me, and I wondered how

many of the people in my vicinity had ever actually been to the castle.

A sinking feeling filled my gut as we drew ever closer. The insanity of what we were doing pressed down on me. I didn't want to bet my everything on Karen and the Red Prophet.

"It's probably wise if we nix this whole idea and just go into hiding," I murmured as I drifted back between Penny and Emery, just in front of the older dual-mages. Halvor glanced back with a scowl. I waved him away. "You do you, bub. I played your game on the way here. Now I'm looking for a safer bet." I lowered my voice and said out of the side of my mouth to Emery, "But seriously, probably better if we peel off now, run for it, and spend our lives in hiding."

"I would never do that to Penny," he said. "It's no kind of life for a person like her. Or you. You remember that island—you were going stir-crazy. We all saw it. If Cahal hadn't been there to train you—to *challenge* you—you would've swum out of there just to get a little action."

"Don't burst my bubble." I felt my magic thrumming within me, responding to the mounting stress. More eyes found us as we approached the wide double door at the end of the path. Elves lurked by the walls, their hair as still as their bodies, watching us silently. They didn't have weapons strapped to them, which wasn't reassuring. They clearly thought *they* were weapons enough.

At the double door, one of the elves stepped forward, cloaked in a green tunic and purple breeches.

"Second, you have come to visit," it said.

"I am now the First," Romulus said, and I barely saw his bow through the thicket of people around us. "My mother is in good health, but she has decided she would prefer to stay within the Flush, governing the people there, than join the rest of us in resuming our duties."

"Ah, I see," the elf replied, and it didn't seem like he really did. That, or he was relaying some subtle context that I wasn't programed to pick up.

"Emery," I whispered, and Halvor glanced back with a hard stare, no doubt to shut me up. Emery glanced over. "You're going to have to start thinking things at me so I know what's going on. I've gotten used to it, and now I'm flying blind. No one wants me to get bored."

He nodded, and his thought message popped into my head. *Can you hear me?*

"Yeah. Good. What—" I zipped my lips as the elf continued.

"Your wing has been prepared, of course." The elf fell silent as Roger made his way up the side of the procession with a confident swing of his shoulders and a commanding bearing. He was being professional. "Ah. And Roger Nevin. Yes, I had heard your two factions...connected once more."

"Yes, it has been a remarkable pairing," Romulus said, pretending the elf's words didn't drip with disdain. "Very effective."

"Quite." The elf paused, and no one rushed in to fill the gap with words. "Well. I'll show you to your wing. Roger Nevin, your rooms are always available, as you know. My associate will show you the way. Romulus, you have some...guests with you, do you not?"

"Yes, as a matter of fact, we do. We will be presenting them, in person, to the king and queen. Rooms within our wing will be sufficient for them."

"Yes, except for the fugitive, of course. He'll need to come with us."

Penny shoved me out of the way and slipped her hand into Emery's. "They won't take you. If they try, we'll resist."

If they take me, make sure she stays safe, Emery thought, and I opened up my brain to all the voices around me. Thankfully, the shifters had taught the fae how to shield their thoughts, and I didn't have dozens of voices battering me. *Don't let her try to rescue me. If they kill me, look after her. She'll feel like dying. Don't let her.*

"If you die, we all die," I said with zero sentimentality. It was a fact. Penny would resist, I'd help her, and we'd either all live and walk out, or all die for our efforts.

But if we were going to die, I intended to take as much of this castle down with me as I could.

"I am quite appalled by the lack of communication within your establishment, I must say," Romulus said. "On our way out of the Flush, we left one of your smartest foot soldiers alive explicitly so that he might tell you our position on young Westbrook. I really dislike repeating myself, and I have had to do it far too often with your faction. Once and for all, he merely played a trick. Hanging does not fit the crime, not by a long shot. Moreover, anyone that is to be executed must have a trial with a high-standing *custode* present. Given he has not had a trial, he will not be executed, per the laws set forth long ago. I have brought him here in good faith so that he might have that trial, and I will stand up at it and wager his punishment, as is proper. Until then, he will remain in my care."

"I understand, First, it's just that… Well, that's not how we do things anymore. Since you and yours walked away and left your positions empty, we've had to come up with other means by which to police our lands. The sun has set on your usefulness, something your kind brought on themselves."

He just laid out exactly where the custodes *stand in*

the Realm, Emery thought. *On permanent vacation. They aren't even going to pretend to honor the original agreement.*

Darius had anticipated that, but he also believed Romulus would try to force the issue. I was safer with the warrior fae than without them, so said the *Seers*, but I'd be safer still with a big host of them away from the elves, in a place we could defend against Lucifer.

I just hoped I didn't get kidnapped before any of that could happen. We were entering the belly of the beast.

CHAPTER 20

"WE HAVE COME in good faith," Romulus said to the elf, who had not budged. "We will keep Mr. Westbrook to his room until you can see him."

"I think I'll just take him with me."

"We both know that isn't wise, just as we both know what happened to the war parties that tried to do exactly that. I assume *that* message was delivered?"

Despite myself, I felt a smile budding on my lips. Romulus was pretty bad-ass. Those manners really shone when he was issuing threats.

"You have a girl in your vicinity," the elf went on. "We wish to question her."

Romulus won that round, Emery thought, his shoulders and arms relaxing slightly. *I won't be killed today.*

"Yes, so we do. And we will present her and the Second Arcana at the same time. Until then, she will also stay to her room. Have no fear—she cannot fly. She'll be quite safe until the king and queen can fit her into their schedules."

Silence met his words again.

This elf doesn't have the authority to force the issue, nor does he want to lose his head for trying. It's interesting they haven't tried to charge the fae themselves with murder. I wonder if the king and queen will bring that up.

"Yes. Please, follow me," the elf said.

And then we were moving, passing a stone-faced Roger. His dual-colored gaze caught mine for a moment, and I heard, *Watch yourself, Reagan,* before I was swept through the doors and out of his sight.

No Darius, and now no Roger. Another of my protections stripped away.

"When you give up the solitary life, it turns out to be no fun going back to the solitary life, especially when danger is mounting all around you," I murmured.

Halvor dropped back beside me again, leaving Penny and Emery directly behind me.

"Why are we in formation when we won't be fighting?" I asked him.

"You never know when you will, or will not, be fighting," he replied, and regardless of Romulus's hopeful outlook, it seemed Halvor was no dope. He expected the worst. He probably didn't understand why we were here any more than I did. Except it was obvious the fae trusted their prophet, drug habit and all.

The wide, curving staircase took us up to the third

floor, and no, I would not be flying out of the window at this height, but it surprised me that no one had suggested that I could hover my way down. Maybe they didn't realize I had that talent. From what I'd been told, the other heirs of Lucifer hadn't possessed the full range of his magic.

A red carpet cut down the middle of the wide hallway, chandeliers dotting the way, sparkling in the orange light from the windows. Large oil paintings hung on the cream walls, elves in battle dress, or picking grapes, or tending odd-looking animals I'd never seen while passing through the Realm.

"I see you have redecorated," Romulus commented flatly.

This hall used to be full of paintings of the fae fighting beside or working with the elves, Emery thought, glancing first at the paintings, and then at the window across from us. *This is quite the statement they are making.*

"Not a good statement," I murmured.

No.

"What?" Dizzy whispered, pushing through Emery and Penny to get closer. "What's up? Is it just me, or is everyone tense? It's making me nervous, Reagan. Thank God we came, huh?"

I didn't know about that. I was certainly glad for more firepower—I was sure we all were—but I didn't want them in danger, either. I hadn't trekked through the Underworld to spare them just so I could force them into a similar situation down the line.

My heart thumped wildly as we reached a wide archway with a heavy wood door I would definitely try to kick in at some point. I had a feeling it would be a serious challenge. The elf stopped at the door, the procession stopping with him, and I was forced to do the same.

"If you need anything, just ring for assistance," the elf said.

"Yes, of course," Romulus replied.

We started up again, the fae pushing in tighter around me as we neared the entrance. Not many could fit at a time, however, and when I passed through, I got a good look at the tall, slender creature with the magically flowing white hair and hard, nearly black eyes. Its power pulsed, like needles prickling every inch of my body. Halvor hissed through his teeth, and my magic swelled, ready for action.

Do not respond, Emery thought, the words barely registering beneath the rush of magic.

"I will see you soon, Rogue Natural," the elf said softly as Emery passed it by. "It will be a pleasure to watch you swing."

In that moment, it took everything in me not to kill the elf on the spot. As I continued on, it wasn't his stare that stayed with me, or the threatening pulse of his magic. It was the elf's assurance that Emery would die, sooner or later.

I sucked in a deep breath and let it out slowly.

It didn't help.

"That will happen *literally* over my dead body," I ground out, red tingeing my vision. "We'll burn this place to the ground if they go after you, Emery, don't you worry. We'll leave a pile of rubble with all those nasty bastards trapped under the stones."

"See?" Penny said to Emery. "Told you."

The solid door closed behind us, and one of the fae slid the metal bar into place, securely locking them out. Halvor sighed, and it was the first time I'd seen him react to stress.

"Well." Romulus looked over the finery around us, the gold filigree on the trim, the solid and artistic woodworking, the plush rugs underfoot. "This is much, *much* worse than I thought."

"The king and queen are going to charge you for something," Emery told Romulus, looking out the window in the grand sitting room. Down the hall, several doors stood open, clearly leading to the bedrooms. "They'll offer you the option to be punished, or to head home and stay out of their business. It'll likely be an offer you can't refuse. I'm not positive, but that's my guess."

"What sort of offer?" Romulus asked as the fae spread out, some heading down to the bedrooms, some peering out the windows as Emery was doing. They were getting their bearings in case of attack.

He pulled back from the window, his eyes shadowed. He was worried.

"I don't know. I was never given one." He smiled humorlessly. "I've just heard that's their way of doing things. It won't look good to the rest of the Realm if they kill you. Of course, they can't let you police them either, even if they're the ones who made the rules you're trying to follow. It'll look like you had to come out of retirement because of how bad things have gotten, which is true, and everyone will know it. They'll want to pass it off like you came, you told them about Charity, delivered me and Reagan, and you left. Amicable. That'll look best for them. They can use your attack on the foot soldiers as a reason to work you around."

Romulus stood with his hands behind his back for a moment, staring out at nothing. "In our position, my mother would certainly leave. And I might have once been tempted, simply to save our people. But seeing the shifters carry out their duty has inspired me to do the same."

"Your people do not wish to be saved, sir," Halvor said, and bowed. "We wish to fight. It is what we were born to do. It is in our blood. In our heritage."

"Yes, yes, I realize that." Romulus stepped away from the window. "And we cannot just hand over two innocent lives. Because no matter how grievous they thought your offense, you merely played a practical joke, Emery. What an absurd overreaction. I cannot believe they are so up in arms about it. What a lack of humor this place currently possesses."

He took a deep breath and sighed it out slowly. I wondered if it would help him more than it had me.

"Well," he said, looking Charity over and crinkling his eyes. "Here we are. They will likely give us tomorrow to rest after our long journey. After that, we will introduce you, and see about the others. From there...we will play it by ear. We have no choice."

"Sounds perfect to me." I peered down the hall at the rooms. "That's my preferred method of handling things. Which room is mine?"

BUT THEY DIDN'T give us a day to rest. Not even the next morning to recover after a single night's sleep.

A knock sounded at the heavy door. Romulus stood from his seat, his steaming cup of tea in hand. Charity walked in from the hall leading to the bedrooms, fiddling with one of the strange bands on her tunic as if she'd only just finished getting dressed.

"This is highly unusual," Halvor said, the first to the door.

"Yes. Highly," Romulus said, his tone dry. He set his tea on the table beside him.

"I can stop them from getting in." I tucked my feet into my boots and started doing up the laces.

"No." Romulus glanced behind him at his people, who'd sped up the getting-ready process. "Let them come. We will play by their rules."

...for now...

His thought curled through the air, and a grin stretched across my face. Adrenaline rushed in to fuel my body. I'd never cared for sneaking around and taking stock of a situation before making a move. That was Darius's department, which was one of the reasons I'd been so loath to lose him for this.

But the elves had just tipped things into my comfort zone. If they planned to throw unpleasant surprises at us, I was happy to lob the unpleasantness right back.

The heavy metal bar slid back before the door shuddered open. An elf stood in the doorway, long blond hair flowing down its back, rippling as if it were out in a breezy meadow. Its heavily embroidered blue tunic stopped just below its waist, and the forest-green satin garment it had on beneath flowed to its ankles.

"Slippers, huh?" I stood and adjusted my pouch, spells inside at the ready in case Penny or Emery needed a magical hand. "We going to a pajama party?"

"First Arcana," the elf said, sparing a glance my way.

"The king and queen request your audience. You are to bring the Second Arcana, Emery Westbrook, his dual-mage partner, and the girl with whom you travel."

I pointed at the center of my chest, walking out from within the fae and stopping beside Romulus. "I'm the *girl*, right?"

The elf, with light eyes so pale they almost looked white, glanced at me. "Yes."

"All this time at your disposal and you couldn't figure out my name?" I whistled and adjusted the sword at my back. "You mustn't be as powerful as you think. That, or you don't have many friends."

Disgusting disease of a half-human, it thought, and I wondered just how much they knew about me. They didn't seem to realize I could levitate out of here, and it was now evident they didn't know I could read thoughts. Or maybe that particular thought just got away from it. My ability to get under people's skin was one of my superpowers, as Cahal had found out the hard way.

"Well, anyway, let's get this circus started, shall we?" I pulled my long blond locks into a tight ponytail on top of my head.

"We're obviously going." Callie stepped forward, zipping up the sweatshirt of her bright orange track suit. She turned to grab her satchel, and I noticed "Werking it" written across her backside. Where did she find those things?

"No, that won't be necessary," the elf said, taking a step back, indicating it was time to go.

"Don't be as ridiculous as the clothing you're wearing." Callie huffed and filed in with the rest of our crew, Dizzy joining her with a pleasant smile.

"You are not on the list," the elf said loftily.

"Yeah." I turned to Callie and Dizzy. "It's a VIP party that you will want to miss, I'm sure of it. Why don't you stay here?"

"Reagan Somerset—" Callie started.

Dizzy put out his hand to stop her, and I was thankful he had sense. Until I realized he didn't.

"Let me, hon." He turned his pleasant smile on me. "We didn't come all this way to sit out in the final hour. We're going with you even if we have to fight our way there, so the best thing you can do is just accept it."

"I am only instructed—"

"It's fine, Bobo," I said, sighing and motioning him on. I didn't honestly think they would back down—they'd forced their way into this journey in the first place, and clearly didn't care whether they were welcome—but I had hoped. I didn't foresee this next phase going well. "They're with me, and I won't be going anywhere without them. You're welcome to try to force me, of course." I flashed him a grin. "But you'll die first."

"Yes, she does make an excellent point. Please." Romulus put out his hand to get the elf moving. "The king and queen are waiting, are they not?"

"I—" The elf cut itself off, clearly at a loss, and just turned and walked through the door, his guards stepping back and to the sides so we'd pass through the middle of a guard twenty deep.

Halvor stepped up next to me.

"No." Penny pushed him away. "For the love of lollipops sucked on by bucktoothed men, be with your own people for this one. The triangle of power needs to stick together or we're all going to die."

CHAPTER 21

I LOOKED AT Penny, surprised Halvor had relented, falling into the middle of the formation that included both Arcanas, the secret weapon that was anything but secret in this castle.

"What's this now?" I asked her with a grin.

"Go, go." Callie shooed us onward as the gap lengthened between us and the fae. Only the Arcanas' assistants and a couple of others were going with them. Apparently it was understood that Arcanas couldn't do things for themselves, probably like elf royalty. "We don't want to get separated. That's when they'll attack."

"We should've called a demon or two, hon," Dizzy said softly, eyeing the elves lining the sides of the hall. "Just to create a little pandemonium, you know? This is too smooth sailing for these elves."

"*Shh, shh.*" Callie batted at him. "Don't give them any ideas."

"I doubt these are new ideas," I murmured, reaching the end of the hall and hitting the stairs. Down we went to the first floor, and from there to the back of the castle, decked out in the same style as that in the front, with red carpet lining the halls, large crystal chandeliers, and finely wrought wood and metal. "How you doin', Emery? Hanging in?"

The elves who'd been waiting to the sides now filed in behind us in two neat columns. There were elves ahead, elves behind, and walls to our sides. Whenever we passed a doorway, someone was standing there, blocking it off. They wanted us contained.

They didn't seem overly worried about the windows, though. Did they not think I'd break through one and jump through at a moment's notice? Because it wouldn't be the first time.

Thanks for the easy exit, fuckers, I thought, wishing I could send the thought to the mages.

The space opened up into a huge sitting room decked out with conversation areas, couches arranged around tables holding bowls of fruit, little pastry-like foods, and beverages. At the back of the room, two enormous double doors stood closed, nestled in an archway that reminded me of the castle's entrance.

I felt magic balloon around us, the spell giving us some privacy from eavesdroppers.

"They won't let me walk away a second time," Emery said softly. "And it's clear they'll take Penny with me."

I huffed out a laugh, and my blood boiled fire.

"Nah. They won't." I stopped with the others, the lead elf pausing and then putting out a hand, indicating we should have a seat and wait for an audience. "On the off chance you guys are pardoned, what are my odds of heading back to the rooms after this, do you think?"

The mages and I clustered together as the fae pretended like this was a polite visit and there was a chance they'd have some refreshments while they waited.

"Next to zero," Emery said.

"And the fae?"

"Almost certainly they will get to go back to their rooms and think over the offer they receive, whatever that might be."

"So you're basically saying they are going to drag you, Reagan, and Penny away?" Callie asked with a hard set to her jaw.

"Karen should've come." Dizzy lifted the flap of his satchel and peered in. "We tried to get her to, but she said she had to remain with that nut ball fae *Seer*. If she'd come, we'd have some insight into what happens next."

"I don't think we're supposed to know what happens next," Penny said, chewing on her lip and looking around with large, worried eyes. "My mother once told me it's impossible to see the right way when too many paths lead from a certain point. You need to wait until a step is taken in one direction or another. We're at the crux, I can feel it."

I knew that look. "What's that Temperamental Third Eye saying?"

"Fight." She put her hands on her hips. "I mean, I personally want to run, but where to? There's nowhere to go. We need to fight. Moreover, we need to initiate." Her eyes came to rest on me, and she shrugged. "I can't tell if that's my Temperamental Third Eye speaking, or just my response to Emery being in danger, but..."

Emery shifted his stance and glanced around. I noticed a shocking lack of shifters at the party. Clearly they weren't in the doghouse. Or maybe they'd get their audience later. It was too bad telephones didn't work in this place, because I had a feeling Roger and Devon would like to hear what was going down.

I turned my lips down and lifted my eyebrows, taking one second to think everything over just so I could tell Darius that I hadn't acted completely without thought. My thoughts weren't actually on what came next, or how I might deal with the situation differently, but I didn't plan to tattle on myself.

"Right then." I burned away Emery's privacy magic and turned.

"What's happening?" Dizzy asked, removing some herbs from his satchel. "What sort of thing should we create?"

What's our end game? Emery thought.

"You will remove all weapons before entering the Royal Hall," the lead elf announced, standing in front of the wide doors. He was preparing to usher us in, which meant the king and queen were in position.

"End game: to be determined," I said, strutting forward.

"No, wait," Charity said, standing quickly. She knew me better than Romulus did. She knew the show was starting before the curtain had been raised.

This was why I hated *Seers*. They got you into these messes, but they didn't often give you a way out. My fate, and Penny and Emery's fate, diverged from the fae right here. I felt it in my bones, and Penny's Temperamental Third Eye affirmed it. The elves planned to give us different treatment, and nothing Romulus said would help us. Not now. We couldn't play polite anymore. We had to be bold.

"Step one: make oneself known." I swept my hand through the air, and the lead elf got caught up in my magic. Its eyes widened as it rolled to the right. It fought to lift its hands, but before it could get off a spell, or whatever it was planning, it bonked its head against the far wall and then lay still. I doubted I'd killed it. Probably just knocked it out. It was nice to know they were as fragile as humans and not so hardy as shifters. That would make things easier.

"Step two will likely be to fight our way out of here,"

I continued. "Then we should get back to Karen and the Red Prophet. Cheat to win."

I paused in front of the wide double doors just long enough to balance on my left foot and kick with all my strength. Metal squealed. With a loud crash, the doors flew inward, even as elves rushed us from around the room. I blocked them with air, shoving them back without looking. The doors slammed into the sides, and one pulled free from its jam, teetering.

We...cannot follow you in this, Romulus thought, standing. I almost felt his confliction in his thoughts. He knew the "right way," but also knew his duty. *We cannot begin a meeting this way. It is not how things are done. Please, come back. Let me lead.*

His illusions wouldn't be long in dying, but I didn't have time to wait.

I ignored him, stalking forward with my weapons intact. Penny and Emery were right behind me, in it to win it. I heard Callie and Dizzy following us. After we made it through, I blocked off the door so the elves couldn't follow. They were standing between us and the fae anyway.

A red carpet ran down the middle of the space, columns on either side of it, and the golden dome above us had to be over two stories high, with pictures painted on the ceiling and an enormous chandelier hanging down from the middle. There were ten rows of seats to one side, filled with spectators who'd shown up to watch the proceedings. That wasn't ideal. In front of me, five steps led to a wide, raised area on which sat two golden thrones. The king and queen both had long, straight white hair, rustling in a nonexistent wind, and wore matching cream-colored robes. I honestly couldn't tell them apart.

"Question—is it normal for elf royalty to marry their twin?" I stopped in front of them, feeling magic take shape around me. The natural dual-mages were readying for an attack. "Because you two look almost identical." I snapped my fingers. "It's a narcissistic thing, isn't it? That's what this is about. You love yourself so much you want to see yourself reflected back to you. Dude, that's gross. You need someone around that will actually tell you the truth from time to—"

"Silence," the one on the right said, and power curled around me, stronger than anything I had felt before, pressing into my flesh and crawling along my scalp. It forced my mouth shut and pressed compliance into my limbs.

Which pissed me off.

There was a lot I could handle, but being compelled to do something I didn't want to was on the short list of hell fucking no.

Power rocked through me, sweet fire licking at my skin. Ice crackling the air.

I sent out a shock wave of it and shook free of the oppressive magic weighing me down.

"Nope," I said, no humor in my tone. In my body. "What do you want with me? Speak quickly, because I'm about to leave."

The elf on the left surveyed me with narrowed eyes. "You insolent scum," it said. "You dare—"

"Yeah, look." I pushed fire into the pew-like seats on both sides behind me, and shrieks crowded the air as flames raced along the base of the structure and licked up the backs of the seats. Power swirled in the room. I increased the potency of the fire, forcing everyone out of their seats, lest they be burned. A spell washed through after my efforts, incredibly powerful and horribly vicious, intending to melt skin from bones. Penny felt the danger and was not fucking around. She'd nabbed that spell out of my most advanced spell book at some point and managed to make it even worse. "I'm not here to be kicked around by a couple of narcissists with a hair complex. You've been looking for me. Here I am. What do you want?"

The elf on the left tapped its fingers against the golden arm of the throne. "You are Lucifer's heir. I can feel the disgusting slide of your magic over ours."

"We had so hoped she would be born of a high-level demon," the one on the right said, with slightly shapelier brows and thinner lips, looking over at its partner, "so that we might kill her along with her friends. Sadly…"

"Yes, I agree," the first said, and unfortunately, I didn't hear any thoughts. "We cannot hope to pass her off as less than the heir. We must…reflect."

The chairs burned wildly behind me. People pushed against the walls to get away, because the elves had invited their social elite to witness our "interview," not their fighters. Not anyone who could subdue us.

"You fuckers are sure arrogant," I said, which brought their focus back to me.

"Your manners are fitting of your origins," said the elf on the left.

"Thank you. Honestly, that is a huge compliment." I hooked a thumb behind me. "What is your plan for the Rogue Natural? Do you intend to honor Romulus—the Second Arcana—"

"First Arcana," Emery corrected me.

"Right, right. Do you plan to honor the First Arcana and give the Rogue Natural a fair trial?"

Bodies crowded the busted doors, some trying to get out, the guards trying to get in. I felt their magic pulsing into the room.

We need to get out of here, Emery thought. *Penny and I are working on something.*

I knew that. I could feel it collecting above our heads, spicy and intense. It was taking shape slowly. I needed to keep talking for a moment.

"The fae are eager to resume their rightful role and help get your kingdom back on track," I finished.

The one on the right laughed, a tinkling sort of sound. "Back on track—do you hear her?"

The one on the left raised its voice, presumably so it could be heard throughout the room, "Our kingdom has never been more prosperous. Our subjects have never experienced a more pleasant lifestyle than what we are currently providing them. It is only vile creatures like you who seek to bring it down. It is people like you who interrupt our perfect harmony."

"Perfect harmony? Holy hogwash, Batman." I laughed and hoisted the fire higher. They weren't trying to put it out, so I would push the issue. "Who are you trying to fool? You idiots try to kill anything that pushes back while brutalizing common folk. You abuse power, think you're above the law, go off the handle in response to any perceived threat, justified or not, and cannot find something so simple as a name to a magical person affiliated with a great many creatures right under your nose. You are losing your grip on—"

Magic crushed down onto me, twisting my guts. It felt like a white-hot blade dug into my stomach and tried to rip out my heart. Someone screamed behind me, and I thought it might be Penny. A body hit the floor, then two, and I wondered if it was Callie and

Dizzy.

I stood my ground, taking the pain. Owning it. Pushing past it. When bonding Darius, I'd been on the brink of death. I'd nearly bled out, a necessary part of the bonding process. I'd felt what it was like to walk the line, and I'd come out the other side stronger for it. Not easily ruffled. Not apt to panic.

Harnessing my inner fire, wrapping myself in ice, I rose to the challenge. I rose to their magic. I was my father's daughter. Running through my veins was the blood of the ruler of the Underworld and, with it, the blood of gods. My power equaled theirs, but my might didn't stem from that. It stemmed from my experiences. My ability to survive. My ruthlessness when threatened and my undying loyalty to my loved ones.

I was the Underworld—I was love and lust, hate and violence. I could forgive, but I could also wield my wrath with no impunity.

In a blinding flash of power, I struck back. The ground rumbled. The windows shook, then exploded outward. Those by the walls quailed, sinking. The magic all around me throbbed, fighting.

Run, Emery thought, and I knew the best I could hope for was to get out from under these elves. They were more experienced, and experience would ultimately decide the victor, but damn it, I wanted to go head to head and come out swinging.

Run! Penny thought.

The spell they unleashed widened my eyes. It filled the room and then some, blistering in its intensity, nearly as powerful as the magic coursing through me and the elf royalty. The natural dual-mages had godly power, and they were showing their might.

The spell slammed into the onlookers before rushing for the thrones. Agonized screams drowned out the crackling of fire. Eyes popped out and bodies twisted. Bones broke, snapping as arms and legs curled in on themselves. Skin continued to melt from the other spell, and now it peeled away in strips, like from an invisible potato peeler.

"Go," Emery said, grabbing my arm and yanking. "Go!"

I spun and pushed Penny forward before bending to haul Dizzy up to his feet. Emery helped Callie, and we sped for the door. A wall of elves waited for us, trapping us in.

Our magic together, Penny thought.

She'd handle the togetherness part, I knew, so I swelled my ice magic and readied to shove it in front of us. A spell wafted up, latching on to my power and adding it to the might of the natural dual-mages.

"Ignite with your fire," she yelled back, clearly forgetting she didn't need to verbalize her thoughts.

I did, starting with a spark and burning hot. That

spark turned into an electrical explosion that likely meant Penny was close enough to Charity to borrow her magic too. A concussion of air blew out from Penny, crashing into the wall and flinging it backward. The doors got caught in the push, ripped from their hinges and frame. They banged and tumbled into the room beyond, squishing bodies as they did so.

In the waiting room, power surged and swords swung, four elves to every fae, and more coming into the room from the other side. The elves were attempting to subdue the fae somehow, maybe tie them up, I didn't know, and I didn't plan on sticking around to find out. The fae wouldn't be killed. We would.

"I blame the *Seers* for this," I said to absolutely no one, wasting no time, hefting Dizzy into a wedding-night hold and sprinting for the hall. Penny stayed close behind me, a natural runner, and Emery thankfully kept up, carrying Callie.

More elves ran our way. I crushed them with air, in no mood to spare anyone. They squished against the rug, and I jumped over the bodies. I heard Penny gag behind me. Around a bend and into a larger room, I eyed the windows.

"We need to get out of the castle—"

"Look. Watch out!" Penny screeched.

A jet of magic hurtled our way, ripping through my middle and trying to come out the other side. It wasn't as strong as the royals' magic, though, and I counteracted it with my own power. Spells rose from Penny and Emery even as Penny groaned and sank down. The spells must've been the tracking type, because they seeped through a cracked open door in front of us. Screams ensued.

"Let me down to fight," Dizzy said, struggling out of my grasp.

"No! We're not fighting, we're running, and you don't do that fast enough." I squeezed him tighter.

"I feel ridiculous," he shot back.

"You also look ridiculous. Just go with it!"

I barely stopped when I reached the tall but fairly thin doors, jumping with Dizzy in my arms and kicking. The wood cracked into the head of someone who was already sinking from Penny's spell, the damage clearly internal, because I couldn't see the effects.

"Using their magic against them. Nice, Turdswallop," Emery said with pride.

The next room opened up to a space as tall as the throne room. It had tall windows along one side and doors on the other, plus a second-floor balcony looking down. I skidded to a halt, my eyes widening, my stomach dropping out of me.

"Turn around," I yelled, trying to back-pedal and bumping up against Penny. "Turn around! This is a kill zone!"

"Too late." Emery's voice was suddenly rough, realization dawning.

Doors opened and bodies entered, their swishing clothes moving in the unseen wind, their outfits form-fitting and made from tough material that would undoubtedly make them more difficult to kill. They stood in a line on the railing above, their position giving them a clear advantage. They poured in through the downstairs doorways and spread out in numbers.

This was the fighting force, and they had us surrounded.

CHAPTER 22

"WHEN I SAY go, run for the windows," Reagan said in a low tone that made Penny's small hairs stand on end. "Jump through and get out of here. They can't have much of a force on the outside if they have all these people in here."

She gave Penny a shove that also jostled Emery and Callie, who was uncharacteristically quiet in his arms. "There is no way we're going to get through the windows," Penny whispered at Reagan. "They'll grab us before we do."

"I'll make sure that does not happen." Reagan set Dizzy down and ushered him behind her.

"Right, fine, but then they'll just chase us down. We need a new plan. We need to think—"

"No. Not all of us. Just you four," Reagan said, and Penny knew she was speaking to Emery. "It's me they want. They want you too, but they'll let it go if it helps them get me."

"No." Penny grabbed Reagan's shoulder as even more elves crowded into the room, their hands in front of them and their magic building. Penny could feel it. *Trap. Kill. Destroy.* The elves had a different goal for each of them, and none of them were good. "No, you're coming too. We can get out of here. All of us can. Maybe if you yell for the shifters or—"

Reagan whirled and leaned in, her face now a foot from Penny's, eyes lit with fire and determination. "You are here because of me. I will not let them have you," she said, and Penny knew in her heart of hearts this was the start of a goodbye. Heat prickled her eyes as Reagan kept talking. "They won't kill me right away. They see value in me. They'll keep me alive until they figure out what to do with me. They *will* kill you, though. All of you. You cannot be caught, do you hear me? *You need to run.*"

"But…" A tear slipped down Penny's cheek.

"Miss Somerset," one of the elves said, stepping forward, and Penny harnessed their magic and cut out that blasted fake wind tousling their hair, ripping it from the room and exploding it upward. The elves on the balcony flinched, but they didn't crouch, squeal, or duck. These were trained forces, and there were definitely too many of them for their small crew to take on. Even if they managed the impossible and defeated this many elves, reinforcements would arrive before they could escape. "Give it up. You must know this is the end."

"You need to go," Reagan told Penny urgently. "Get Darius. He'll figure something out."

Penny nodded mutely, her heart breaking, sobs threatening to overcome her. Because Reagan was sacrificing herself to save them.

"You are one of my best friends," Penny told her. "I *will* return the favor and rescue you."

Reagan smiled, her velvety brown eyes softening a little. "I knew it." She stuck her finger in Penny's face. "I knew you would grow to like me. See? I'm always right."

"Okay, but"—Penny wiped her face with the back of her hand—"don't gloat about it or anything."

"I am going to gloat. I'm going to gloat all day long."

"Reagan." Dizzy's eyes were mournful. He shook his head, also at a loss. Callie didn't utter a sound. Her face was closed down in a bulldog expression, but her eyes were glassy. Helpless.

Surprisingly, Reagan laughed. "You guys need to lighten up." She shrugged. "It's good. I'm going to blow this bitch sky-high. I'm going to be the absolute worst prisoner they've ever dealt with in their lives. They will loathe the day they made this decision. In three…"

"This has to be part of the overall journey some-how," Penny said, partially to herself, clutching Reagan's arm. It had to be. Her mother wasn't wrong. Not on big things. And both she and the Red Prophet had told them to come here, and to do it without Darius.

Except what if they'd been wrong? Or what if the crux of the crossroads had been in that throne room and they'd gone down the wrong path?

The elf said something that Penny couldn't make out in her panic.

"I'll be with you in one second, fancy dresser," Reagan said. "I'm just saying goodbye to my friends before you kill them." She glanced the elf's way. "You *are* going to kill them, correct?"

"If they come quietly, we will hang them, as befits enemies of the kingdom."

"Yeah. That's a real good reason for them to come quietly, sure. Tell me, are all elves this stupid? Because I haven't actually met a smart one." She held up her finger. "Wait, don't answer. It'll just annoy me, and I'm busy."

Penny felt Emery's hand on her shoulder. "We will stand together at the final battle," Penny continued, thinking of her mother's first vision of the three of them, together at the end. She had to believe in it. She had to. "My mom wouldn't send you to your death. This has to be part of the plan. It has to be."

"Whatever it is, it will be." Reagan's smile was serene, and Penny knew that meant she was about to partake in one of her favorite activities: demolition.

"And that'll happen in two…"

"We'll be back," Emery told Reagan, or maybe it was Penny, because she couldn't bring herself to budge. She didn't want to leave her friend to this. She didn't know if she *could*.

Reagan paused in her counting. "You're only allowed to say that line if you use an Austrian accent."

"Get ready to run, Penny Bristol," Emery said in Penny's ear. "They won't kill her. We'll get out, round up Darius and Cahal, and regroup. We *will* be back for her. We might be running now, but we will come back. She needs you to stay alive. That's the only way she gets out of here. You are the yang to her yin. You *need to stay alive*."

"I hate to say it, but he's right," Callie said, leaning in. "If there was any other way, we'd take it."

"There's no time to call a circle right now, or we'd summon a demon to fill Lucifer in on the situation," Dizzy added, and he'd kind of missed the mark on acceptable solutions. The whole point of coming here was to avoid Lucifer.

"One… *Go!*" Reagan spun, and then Emery was jostling Penny, yanking at her, running with her, corralling the older dual-mages.

"Use her magic and bust us out of here, Penny," he yelled as elves swung up swords in a neat sort of unity and prepared for battle.

"What's up, fuckers!" Reagan shouted, her voice echoing through the room. "Come at me!"

Air punched out in all directions, hitting all the windows at once, knocking the glass out. The elves standing in front were thrown against them. Another blast of air took out the frames. A third blast blew out the walls and the elves with it. The power built, expanding, growing, filling the room with such unspeakable menace that Penny felt her limbs shaking. She'd stopped without realizing it. So had Emery and the older dual-mages.

"Come on!" Emery got them moving again, but bright light made Penny look back, her heart in her throat, tears streaming down her face. Reagan bent at the knees, slapped two hands together, and shot a thick stream of hellfire at the columns above. It sliced through stone like it was water, bodies like they had always been two halves, the walls beyond with just as much power.

"If I'm going down," Reagan hollered, "you're all going down with me!"

"Oh crap, she's really going to do it," Penny said, dragged out through the gaping side in the building.

Fire blasted out all around Reagan, the heat forcing Penny to duck away and throw an arm over her face. Glass crackled under her feet. Shouts rang out outside. A roar reverberated off the building. The shifters were outside.

"Go toward the shifters," Emery yelled. "Penny, come on! You can't help her now."

Penny looked back one more time. Reagan stood within a bonfire, holding elves with her air magic and burning them alive while she cut down the top floor and punched at the walls and the ceiling. She was going out in one hell of a fight, and Penny doubted there'd be anyone left. Not in that room, anyway.

"We could've stayed," she said, pulling to go back. "She can handle them. All by herself she can—"

But the fire was being pushed back on one side by unseen hands, the powerful elves now fighting back. The hellfire lost potency, winking out. Reagan sagged but didn't stop. Spells were next, and she started throwing them before faltering, sinking to a knee, fighting what Penny knew had to be powerful waves of magic. Reagan hadn't held anything back. She'd started with everything she had. She didn't have the energy to keep going—she only had the energy to give her friends a chance to escape.

Resolve hardened, and then Penny was running for all she was worth, throwing spells, hurling insults replete with the worst actual swear words she knew, all while blinking back a stream of tears.

"I will avenge her," she said as she turned a corner and tore down three elves trying to stab a lion. "I will avenge her and make the elves pay for this!"

"First, you need to live." Emery pulled her toward the pack of wolves organizing, Roger at the front. They were clearly under attack too, but they'd made it out of the castle. "Callie, Dizzy, get into the Brink and tell Karen what happened here," Emery said as they ran, moving much slower with the older dual-mages. "Do not get caught."

"What do you think we are, stupid?" Callie clapped back.

"Penny and I will get Darius. We'll call you when we can."

"Good."

Emery put on a burst of speed, and Penny caught up. He glanced at her as they ran. "The shifters will get the fae out, or they'll bring in more people who can. I still don't think the elves will try to kill the fae. They'd be incredibly stupid to do that. If I were a betting man, I'd say they were keeping the fae contained, and the shifters out of the way, so they could grab Reagan. And us. They'll probably try to talk Romulus around. We need to get out of here. We need to let them handle it."

"Are you sure they won't kill Reagan?"

"If they do, there will be war."

"There'll be war anyway."

"Not if they can talk the fae around and make some sort of deal with Lucifer. They are ten times more conniving than the vampires, Penny. Their best interest is to keep Reagan alive and use her as collateral."

Either way, their friend would be lost.

"We need to get Darius," Penny said.

She hoped to hell he'd be enough.

CHAPTER 23

L UCIFER STARED DOWN at the blueprint for the new resting area without really seeing it, his mind churning. There had been a lot of turmoil in the Dark Kingdom of late.

Time rippled out behind him, a river of it, and over the many, many centuries, there had been natural rises and falls in activity as various factions or individuals fought for placement or peace, but this was different.

The traders across the river had suddenly become much more sophisticated. Squabbles for goods or power had turned into organized plays for strength and power in the Edges. The quality of trade had risen, and in turn, the riches had quadrupled. Because of that, those in the kingdom looked outward with interest, making more frequent trips, staying longer, and returning with a heightened sense of ambition and purpose. His people were fighting for larger territories, requesting larger sporting battlegrounds and leisure sex huts, and seeking more robust entertainment...

Something had stirred them.

He tapped his charcoal stick against the parchment, leaving dots of black along the edges.

Magic had worked its way into the kingdom as well. Hardwearing, complex, powerful magic, the likes of which Lucifer had rarely seen. It was being brought in through the Realm, but sources said it was created in the Brink and transported through a series of intricate steps that had completely slipped the elves' notice. Rumor had it that a mastermind elder vampire was behind the scheme.

Lucifer dropped his charcoal and stood, strolling across his workroom, watching the play of light against the marble floors. He stopped at a large window that overlooked the garden dedicated to his most recent love, a woman who could bloom flowers with her laugh and wilt men with her glare.

Instead of lingering on her memory, a pleasant distraction, he lifted his gaze to the sky, summoning images of the various areas in his kingdom—a magical form of surveillance he'd instituted after getting the idea from the Brink. The Brink had such remarkable ways of tracking and spying on its subjects. It had been incredibly useful. He couldn't believe he hadn't thought of it before. Even now, after an endless life, he could still learn from others and benefit from their efforts.

This mastermind...

There were two elder vampires at work in his outer

kingdom, he knew. One had been weaving threads together for some time—decades. Only a few stray threads at first, but he'd woven them together over time, creating tapestries. Vlad, his name was. A well-known vampire who was also well positioned within both the Realm and the Brink. He had amassed quite a lot of power and had more than a few eager ears listening to his ideas about revolts. His dabbling in the Underworld could not go ignored, however. When Lucifer had finally agreed to an audience with the vampire, he hadn't known what his next move would be: issue a strong warning, or just kill the vampire and be done with it.

Amazingly, neither had happened. The vampire was incredibly clever, with a well-established network Lucifer could use. He would be difficult to govern but worth the effort.

The other vampire, though...

Darius Durant, if rumors could be believed. Vlad's child.

Lucifer glanced up, summoning images of the toughest dwelling area in the Edges, a place where death haunted its citizens, and a single misstep would cost someone their life. The second vampire had set up shop there, forming alliances with some of the toughest residents in the Edges.

This other vampire worked altogether differently

than Vlad. He hadn't attempted to bring any sort of sophistication to the Edges, nor had he tried to change the culture in any way. Because of it, his business thrived. More than thrived—it had spilled over into the areas surrounding it, including those already infiltrated by Vlad, and spread into the very heart of the Dark Kingdom. The vampire knew his market, so to speak.

He knew the Dark Kingdom.

He'd set up trading stalls catering to Lucifer's subjects. He'd even found someone who could thread Incendium and Glaciem magic into the spells.

An image crystalized in Lucifer's mind. A blond woman in black leather pants and heavy boots, a sort of pouch around her waist. Lucifer hadn't been able to make out her face, but he would forever remember that bearing. Strong and straight and utterly fearless, even in the middle of a battle. She'd looked his way in challenge.

And that vampire had been beside her.

Darius Durant.

Lucifer threaded his hands into his pants pockets and turned from the window.

He'd only recently found out the woman's name: Reagan of the Brink.

She had no records. No friends he could discern. No listed home, no birth certificate, none of the records attached to normal Brink citizens. It was as though she did not exist.

The woman the *custodes* had recently found had all of those things and more. Every inch of her life could be accounted for, from her mother's death to her move to Santa Cruz for school and eventual assimilation with the shifters. She'd destroyed Lucifer's subjects in the Realm, so he'd thought for a time that she might be the one he'd seen. But he'd sent his subjects to check it out. They hadn't sensed any Underworld magic from her, and her party hadn't noticed the *amare interiorem* perched on the roof above them, watching it all unfold.

She was not the one. But she had helped flush out the one.

After an extended absence, an absence not even Vlad could penetrate, Darius Durant had resurfaced. And with him...her.

Her. The woman who was possibly Lucifer's heir.

The door clicked open, and Lucifer turned as Victoria entered in human form, her legs a little too long but overall well shaped, and the rest of her proportioned perfectly. She maintained that humans liked longer legs on women for some reason and had not been dissuaded from the choice.

"Sir," she said, sounding harried. "I received reports from our spies in the Realm. Reagan Somerset is being held by the elves. She arrived three days ago with a band of *custodes*, four mages, and a pack of shifters led by Roger Nevin, the wolf. They detained the *custodes* and chased out the shifters in an effort to acquire Reagan Somerset. Their plan worked almost to their liking, as far as I have heard. They *did* acquire Reagan Somerset, though whatever they'd hoped to achieve with the shifters and *custodes* did not pan out. The two factions successfully left the castle. Most of the *custodes* and shifters successfully escaped to the Brink. The elves are sending people after them, though we aren't sure what they plan to do. They don't have enough forces to cross into the Brink and disband the traitors, as the *custodes* and the shifters are being called."

"The elves are trying to save face. The *custodes* have always been well loved. Their absence has only created a deeper fondness. This will create turmoil for a kingdom already harvesting unrest."

Lucifer thought back to all that Vlad had said. His plans for striking at the heart of the elves. His assurances of success. His confidence in the players at his disposal. He only needed the might of the Underworld to see his plans unfold, he'd claimed. With Lucifer's help, their victory was assured.

Had Vlad suspected these events would transpire? His hints seemed to indicate it was so.

"And the woman?" Lucifer asked, calmly collecting his thoughts so as not to react hastily. His actions now would create lasting ripples. One misstep and he could be pushed further down the ranks in the magical world.

But if he pushed an advantage, perhaps he could right old wrongs.

"Without a doubt, the rumors are true. She has both *Incendium* and *Glaciem* magics, has merged them, and uses them both. The working of her magic is rudimentary at best, but her power level is that of a mid-level five with room to grow."

"With room to grow?"

"She is but mid-twenties in human years. She has many long years to fruit."

Lucifer stared hard at Victoria.

She nodded. "She could reach a level six. And more, she looks quite a bit like her mother."

"Her mother?"

"Yes." Victoria didn't look away as she pointed at the window overlooking the garden. "The inspiration for the statue down there. There can be no doubt she is yours."

Lucifer said nothing for many long moments, taking in that information. He'd always hoped for another heir. A child who could survive this world. An heir the Underworld could be proud of, and who would take his place when he desired to visit the Brink. Someone to help him work his creations.

"She has been in the inner kingdom," he said, his voice devoid of emotion. He'd had many heirs in his never-ending life. He'd lost them all. No father should have to magically freeze their child for all of time in the pits of fire. A child was supposed to do that for the parent. If only he could keep one. Just *one*. "She can at least survive here for a time."

"The vampire Vlad has been in touch. He has apparently done some digging." Victoria narrowed her eyes. She wasn't too keen on that vampire. It was wise of her not to trust him. "Reagan Somerset's mother—"

"Amorette."

"Yes. She is said to have had godly power."

"Godly power?"

"A human notion. We know it as the touch of angels."

Lucifer hissed. Angels were nothing but meddling, troublesome creatures that could stay holed up in their "paradise" for all he cared. They kept their so-called gifts to themselves, for the most part, which was the best idea they'd ever had. His kingdom had been plagued with much less riffraff because of it.

He thought back to his powerful attraction to Amorette. It hadn't been logical, his need for her. His ardent desire. One look at her beautiful face, and he'd been caught. He hadn't been able to get enough, always begging for one more smile, one more touch.

"She beguiled me with an angel's kiss?" he asked, trying to conceal his reaction to that thought.

"No. It was in her heritage. In her blood. It would

not have a direct effect on a dark ange—"

His look cut her off. She'd nearly forgotten herself. He would not suffer his person to be spoken of in the same sentence as those fools, regardless of his origins.

"The blood will act as a crutch to keep her human elements from deteriorating," Victoria went on. "We already know she does not need oxygen, assuming she was the woman you glimpsed, and I feel we must. There could be no other. Now we can assume that many long years here will not break her down as it did with the others. Something the elves do not yet know."

"And why is that?"

"The vampires clearly know it, but they and the elves have been at odds for centuries."

"Yes, of course."

"And two, the elves' questions are going unanswered."

"Their questions…" He'd heard what the Realm had devolved into. What the elves had devolved into. He'd seen it himself on his visits. Despite his power and might, they always treated him as lesser. Mocked him. "They are torturing her?"

"Yes."

"They suspect she is my daughter?"

"Yes. That is the only reason she lives."

"And yet they are still torturing her?"

"Yes, sir. So far—and this news is half a day old due

to travel time—she has not broken."

Memories crowded him. Of a glowing, dewy-faced Amorette, so serene and content even after losing her breakfast every morning for a month. It hadn't bothered her, the human sickness, and she'd looked so radiant in those final days he was with her, so earthy and peaceful, resplendent, that he hadn't pressed. She was everything the Brink could boast for beauty. It had given him countless ideas for new creations.

He'd assumed she was ill, that she would succumb to human fragility, the way his children had. When she'd demanded he leave, he hadn't pressed. He hadn't wanted to see her downfall.

She'd been pregnant.

The possibility should have occurred to him, but most magical beings didn't get with child so quickly. So easily.

"It has been a while since we last stormed a castle, has it not?" he asked Victoria, his thoughts turning to action.

"Yes, sir. Far too long for my taste."

"I agree. Ready the forces. There is not a moment to lose." He strode for the door. "We will retrieve my daughter. And call the vampire Vlad. This calls for a war, I think. The elves can expect no less, after this."

"Yes, sir."

"And let my subjects off their leashes. They may

tread wherever they will. No more restrictions."

"And the fog, sir?"

He paused at the door. "Keep the fog. I do not want my enemies knowing what sort of forces I've been preparing these many long years."

"Everyone likes surprises, I hear."

He tilted his head. "I guarantee they won't like this one."

EPILOGUE

CAHAL MOVED QUICKLY, pausing beside a stone column as an elf flounced by, an absurd waste of movement for any creature, but ridiculous in a guard. It was no wonder he'd infiltrated the dungeons with very little effort. The elves had been mighty at one point. Fearsome but fair. He'd snuck into this place plenty, but it had never been this easy. No one had sensed his magic or his presence. Not one guard had so much as stiffened in unease.

Sheer numbers were the only reason they'd been able to capture a woman as promising as the heir, especially with those natural dual-mages at her back. It was the only explanation. The elves were ill-prepared for what they'd set in motion.

He slipped over to a shadowed doorway as his senses went on high alert. A smell reached his nose, coming from the way he was traveling—ancient but familiar, although he couldn't exactly place it. His small hairs stood on end, and he knew it was someone with power. Someone dangerous.

Using his tools, he quickly and silently unlocked the nearest door and slipped through, leaving it open a crack so he could peer out. He wanted to see who haunted these halls.

Magic swirling, blocking his presence, he waited patiently. Reagan had been locked up for nearly four days. If she was going to crack, she would have done so already. She could handle a bit more pain so that Cahal could do the smart thing and see who or what was dogging her heels before he showed himself.

The being's shadow announced it before a shape filled the archway leading to the cells within the bowels of the castle. It stalled, as though it sensed him.

He waited. It waited.

Finally, a shoe slid across the ground, a foot pivoting, grinding straw into stone. Light steps announced the being was moving forward, but it quickly stalled again. Flickering fire from a nearby iron torch holder illuminated a slight frame. Short, thin, petite—the woman stayed still again, unbothered by the patrol that should've been walking through about now. The elves were ineffective, but at least they were punctual. It was nearly all they seemed to get right.

Cahal recognized her about the same time as she clearly recognized the presence she felt.

"She has mighty friends, it seems."

He remembered that silky voice, dripping lust and

passion and things humans could not resist. Thankfully, he was not human.

"Ja." He didn't bother moving from behind the door, and she didn't turn in his direction. There was no need. "You are not someone I would've expected to see down here."

"Nor I you. You must have a fascination with the heirs of the Underworld."

"For the magic." Specifically, he liked watching the heirs learn to use the full range of their magic, but she didn't need to know that. Knowing her, she'd somehow figure out a way to make that work against him.

"Yes. It is magnificent," she replied. "As is its origin."

"Is that your play in all this, then? You hope to regain access to one of your homes?"

"We all long for our homes in the end, do we not? Except for those of us without homes, of course."

It was a dig at him. This vampire had always been one of the most cunning power players in her species. She'd navigated times that had made a quick end of other strong people, magical or otherwise, a journey made harder by being female. Sometimes the social realities of that had slowed her, but they'd never stopped her.

"And what is your play, Mr. Shadow?" she asked. "Or do they call you *Eliminator* now?"

"I have many names."

"So you do. As do I."

He paused for a moment, carefully collecting his thoughts. "You have set me on this journey, by contracting me to her friend, and allowing me to witness, firsthand, her power," he finally said. "The power of Lucifer's heir. I am bored with my long years. I might as well walk the path for a while."

"The path of the righteous?"

"The path of the forsaken. It's more interesting than that of the righteous."

She laughed. It was an answer she might've given herself. When Ja had approached him, he hadn't needed to do his homework on her. Before she'd semi-retired, he'd watched her maneuverings, surprised when she'd taken a step back, not at all surprised when she'd burst back onto the scene.

"Why are you here?" he asked her. "She is not with you, so clearly it is not to let her out."

"Oh my, no. If I did, how would she learn?" She laughed again and continued forward. "Good luck, Mr. Shadow. I'm sure I will see you again."

He rather hoped not.

He shut and locked the door behind him and then hastened down the hall, flitting through the shadows. A guard lay dead in the center of the floor behind two cells, the prisoners within long since dead, nothing but bones now. The neck of the guard had been torn out. Ja had wanted to make a show, ensure the elves knew a vampire had been down there.

He slowed for a moment.

Had Ja known he would be coming to rescue Reagan? If so, she might be trying to set the stage to make it look like the vampires were the ones who'd broken in, killed everyone, and then rescued the prize.

No, that couldn't be it. She hadn't known right away who was waiting in the shadows. If she'd been expecting him, she wouldn't have paused for so long. She was not a showy vampire, like Vlad, but all vampires liked to play with their food. It was in their nature. She would've made a quip or two about being way ahead of him.

...how would she learn?

He shook his head and continued on. He was not clever enough to figure this out, not with so little information.

A man sat in the last cell on the right, ribs clearly showing and wiry muscle lining his nude form. He sat hunched over propped-up knees, his head hanging low.

Another guard lay half in and half out of the doorway up ahead, the door standing open. Heavy wooden doors lined the other side of the hallway, closed off, darkened, single-person cells designed for confusing the mind. Food would come at random times, sleep would be interrupted, random water tossed in, and the prisoner would be kept in continual darkness unless he or she was being tortured. That treatment would break someone. Most of the time, anyway.

"Hey," Cahal whispered, revealing himself to the man in the cell.

The man didn't move, staring at nothing.

"Hey," Cahal repeated, raising his voice.

Still the man didn't look around. Spit dribbled out of the side of his mouth. His mind was gone. He wouldn't have noticed the vampire, probably, and if he had, he likely didn't have enough sense to coherently remember what she'd done here.

Cahal moved on, stepping over the guard and quickly checking behind him. There shouldn't be a change-out for another hour, at least. Food had come not long ago. The torturers had already been here twice. He should have a big window here, but one could never be too sure.

Within the second part of the dungeon, he had to but smell his way to the cell he needed, following the scent of fresh blood in the stagnant air. Last door on the left, charred and leaning awkwardly, with a few chunks taken out at the bottom and a hole burrowed through the top. They didn't look like escape attempts, but the result of a temper.

"Reagan," Cahal whispered, no idea what he might find beyond that door. Not really wanting to find out, if he was being honest. He'd been tortured for a year, but never with such vigor. He didn't know if he could stand seeing her like the man in the other cell. "Reagan?"

"Knock, knock…" came the reply.

He heaved a sigh of relief.

"Who's there?" he answered, working at the lock with his tools. He didn't want the elves to know what manner of creature had broken in. When he locked it back up after they left, there would be zero evidence of how she'd gotten out.

Except for the dead bodies with their necks torn out by a vampire.

He paused and looked down at the lock. Once he'd been good at this. He was clearly rusty. He was helping Ja frame vampires…if that was what she'd set out to do.

"Orange." Her voice was weak and scratchy. He could barely hear her through the wood.

"Orange who?" The lock clicked over.

He dropped one of his tools on the ground. They'd now know it was a burglar, not a vampire. That would confuse them a little. Maybe upset Ja's plans. She was too cunning for her own good. All vampires were, but she was worse than most. Her intelligence made him feel like an amateur.

"Orange'cha glad you're not the one in here?" A wheeze of laugher floated out of the cell, followed by a wet, hacking cough. "Ow."

He grimaced as he pulled open the door. A long, low groan issued from the wood.

"They keep trying to repair it." Her voice hung heavily in the liquid darkness. He could barely see her form in the corner, like a body dumped there after it had been dismantled. "I kicked it in when they were bringing me in here. That confused them. Then I kicked it out after I killed two of their guards. They swarm the place like rats, though. Can't get past the buggers. Too many."

"How you doin'? You good?"

"Oh sure, yeah. Fucking amazing. How are you doing?"

He pushed the door open wider and brought in an unlit torch from the outside wall. "Can you light this so I can see what I'm working with?"

"Take a deep breath, bud. I am not the same girl you saw last time. Also, can't you see in the dark?"

"To an extent. This is beyond—" He lost his words when the torch flared to life.

She sat on the cold stone nude, deep blue and purple bruises covering her body, broken by bloody slits and spots where they'd torn off chunks of skin. The bone on her lower right arm stuck out through the skin. Her left hung limp from what looked like a badly dislocated shoulder. Her right eye was swollen shut, and her right foot at an unnatural angle. On her right hand, not one finger was lined up correctly.

"How's my hair?" she asked, her head resting back against the stone wall smeared with blood. "I didn't get a chance to style it today. The elves have kept me busy. So sweet of them to visit so often. They don't seem to like my jokes, though. Probably because I make them at the elves' expense, huh? Sensitive fuckers."

Cahal knelt beside her, at a loss. He hadn't thought there would be this much damage. Not so soon. They were clearly trying to fast-track the process, a sure way to kill someone rather than break them.

"What are they after?" he asked, leaning closer to her chest to see if there was any rib damage that might indicate internal bleeding.

"Oh...you know. Nothing much. Just my life story. Very nosy, these elves. They seem to think I'll tell them my history. What dopes, am I right? At least they didn't cut anything off. Awfully hard to heal it if it isn't there, know what I mean?"

"Yeah. I do."

"Right, yeah, I forgot. You know the deal. Another day in paradise. Not sure I'd want to do this for a year, though."

"I didn't have it as bad as this. Not all at once." He couldn't help his breath hitching. "Not even close."

"Nice. I win. Where's my prize?"

"Here's what we're going to do..."

"Crack everything back in place so I can heal it up—eventually—and then run me out of here, I hope?"

"Yes. It's going to hurt like hell."

"Nah. It'll hurt worse than that." Her bleary eye came to rest on him. "I am really, *really* glad to see you. Did you know that the elves can dampen a vampire bond?" He grabbed hold of her pinky. It was as good a place to start as any. *Crack.* "Elephant dongs in a singalong! Damn it, I sound like Penny." *Crack.* "Holy fuck tarts!" She breathed through the pain. "Anyway, turns out they can dampen a bond. He's there, I feel him, but he's so muffled that I can't feel any emotion from him. Don't worry, I will kill the king and queen for that. Mess with my limbs? Not good, but we all have our issues. Mess with my bond to Darius? I will rip your head from those bony shoulders and shove it up your ass." She paused as he tackled the rest of her fingers. "Just as soon as I can work my limbs, obviously."

"At least you're in good spirits."

"Yeah. I was singing bottles of beer on the wall through the last session. They really hate that song, it turns out."

The ground beneath them rumbled. The walls groaned. A push of air disturbed the stuffy silence.

Cahal paused, her shoulder in his hands, listening.

Somewhere in the castle, a large load of power was sinking into the very foundation, tremoring through the stone.

…how would she learn?

He turned back to Reagan in a rush. "We need to go for 'good enough' and get you out of here."

"Why, what is it?"

"Someone you're in no shape to meet."

LUCIFER BLEW OFF the front face of the castle, sending stone and brick raining down. His subjects erected a ceiling of air so he could pass through the debris without being struck. His subjects hurried out in front of him, all different forms, ghastly creations that had been forbidden to show their faces in this poor excuse for a castle.

Elves rushed toward him from the front hall, only to fall back again.

His black, feathery wings snapped out behind him, filling the hall, the edges raking down the walls. Fire pulsed around him, burrowing into anything wood, flames roaring in his wake. The ground shook as his subjects joined their power with his, their magic tearing off doors, pulling down chandeliers, scraping up the floors.

"In the dungeons, sir," Victoria said, flying in her demon form in front of him, half his size and adept at handling tight spaces and ghastly surprises.

He tore the next door from its hinges and threw it aside. With an extra little boost of magic, it tore through glass, brick, and mortar. Through the archway, which he'd left intact for his subjects to rip down, he let surprise hinder his step for a brief moment.

The large room, two stories with a viewing balcony, had been utterly destroyed. Huge, gaping holes punched through the left wall and the ceiling, clumps of destroyed stone littering the floor. Columns lay in ruin, and half the balcony had been torn down.

"Your daughter, sir," Victoria said.

Pride welled within him, and he laughed. "Finish the job," he said, turning.

At the narrow steps to descend into the dungeons, he felt the unmistakable power of the king and queen. He turned to the right, waiting to see if they would present themselves. His subjects crowded around him, ripping and tearing, making clear what he thought of this insult.

The king's voice reverberated through the chamber. "She has committed grievous infractions within our kingdom. She should be hanged. She was spared solely because she is your heir. Your actions today, however…"

The threat lingered, though the king did not step through the doors. He did not intend to confront

Lucifer face to face.

A smile stretched across Lucifer's face.

"My actions today serve as a hint of what is to come. Brace yourself, you sniveling coward. You have no idea what your actions will unleash." He glanced at Victoria and thought, *Tell them to cover me, and then follow me down. Leave the rest up here.*

He descended, closing his wings with a snap, letting the fire follow him down. A body littered the ground, the neck having been ripped out. A vampire had visited, then, and clearly not one under the employ of the elves. Vlad?

A man in a cell looked up as fire crowded the room, his eyes wide but glazed, responding to the light. There was nothing behind those eyes, his mind utterly gone. He would never come back from this. Only the primal part of him still remained, and that part wasn't enough for any sort of action. This man was waiting for death.

Lucifer stabbed him through the forehead with air, a merciful killing. "Find out who he is and deliver him to his people. Inform them of what the elves did."

He stepped over another guard, killed the same as the last. He moved down the hall, passing closed doors. Only one of them, the last on the right, was open. He slowly walked toward it, anger burning within him. If the vampires had taken his daughter with anything other than the intention of delivering her…

He stopped in the doorway and changed into his humanoid form. Cahal the druid rose from a crouch, his expression flat.

A woman sat at his feet, and a pang hit Lucifer's heart so fiercely that he nearly staggered, nearly rushed to her, nearly commanded his subjects to go to war right then and there.

He knew her face, though he'd never seen her up close. Knew her poise—her challenge—even as she sat bleeding on a stone floor. Knew her magic, since it was his own. Knew her potential, because he could see her strength. She would not break, this woman. Not from life, not from the elves, not from anything.

"You are Amorette's daughter," he said, and it wasn't a question. He could see Amorette in the lovely face covering that hard edge. In her obvious stubbornness. In her immediate ability to wrap him around her little finger, even if this time it would be as a daughter does a father.

"Hey, Pop. Nice to meet you," she said with a wheeze. "I'd get up, but I'm in the middle of something."

He laughed. Though her voice was weak and scratchy, her confidence could not be misinterpreted. Her swagger, her blasé attitude, even while suffering a pain so great it dulled her gaze…

"She reminds me of you, sir," Victoria said, peering

over his shoulder. "And she is already speaking our language, even here."

"I learned when I was in the Underworld. Somehow. That was me, by the way. In the Underworld." Reagan grimaced, trying to keep sitting, but gravity was pulling her down. "Surprise…"

"Yes, I'd gathered," he responded, a feeling of lightness coming over him. Also an urgency to ease her pain. "Give me a moment, and we'll get you cleaned up. I assume you can wait?"

"Yeah, sure, why not. I'm not in incredible pain or anything. Better yet, why don't you head on back to the Underworld, and Cahal will take me out of here as planned."

"Can't, I'm afraid. I'm using you as an excuse to start a war. I'll need to take you with me."

"Super. My day keeps getting better and better," she grumbled.

He grinned. She was delightful.

He eyed the druid before shifting to the druid language very few knew existed. It was the language the druid had turned to when he was praying for strength those many long years ago, alone in his cell. And he had found it. Those accursed, meddling angels had stuck their noses in and hardened his resolve. Lucifer hadn't known then that the druid was a favorite.

"How interesting to find you with another of my

heirs," he said to the druid.

"I was recently hired to protect a mage. Your heir is the mage's good friend. I knew Reagan's magic instantly, and have kept an eye on her since. I trained her as best I could."

"You trained her…"

"As best I could."

"Interesting. Angels again?"

His brow furrowed. He didn't speak.

Lucifer laughed, long and low. "Ah. They have forsaken you, have they? Just like humanity. Pity. Well, Sir Darkness, I am indebted to you for helping my daughter. Will you come with us?"

"Yes. But not as your ally. I will attempt to keep her from going the road of the last."

"Ah, but you see, that makes you my ally, Mr. Shadow."

"Until it does not."

"Leave the riddles to the vampires. They are better at them." Lucifer waved his finger behind him. "You tried to frame them?"

"No. That was not me, and I don't know why it was done, quite frankly."

"But you know who?"

"Will you torture me to find out?"

He tsked and turned toward his daughter. "You bore me, druid. Torture was my last son's hobby, not mine. I just kill and be done with it. But you have some uses, and so I will forget your involvement in his death. It would've happened anyway, I see that now. You merely…sped things up. No, let us look to the future, shall we? My heir will be crowned the princess of the Dark Kingdom, and together, she and I will tear the rest of this castle to the ground, and maybe the Realm with it. It is time for the Underworld to rule all the magical land below the clouds. One day, maybe the clouds as well, who is to say?"

He wrapped Reagan in numbing ice before bending for her and lifting her gently. "Go to sleep," he told her softly, "and when you wake, the pain will be gone."

"But my nightmare will be just begun," she mumbled softly, and her eyes fluttered shut.

The End.

About the Author

K.F. Breene is a Wall Street Journal, USA Today, Washington Post, Amazon Most Sold Charts and #1 Kindle Store bestselling author of paranormal romance, urban fantasy and fantasy novels. With over four million books sold, when she's not penning stories about magic and what goes bump in the night, she's sipping wine and planning shenanigans. She lives in Northern California with her husband, two children, and out of work treadmill.

Sign up for her newsletter to hear about the latest news and receive free bonus content.

www.kfbreene.com

Printed in Great Britain
by Amazon